ABISH
MOTHER
OF FAITH

K.C. GRANT

ABISH
MOTHER
OF FAITH

a novel

Covenant Communications, Inc.

Cover image: Foreground, Mayan Calendar © Hannah Gleg; Background, etching by Frederick Catherwood

Cover design copyright © 2011 by Covenant Communications, Inc.

Published by Covenant Communications, Inc.
American Fork, Utah

Printed in the USA
First Printing: March 2011

17 16 15 14 13 12 11   10 9 8 7 6 5 4 3 2 1

ISBN 978-1-60861-104-1

To "M" and "K"—
my constant inspirations

Acknowledgments

I am very grateful to the many readers who encouraged me to continue Abish's story with their kind words and acceptance of my first attempt. I can only hope this will meet with their approval as well! My thanks to Covenant for their continued support and my undying appreciation to my editors, Eliza and Samantha, for your guidance and helpful suggestions, and also to Kelly in marketing for being patient as I learned the ropes. And to my husband and children, who let me disappear downstairs for hours at a time to type away at the computer, thank you!

"Now they never had fought, yet they did not fear death; . . . they had been taught by their mothers, that if they did not doubt, God would deliver them. And they rehearsed unto me the words of their mothers, saying: We do not doubt our mothers knew it."

Alma 56:47–48

Prologue

Perhaps my story should have ended that glorious day when my life found its purpose. On that day, my Creator saw fit to use my weakness as His strength so the truth of His gospel could surge across the land, enveloping my people from the east to the west, from the sea to the wilderness. That wave of righteousness, I knew even then, would never again be at the mercy of one person's hand. I also knew that I would never again have such a role to play as I did that fateful day in King Lamoni's court.

So I must admit that it is only my own vanity that wishes the rest to be told. After all, how could the fulfillment of a heart's desire compare with the deliverance of a nation? I can only hope that an old woman will be forgiven for her shortcomings because there are things one can't help but remember: the look on a husband's face when he calls you his own, the softness of a baby's skin when he is put into your arms for the first time, and the inevitable joy that comes when the anguish of death is softened by time.

How could I not add these memories to the ones that have come before? Especially now. Especially when the past is all I have left.

Land of Ishmael
87 BC

1

Abish pulled back the worn leather flap and stepped out of the tent.

Tendrils of fog hung thick on the ancient trees that rose above her and blocked out the early morning's light. The mist was so thick that it blanketed her body and left her feeling chilled. Not even her waist-length hair or thick leather tunic could keep her warm from such a fog, and she shivered. Rubbing her neck, stiff from hours of crouching over, she walked a few paces toward a nearby precipice. As she scanned the valley below, Abish could see where the sun was already burning away the haze near the river. Soon morning would come, bringing with it a new start. And new challenges to face.

A figure emerged from behind her, and Abish managed a weary smile for her dearest friend. Teara's countenance was serious as she joined Abish: her soft brown eyes were clouded with fatigue, and her shoulder-length black hair, still damp with perspiration, clung to the sides of her oval face. They stood quietly for a while, aware of the many unspoken words that rested between them.

Abish was the first to breach the silence. "I should have sent you home hours ago. I had no idea we would be with her this long."

Teara crossed her arms across her chest with a defiance that was in direct contrast to her tiny frame. "When I became your apprentice last year, I accepted that there would be many long nights like this. But we did well—and now a new life has entered the world."

"Yes," Abish said softly. "A son. She is very fortunate to be so blessed."

When Abish stopped abruptly, Teara said, "Your time will come."

"Perhaps. But for now, it's their time to celebrate." Abish turned toward the tent. Now a stream of light had broken through the thick canopy and cast a hazy glow where she was looking. Taking a deep breath, she sighed. "I'd better return and make sure they will be well enough off."

"Let me do it," Teara pleaded. "You're exhausted. You should go home."

"No. It's my responsibility. You go." As Teara shrugged and turned, Abish added a quick, though heartfelt, "Thank you."

She allowed herself to hesitate at the tent's opening for just a moment. As Abish reentered, her eyes adjusted to where she could see that the young man was still kneeling on the ground, hovering over his wife and the small bundle at her side. He looked up when she entered and, sensing her reticence to interrupt this precious moment, bade her forward with a nod of his head.

Abish went to him and whispered, "If you'd rather be alone, I'll understand. I just wanted to make sure your wife was well enough for me to leave."

Now the young woman opened her eyes and with an almost heavenly expression shook her head. "Oh no! We couldn't imagine you not being here to share our joy! After all, it's because of you that we have him."

Abish followed the woman's gaze down to the sleeping form and watched with amazement as the baby pursed his lips as if he were already imagining his next meal. She laughed softly and then felt the familiar tug on her heart. The father looked so proud. After all, his wife had given him a child . . . an heir to receive the birthright now that they were part of the covenant people.

"I should check—" Abish glanced quickly at the husband, aware of the delicacy of the situation. "I need to know if things are progressing as they should."

The man kissed his wife quietly on the cheek and left the tent. Another hour passed while Abish cleaned up the small tent and gave instructions for cleansing and purification. As long as the woman's body did not take on a heat sickness in the next few days, she would make a quick recovery.

Fatigue settled on Abish and lulled her to only a half awareness of her surroundings. At some point, the woman's husband had returned and he was talking to her.

". . . Naomi is still my responsibility. I'll do my best to care for her and my son. Thank you again for everything you've done."

Stepping from the tent, Abish found that the day had burst into its full glory, and now she could not help but leave some of her longing behind and smile. She could hear the commotion of the city around her as it awakened. Leaving the small tent community, which had sprung up almost overnight around the established city due to the influx of immigrants from neighboring areas, Abish walked back through the central market. She was still amazed at how Ishmael had changed in these few short years that had passed since the Day of Conversion. She looked around at the bustle of people going about their day, already filling the north end of the marketplace. Though the palace and its impressive stone wall were the most prominent features in the area, dozens of communities had already spread out from this central plaza, keeping it not only the economic but also the social focal point of Ishmael.

Her return home took her first down the Street of the Vendors, where merchants were arranging their wares like a twenty-square board on the blanketed ground. There had been a good early harvest that would hopefully support Ishmael's swelling numbers, especially as the dry season approached. Perhaps hunger could be staved off another year.

As she walked along, she caught a whiff of something that reminded her of her own hunger. The meager offering of manioc and dried fruit she'd been given that morning was far from sustaining, but she knew that the couple had given her all they had. Nearby, a woman was browning some maize cakes on a griddle. Knowing she had a measure of copper that a more established supplicant had given her the day before, Abish couldn't resist purchasing a few. As she savored the hearty texture of the cake and the piquant aftertaste of the lime with which it was flavored, Abish suddenly groaned—*not* from the satisfaction of a full belly, however. It was because she'd realized that while she had been busy with her work last night, she hadn't left any evening meal prepared at home. She changed her course of direction, hoping a quick apology could stave off her feelings of guilt.

At the Street of the Artisans there was little time to admire the works of jade, obsidian, pottery, and bone. Instead, she continued until she came to the far end of the square. As she smelled the familiar combination of cooling steel and human sweat, her heart quickened as it always did. The smithy was always dark enough that it took her eyes a few moments to adjust. When they did, she saw what she had been looking for.

There he was.

Jared sat on a wooden bench, pumping the bellows for the smelting oven with his foot. With his back to her, she could admire his thick dark hair, which hung down to his shoulders again, as was the fashion. Because of the heat, he wore just a leather apron strapped around his neck, his back bare down to a soot-covered linen girdle. Abish couldn't help but stand there and watch his muscles flex as he worked.

"Ahem," she interrupted and then continued her well-rehearsed part. "I do not have much time and need a service from you." She held up her empty hand to mime her role. "This stone needs to be set. Can you do it or are you just . . . well, do you just . . ."

"Tend to the bellows?" came the sarcastic reply. But when Jared turned around, the glint in his eyes belied his supposed words of disapproval. "Stand still," he spoke off script, "and I'll show you just what I can do."

Abish laughed as he came toward her, scarcely noticing the uneven gait that his crooked legs caused. As his arms sought to embrace her, she playfully pushed him away. "You didn't finish your part right!"

"I couldn't help it." He shrugged. "My wife standing in the doorway was too tempting a sight."

When her lips were free, she chuckled. "Then I forgive you."

For a moment Jared's eyes narrowed. "And *I* forgive *you*."

Abish knew to what he referred. "I'm sorry. I forgot to send word. And I can't imagine what you found to eat for dinner last night."

"I managed."

"Am I really forgiven?" she ventured.

"Kiss me again and I think that will help me know for sure."

She obliged. And then, with a weary sigh, she walked back with him over to his bench where she settled on his lap. "It was another long night. Teara and I just barely parted."

His face grew concerned and he asked, "Something you need to talk about?"

Abish shrugged, not wanting to speak of babies—or sons—right now. So she changed the topic. "I promise when you come home tonight I'll have your favorite meal waiting: spicy venison and honey squash. I'll even make some coconut sweets."

"Ah," he groaned with delight. "You are forgiven! I shouldn't be too late. I would be even earlier if some of the council members weren't so full of hot air!" He pumped the bellows as if to demonstrate.

Abish frowned. Jared had been to a lot of these meetings lately. "Are the rumors true then?"

"I'm afraid so. Apparently the Amalekites and Amulonites have decided that it's better to hate us than waste energy hating each other. If enough of our people can be united to their cause, they might come against us."

"*Our* people? Now that we are called Anti-Nephi-Lehies, it's hard to see them that way." Abish walked across the room away from the intensifying heat of the ovens. "To me, they're just *Lamanites.*"

Jared frowned slightly. "When these plowshares are completed I shouldn't have any more large orders for a while. I'll be home with you more."

"Teara's always telling me I should be more optimistic. So I'll try. Perhaps this war talk will be good for business." She looked at all of the unsold swords sitting in the corner. "It's ironic, really. The sad truth that both of us could be busier because of it."

Abish couldn't ignore the disappointed look that often crossed Jared's face at the mention of her work, causing her own countenance to droop.

"Hmmm." Jared's face changed to a look of concern. "I think that long night is taking its toll. You look drained. Go home. I'll see you tonight."

Abish agreed, knowing some problems could not be solved in a day.

2

Even though the sun was now high in the sky, the cooler air outside the smithy revived Abish as she exited the shop. She was almost tempted to make a quick stop at Akah's on the way home. It had been several days since she'd visited the older woman who had been like a mother to her all these years. But then she admitted to herself that "quick" visits were not Akah's specialty, so she resolved to leave the visit for another day.

Abish set out for home again, crossing down the embankment and enjoying the feel of the many varieties of giant ferns and broad-leaf plants that slapped against her bare legs. The plants crowded and clung to the steep down-sloping trail while sunshine sparkled off the damp greenery, glistening like gems. But like any positive aspect of life, she also had to face the opposition that surrounded them—whether it came in the form of annoying insects that hung thick in the air or the season of rain that followed after the time of planting, which always brought with it an influx of sickness to the land. *Why?* She had yet to figure it out. Gone were the days when she thought that the gods or transgression caused illness, but so much was beyond her understanding that she often wondered if she were really helping at all.

But who else could the people turn to? There were few who understood the body and the use of herbs and plants. With increasing numbers, Abish had needed help. That was one reason she had asked Teara to start learning at her side last year. That, and the fact that it might take Teara's mind off the recent death of the queen, whom she'd served faithfully for many years.

Her thoughts brightened as her home finally came into view. The small adobe hut sat on a rise only about a hundred paces from the river and had an air of permanence that set it apart from many of the hastily built pole and tent homes that now shared the area. Its palm-thatched roof was still in good repair, though the stucco would already need another coat of whitewash within the year. The most striking feature was the wood lintel above the doorway, where Jared had used all his skill to carve the symbols that represented their family and his position in the land. And though it was humble compared to what she had been used to most of her life, their hut represented something Abish had longed for as long as she could remember: a place to call her own. At times, though, she felt like it didn't belong to her—almost as if one day she would have to say good-bye to it all again.

To keep her promise to Jared, Abish got right to work preparing the evening meal. *Guilt had its price*, she thought as she put some coconut milk in a bowl out on the hot stone terrace to warm in the sun. Then she took out her grinding stone and began crushing casaba root into pulp for a simple bread—all she had time for. She added lime and salt and placed the mash in a tightly woven bag to squeeze out any excess liquid. The final step would find the concoction rolled out into flat pancakes and cooked on the heated hearthstone. She covered some squash with the ashes of the morning fire Jared had made and placed several large chiles on top then retrieved the venison Jared loved from the smokehouse. If she was lucky, she'd still have time to hang out yesterday's wash and repair the crack in her main water jug by the time he got home.

A few of the other village women passed by, and Abish gave them a quick wave. They nodded politely in return but did not stop to talk to her. She paused on her way around the hut and watched them walk away. One was carrying a large bundle on her head and another had a small infant swaddled against her back. Though both women were commonly dressed, you could still sense the pride they had in their workmanship. The elaborate patterns that had been woven into the cloth belied the fact that these were everyday clothes. Even with the weight they carried, there was a graceful feel to their movements.

Abish sighed and continued walking to the smokehouse. It was unlikely that these women's husbands had ever had to wait for their wives to prepare their evening meals. The stately women probably never left dishes unwashed or forgot to shake out the sleeping mats. Or, as she had just discovered, forget to cover and hang their meat in the smokehouse so that animals would not confiscate it!

Abish's shoulders fell, and she turned back to the hut without the venison. It wasn't that she didn't try. She was just so busy with her healing work that many of her household duties fell to others, which was why Akah was indispensable when it came to so many things. Abish had lost track of the times when she would come home during the day and find a bushel of fresh avocados or melon on her doorstep. Or find her threshold swept clean of leaves and debris. Or find the water gourds freshly filled. She didn't know how the other women got so much accomplished.

As she stirred honey into the warmed coconut milk and set it on a rock near the fire pit, Abish tried to keep her focus on her work, thinking it would drown out other thoughts. But she soon realized that the type of work she was doing required little thinking and thus provided minimal distraction. Almost as if an answer to her unspoken prayer, Abish heard a voice call to her from the front of the house.

"Abish, come quick!"

Only too glad to leave her present duties, Abish rushed to see who was summoning her. It was Taya, daughter of one of the neighboring families. She had an arm around her little brother, Shem, who was whimpering. A large gash on his left leg was oozing crimson blood.

"Let me look at you," Abish soothed as she rushed to them. "What happened?"

Through sobs the boy said, "I—I was climbing and I—I fell down."

She led him into the house. "Let's get you cleaned up. You're going to be just fine."

It shouldn't have taken long to wipe the wound clean and apply a poultice, but Shem felt as if he needed to give her a lengthy description of his adventure and wanted her complete attention. She tried not to grimace as he elaborated on his story. He had only wanted to capture the tiny monkey in the tree near his house and keep it as a pet. How could she explain that a scraped leg would have been the least of his worries if he'd succeeded at his task and the small though feisty animal had had the inclination to fight back?

Finished, she handed him a small piece of honey *pah-lech*—kept for just such a purpose—and reminded him that little boys should stay closer to the ground. Shem threw his arms around her and gave her a sticky kiss on the cheek before running down the path. As she watched him go, she realized that was all the payment she needed. In fact, how much easier life would be if that were the only form of payment she ever received.

When she and Jared had first married, he had made it very clear that he was the provider of the family. This left Abish with the dilemma of what to do with the variety of payments she was often given. Most patrons insisted on giving what they could: a trinket, some cloth, or a basket, which would occasionally be full of produce or bread. Since these were practical, "womanly" gifts, he usually wouldn't begrudge her keeping them for their personal use, though frequently she would pass the items along to families that needed them more than they did. The measures of silver or copper were another matter. This was given for man's work and Jared heartily disapproved, so she tried to make sure he saw as little of it as possible. Maybe, she had thought, one day he would be more accepting of what she did.

As Abish reminisced, she suddenly noticed a strange smell in the air. She sniffed cautiously. "Aaiaee!" she cried, rushing to the back of the house.

As she stared at the charred remains of what should have been their dinner, Abish wondered how she would explain yet another failure to Jared. The squash had exploded because she had forgotten to prick the skin. The coconut sweets had cooked down to an impenetrable, gooey mass. And the chile peppers that she had been roasting were unidentifiable. *Along with no meat*, she sarcastically thought, *this is going to be a feast!* Scraping the remains into a nearby basket, she wanted to sit down on a nearby rock and cry.

"Is anyone home?"

Oh no, Abish groaned as she heard the voice. All she needed was to be called away again and not even be there when Jared returned. Going to see who needed her, Abish nearly cried out for joy when she saw it was just Akah, carrying a large clay pot.

"There you are!" the older woman huffed, coming toward her. "I made too much stew again. You'd think after all these years I'd remember how many I was cooking for."

Abish watched as the pudgy woman came toward her, a strand of graying hair hanging over her brow. Sometimes Akah reminded Abish of the time when she had watched a mother parrot bringing a tasty treat back to her nest, only to discover that half of her chicks had flown away. Akah's family had shrunk to all but her husband and twin boys, who were already preparing to become apprentices in their chosen trade. To think she'd started off with seven! But time and both a few happy and a few unfortunate events had taken care of that.

With a sincere smile, Abish took the heavy pot. From inside came the heavenly smell of rabbit and vegetables in an aromatic broth. "You're an answer to a prayer, Akah."

Seeing the smoking contents in the nearby basket, Akah chuckled. "Burnt offerings again?" Putting an arm around Abish, she added, "No matter. The Lord's blessed you with other abilities, that's all."

"Perhaps," Abish admitted. "But there are times when I think I would give it all up just to be . . . well, a normal woman. Like you."

Akah clucked. "Now don't go envying my life. There are days when I'd give anything to be needed like you instead of having raised a passel of children just to have them disappear, and have to put up with a man like Laban. We all have our roles to play. Don't think less of yours 'cause it's different."

"But why has God not allowed me to do both? Why hasn't He given me . . . ?"

"Children?" Akah painfully filled in. "I don't know. I've seen you with them, so it's not for lack of motherly instinct that you don't have a brood to call your own. I always thought you'd know better than any of us why bodies do or don't work."

"When it comes to that, I'm afraid I know hardly anything at all," Abish sighed. "I understand now how my father felt when he was in the Order of Healers, trying to understand the body: the relation of parts and organs to each other." She grew animated, "You see, he taught me that health comes when there is balance. Disease, then, must be an imbalance, when elements with opposing properties work against each other. Now illness in itself seems to have either hot or cold characteristics. For example, if a person had an illness that was thought to have cold properties, I might treat them with a plant that is known to have a hot quality or characteristic in order to bring him back into balance. But sometimes there are other elements at play—emotional states, perhaps alterations of the soul—that I don't know how to affect. I assume these must be driven out in order to heal the afflicted. But I don't know how."

Abish flushed a deep red as she noticed her companion's expression. "I'm sorry, Akah. This must be boring you."

"Oh, well . . . no."

"I won't let you lie to save face," Abish chastised. "Go on. Back to your family. And thank you for the meal."

"It will get better." Akah smiled. "Be patient."

Be patient. Another area where she was lacking.

Left alone, Abish set out the eating mats and gave the stew a quick stir. Some of the bread nearest the fire pit was done, though she still lamented the sweets and squash. By the time Jared came home, it looked as if she'd been working all day to prepare this special meal. He didn't question the sudden change of menu, but instead was anxious to talk to her about the latest news he had heard circulating through the land.

"There's going to be a council," he explained. "The high king might be giving up his throne and wants to make it official. In a few weeks, we could have a new king. Whether it will be Lamoni or his brother, we'll have to wait and see."

"Why does it make a difference?" she asked.

"In my opinion, King Lamoni was always better at relations between us and the dissident Lamanites, much like his father. Of course, his brother is the older son and entitled to it, but I hear he thinks that we need to more aggressively pursue those who are not of our faith and 'persuade' them to join us. It could increase the tension that already exists between us."

Abish frowned. Somehow, amid all of the conflict around them, Ishmael had remained something of a safe haven. What would happen if the events Jared was speaking of came to pass? He answered her unspoken question.

"It could mean war."

3

Abish was extremely grateful for Teara's help that would come in the following days. They both knew that the influx of visitors to their city had to do with the great council that was to occur two days hence. But along with their hopes, the people brought all manner of ailments. As Abish and her companion walked along after one particularly exhausting case, Teara was still comforting her over yet another loss.

"You did everything you could," Teara said.

"Except arrive in time."

If only she had been by the man's side instead of his wife, who had misinterpreted Abish's instructions and forgot to dilute the sedative she had prescribed. *I should have been there.* She had known the aged man's wife was probably not well enough herself to care for him. Abish had almost suggested he be moved closer to her own home, but where would that end? She could not possibly have all of her worst cases come to live with her. It would take a place with many rooms to care for so many.

A place with many rooms . . .

The thought stayed with Abish as an idea materialized in her mind that just might solve her own dilemma of that morning. Would it work? She could almost imagine how much easier it would be—but could she convince Jared? Perhaps.

When the moment was right.

* * *

Finally, the day of the council meeting arrived.

But thoughts of kings and councils were far from her mind. Instead, Abish was so invigorated with the plan that had come to her that she had a hard time waiting for the right opportunity to speak to Jared. But Jared's work was important, and the fire's glow could keep him working well into the night. It was moments like that when she realized how much she missed the warmth of his body next to hers as she slept. The cold stillness reminded her too much of all those years when she was alone. She prayed that the council would make wise decisions so he could be home with her again.

Abish tried to wait patiently at home for Jared to return, but found after a while that she could no longer stand the silence. As the palace gates came into view, she realized that she was not the only woman anxiously awaiting the outcome. An ambitious vendor had anticipated their arrival and walked around them selling refreshing slices of melon. Abish bought one, but barely tasted the sweet juice trickling down her throat because of her eagerness. At last, a commotion began to surge through the crowd until it became a wave.

"All hail our future king!" the voices began to chant.

So it is decided, she thought. She hurried so she could hear it from Jared's lips. In her search, it was easy to spot Ammon's fair skin and honey-colored hair as he walked through the palace gates. She resisted the urge to question her friend, instead waiting until she saw Jared amid the throng. She ran to him. "Tell me! Tell me what's happened!"

Signaling her to be patient, he linked her arm in his as they walked toward his shop. When she saw the frown on his face, she knew who had won.

"Many of the council felt as I did," he began, "that there will only be an escalation of tension between us if Lamoni does not take the place of his father. But his brother will be our leader, and we must have faith that he will do the right thing."

Abish tried to be comforted by Jared's words. But it was difficult to put their future in the hands of one man. At times she wished that Ammon would be named king—but the danger of that had been ingrained into them all, so they were eager to use Zarahemla's system as a guide: one man to rule the land, the other to rule the church. And God to rule over them all. As long as they remembered that, they would surely be blessed.

* * *

Nobody Abish talked to over the next few days was any surer as to what lay in their future—or at least not willing to share what they thought. Even Ammon merely chuckled when she asked him what was going to happen.

"Abish, you must be patient," he playfully chided, his green eyes sparkling.

"Since when," she teased, "has patience been a part of my character?"

"True enough. But tensions are running high right now, and it would not do for speculation to run through the city unchecked." He must have noticed her scowl. "All right. I can let you know that I am going to go away for a few days. My brothers and I are reuniting in Midian to discuss some of what is occurring. I promise that as soon as I return, our decisions will be made known to all."

"Even the women?" she said, which produced a hearty groan from Ammon, accompanied by a nod of his head. Satisfied with that much of an answer, Abish concluded. "Fine. I guess I have no choice but to wait."

"Good." His countenance grew serious again as they walked along through a more secluded section of the market. "How are things with you? Is all well?"

She shrugged. "Well enough. Business has been demanding, but there is Teara to help. Jared has certainly been busy enough, but . . ." She hesitated.

"What?" he prompted.

She was so desperate to ease her mind and tell him what was troubling her. If only she had women friends who understood this burden, but Teara would never understand and Akah had no insights. Perhaps there was still a way to find some answers. "I have a supplicant," she tentatively began, "who, after several years of marriage, has not been able to have children. Have I . . . has *she*," Abish checked herself, "done something to make God displeased? Is that why she is still barren?"

"Abish. 'Barren' is a strong term to use. I don't know how old this *supplicant* is, but," he grinned, "when she is as old as Father Abraham's Sarah when she conceived, then she has permission to complain."

Abish dropped her gaze. *Ammon is right*, she thought. At only twenty and four years, she had no right to complain.

He put a hand on her shoulder. "God does not punish women by depriving them of their greatest joy. There is so much more we must understand. Tell her to have faith and be—"

"Yes, I know," she sighed. "*Patient.*"

* * *

Some of the answers came as the dry season ran its course.

Ammon had recently returned to Ishmael, and word came that a city-wide meeting was to be held, inclusive of *everyone* who wished to attend.

Word trickled down that their high king was ailing and would not live much longer. It was also said that the newly elected king himself would join them to speak encouraging words. The day of the council, Abish frantically tried to finish up her work, but a difficult case had her reluctant to leave the man's side and so she sent Teara to join the others in the public square by the old Sun Temple. Finally, though, she had set the man's leg, made him comfortable with careful instructions given to his wife, and was free to leave.

The pathway was all but deserted. She quickly crossed the river and made her way to the palace wall. By the time Abish arrived, there was already a massive throng and she had no way of finding Jared. How she'd wanted to be by his side! She tried to push her way through the crowd. It was hopeless, however. She had to be content to watch from the back. Knowing she had probably missed most of the king's address and Ammon's speech as well, she listened to her new sovereign's words, all the while looking for Jared's head in the crowd.

". . . We shall be brought to stand before Him to be judged, that we have not stained our swords in the blood of our brethren since He imparted His word unto us and has made us clean thereby," he was saying. Abish strained to hear all of his words. Never before had she heard such an idea. "For even if our brethren seek to destroy us," he continued, "we will hide away our swords, yea, even we will bury them deep in the earth, that they may be kept bright as a testimony that we have never used them. And at the last day, if our brethren destroy us, we will go to our God and be saved."

A great cry went up throughout the crowd as the Spirit testified of this. "Yes! Yes!" the people shouted. "Let us bury them!"

At first, Abish wondered why this outward act was even necessary. They had already decided to lay down their weapons and not fight against their brethren anymore. But then she realized that perhaps that was the only way for them to truly testify that they had changed as a people: to bury their weapons just as they had chosen to bury their sins. The Spirit testified this so strongly to her that Abish wanted to cry out as well.

Abish finally saw Jared as the crowd cheered the king's name. He was raising his fist and cheering with the others. But as she watched him walk with the other councilmen through the multitude, gathering the swords and weapons that hung at the men's sides, she suddenly realized the sacrifice that he was making. As the pile in the midst of them grew larger and larger, she could not look upon them merely as weapons of destruction being buried, but Jared's workmanship, his skill . . . his pride being destroyed! Thinking she would find him when they were finished, she instead saw that he was no longer part of the crowd.

After some searching, she found Jared alone in his shop, destroying his unsold wares.

As the acrid smell of melting steel assaulted her nose, she could barely see him amid the smoke and steam. "Jared," she called gently. "I'm . . . I'm sorry. All your work."

He turned to her and smiled a bit sadly. "That's not why I left so quickly. I was ashamed that I ever thought these would be needed. Apparently my faith is weak enough that I thought we might still go to war."

But Abish knew that wasn't true. Some days Jared had enough faith for the both of them.

"Are you coming home?" she asked, sensing the hurt he was trying to hide.

"In a while. I think I need to be alone."

Trying to hide her own hurt, she kissed him gently and left.

4

In the months that followed, while the people both rejoiced at their decision and then mourned the high king's death, Abish watched as Jared's business began to suffer under these latest political instabilities. Under the watchful eye of the Lamanite armies, trade had become difficult with the neighboring cities, making it difficult to procure all of the supplies Jared needed. He tried to act as if it didn't bother him—but she knew it was taking its toll. When she found herself anxious to receive the small tokens of food and supplies from her patrons that before now she had been quick to give away, Abish knew she needed to finally discuss her plan with him, to make him see there was perhaps no other way.

"I'm at the mercy of the expanding areas," she explained as they shared a meal one evening, trying to work reason into her argument. "I can barely walk the distance from the Old City to the new settlements at the northern wall in the course of a day. And when there is a particularly difficult case, one that I must spend hours with, I'm lucky if I see one or two other patrons that day."

"What are you suggesting, Abish?" Jared asked.

"I need a central location. One where I can keep the most critically injured and where others can come to me. As the city grows, I can see no other way."

"And where would you suggest you do this? There's not enough room here and I doubt the king would appreciate the palace being turned into a sick ward. Where else would you go?"

"I know you were opposed to it when we first married." She tried to rein in her enthusiasm and took a deep breath before starting again. "But, you see, once the Order was dissolved, my father's possessions were rightfully given back to me. It's a waste that my childhood home should sit abandoned, unused, when it could do so much good."

Jared frowned and spoke quickly. "I know that you grew up differently than I did as the daughter of a powerful healer and that you are used to luxuries. I thought you could accept being married to a *poor* blacksmith."

Abish bristled. It had been many years since she'd lived that way and she had never complained about their life before. "That's not fair, Jared. And my marriage-rights state that everything I own belongs to you anyway."

"I don't need charity."

"There is no charity in this decision." Abish stood and began to clear away the remains of their scarcely touched evening meal. "It's the perfect solution. Besides, the way things have been going lately—" She stopped herself by biting her tongue.

Jared stood and walked toward the door. He said, "I am still the man of this family," before closing it behind him.

* * *

Abish tried to keep busy the remainder of the week so that she wouldn't have time to see much of Jared. He seemed to have the same goal in mind because aside from a few moments in passing, they'd scarcely said two words to each other. And they wouldn't, Abish fumed, until Jared started to be more reasonable. Anxious for someone to commiserate with, she spoke with Akah, who nodded politely but could hardly understand Abish's position, since it had always been obvious that in Akah's family, Laban had the first and final word.

When she tried to talk to Teara one day about her frustration, it wasn't much better. And it wasn't just because her friend was younger and unmarried. Abish couldn't imagine Teara ever questioning her spouse's judgment. So how could she get Teara to understand that if Jared would only let go of some of his pride, everything would be so much better?

"He's just hurting," was Teara's response as they finished up their work day. "Ishmael's struggles have been hard on many of the men."

"I know." Abish shifted the heavy bag of supplies on her back, thinking this only proved her point. "So why won't he even consider it? I could help twice as many people this way and, well, we could sell our present home to one of the immigrants. With the money we earn from the sale and from the increase of patrons I could help, there would never be a need to worry about where our next meal would come from again. In fact, you could even come and stay with us. Think how comfortable we'd all be."

"Now who's being proud?"

Abish wasn't sure if she could take hearing the words that came next, even from Teara. "Jared has always felt like you didn't need him. No, don't try and deny it. And now, his worst fears are coming true. Living in your parents' home would be the final measure of defeat for him. He needs to feel like a man."

"The way I feel like a woman?" She ignored the hurt in Teara's eyes at her outburst. "Do you think it has been easy for me? I move freely around the countryside practicing in a man's profession." She gulped. "With no children to call my own. Do you think I don't see how the other women look at me? Like they're not sure if they should associate with me because I'm so . . . so unnatural."

Teara paused before answering. "And would you change that? Would you give up what you are—*who* you are—to be like them?" She spoke softly. "And yet, by making these demands, you're asking Jared to give up who *he* is."

Abish frowned, feeling like she was being pushed into a corner and forced to make a decision she wasn't ready to make. And so she said nothing more.

* * *

As if to prove that she was more independent than she felt, Abish left the next day without saying a word to Jared. She packed a light lunch and climbed up the mountainous pass. When her childhood home came into view, she paused only a moment at the crumbling rock arch that bordered the property before crossing under to find herself in the untended gardens. The scent of hibiscus mingled with the morning's fresh air as Abish walked between the overgrown rows of hedges and flowering shrubs. She reached out and stroked the soft petals of a nearby bloom and sighed deeply. The emotional distance she had felt between her and Jared now coupled with the reality of their physical separation, and she suddenly wasn't sure if she should have even come here. Perhaps she'd acted like a child, running away when things were difficult.

But she wasn't ready to be reasonable. Not yet.

Her favorite bench was still tucked away in a corner of the garden. She sat and ate the corn cakes she'd wrapped up. It was nice to have a moment, she thought, without any demands. With no one needing her. She would have to do this more often. Wiping a few crumbs from her lap, she stood and made her way back toward the house. When she found herself at the front door, she chuckled, realizing that she was again hesitating to open it, just like she had when she had been sent home from the palace after being a playmate to the king's daughter for many years. She hesitated then because she had felt she didn't belong there anymore. For some reason, that feeling had not entirely changed.

The house emitted a musty odor as she stepped inside. Small swirls of dust flew up as the hem of her dress swept across the floor, and she coughed slightly. Abish immediately went to one of the windows and opened it. The fresh air and sunlight immediately cast a different aura on her surroundings, and as she walked through the halls, Abish found she could still evade most of the ghosts that lingered there.

Her father's room was now devoid of all of his inventions and healing implements. Some of these Abish had taken for her own use. It made her happy to think that they were still being used to heal and succor her people, because that had been her father's mission while he was alive. The compassion her father had always shown to their people, even in their wickedness, had always had a great impact on her own work. And it also must have been the reason God had been merciful and shared such great truths with him in a vision before he died. He had not been a perfect man by any means, but surely God knew the intent of Shelem's heart.

Her mother's room had also long been cleared of all of its belongings. They had given them to some of the poorer residents of the city—a thought that would have made Saranhi grimace—but there was still a slight hint of the sandalwood and cedar fragrance that had clung to her clothes. Abish began to wonder if that was the true reason why she had wanted to keep, or even stay in, this house—the thought that perhaps her mother would come "home" one day. But there had been no word of her after that eventful day when they had been reunited in King Lamoni's palace.

Abish stood still and let her mind think back. It had been a shock to see her mother after all those years apart, but an even greater shock came when Abish learned that Saranhi was now married to Lehonti, the wicked commander of the Lamanite army. They'd had only the briefest time together to undo some of the animosity between them, and then her mother had fled to keep her husband from discovering Abish's presence and exacting revenge upon both her and Jared. So this meant no further reconciliation. No chance to share with her the gospel message.

No time to relearn what it was like to have a mother.

It took Abish a few more minutes to wander through the many hallways, and with each step she felt her frustration over Jared's attitude returning. To think that all of this was going to waste! But no matter how hard she tried, she couldn't think of any way to convince him that she was right. He could only see this as charity—a blow to his pride. It didn't matter that she was giving it to him as a token of her devotion to him. In fact, he had never truly accepted what she did, even though it was so much a part of who she was. Maybe that meant he didn't really accept her as she was.

As the imaginary argument played out in her mind, she almost believed that she could hear their voices echoing through the empty hallway. She stopped just outside her old nursemaid's room and hesitated. No. There were no voices. She was only imagining things. And yet . . .

How often she had heard her parents' heated words coming down these same hallways, their angry words weaving themselves around the corners like a sinister omen until they finally found her huddled under the covers in her room. In a habit-like gesture, she flung her hands over her ears as if to stop the memory.

Oh, Jared!

Now a part of her was glad they didn't have children. What would they have thought of their arguments lately?

Feeling duly chastised, she made the short walk to her father's grave. As she cleared away some of the dead plants and debris, she found her vision growing blurry. "I'm not very proud of myself right now," she said softly. "You taught me so much, Father. But there were some things you didn't teach me." Then she looked up through the trees and addressed a different parent. "Heavenly Father, when will I learn patience and become humble? Why is it so hard for me to forgive?"

A brilliant white macaw burst out of the tree and let out a loud squawk. It was not quite the answer she was looking for, but she laughed and wiped away her tears. Then, she went back to her true home.

* * *

It was dusk when Abish found herself within the city proper. Fortunately she didn't need more than the light of the fading sun to find her way back home.

As she opened the door, her eyes took a moment to adjust to the light of the oil lamp that shone dimly in the corner of the house. Soon, she recognized Jared's strong frame standing by the opposite wall. He was hanging up some of the more expensive tools, which he dared not leave unattended in his shop, but turned almost immediately when he sensed her presence. In the darkness, she strained to make out the look in Jared's eyes. Was it happiness . . . or mere surprise?

All doubts were instantly washed away as he came toward her. His hands rested tenderly on the sides of her face, stroking her brow, her cheek, her lips. As his hands cupped her face, she met his eyes and saw love and forgiveness there. She knew that in this moment no words of explanation or remorse needed to be spoken.

Later, as they lay in the darkness, Abish savored the warmth of Jared's embrace. Then she took a deep breath and hoped the words she had been rehearsing on her journey home would do her feelings justice. "Jared, I'm sorry about these last few weeks. I know how hard things have been for you lately and my stubbornness only made it harder. I've had some time to think and I realize that it was *my* pride that kept getting in our way. I cared more about being right than I did about our feelings for one another. Will you forgive me?"

Now she heard Jared take a breath as well. "Oh, Abish. I'm sorry too. It's just that, with all that's been going on lately, I'd begun to wonder if . . ."

"I still needed you?" Abish finished.

Jared sighed. "I doubt you've ever really *needed* me. But I was beginning to wonder if you still loved me."

Abish sat up, crying out, "*Love* you? How could you ever doubt that? You are my heart, my life! I remember all those years ago when I thought you had drowned. I felt as if I had died that day as well. And does it really matter that through my skill I have the means to support myself? If anything, it should prove my love to you even more—that I don't *have* to be with you, I *choose* to be with you."

She could hear Jared shift in the darkness. "I don't know how to explain it. To no longer be able to provide for you, along with us not having any children . . . I feel as if God is displeased with me."

Glad for the darkness so Jared would not misinterpret the smile on her face, she said gently, "You don't think I have had the same feelings? Ammon told me, though, that God doesn't punish us that way and that there's a reason for the course of our lives. We have to be patient and believe that He will bless us with all that we need when the time is right."

"I just want us to always be together," he whispered against her cheek.

"We will. Always." Abish brushed his lips with hers.

5

It had been the hottest dry season anyone could remember, and even though she waited anxiously like the others for the cooling rains of summer that would soon come, Abish was happier than she had been in a long time. Teara had accepted her apology, and it was as if she and Jared were newly committed to each other. It reminded her so much of their courtship that she often found herself blushing like a new bride. Even Jared commented that he felt the same way he had the day she had stood before him to become his wife.

She would never forget that day.

She had scarcely been nervous at all that morning, considering that Jared was her best friend. But when she'd heard the shouts, "The bridegroom is coming! The bridegroom is coming!" Abish had suddenly felt more nervous than she'd ever been in her life. The cries prompted Teara to quickly tighten up the remaining stays on her embroidered tunic and assure Abish that none of the flowers had dislodged themselves from her lustrous hair.

"You look beautiful," her friend had assured her.

Touching her scar on her left cheek, Abish smiled when she remembered that she had once thought it would make her too hideous for anyone to consider marrying her. But that thought had been dispelled more than once, to where she often forgot it was even there. "Am I ready?" she asked.

"Only you can answer that."

Abish embraced her friend and smiled. "Tell them I am ready."

As her thoughts returned to the present, she turned to finish up some mending that she had been putting off—her time having been spent in more enjoyable endeavors recently. While she sat outside in the shade that the house was now providing, Abish felt glad that she had turned over much of her healing responsibilities to Teara. Even though she missed her work, seeing the contented look on Jared's face more than made up for the loss. Jared had used his ingenuity and skills and had discovered that he was just as adept in working with wood as he was with metal, leaving him almost as busy as he had been before. This meant a few more lonely hours at home again, but she would survive.

Soon she was sore from hunching over her mending and was relieved when it was time to make her daily trip to the market.

As Abish walked along past the dwindling stalls and vendors, however, she was disappointed that fresh produce was becoming scarce. She would have to take some more lessons from Akah and try growing her own small garden behind the house. Stopping next at the butchers, Abish saw that the usual cuts of meat were also difficult to find. How much longer could Ishmael support its swelling population? Staring down at her nearly empty basket, Abish shrugged and returned home to prepare yet another meal.

Gratefully, Akah had brought by some "extra" corn cakes that morning. Along with the venison she had just purchased, it would make a plain yet satisfying meal. But as Abish began to season the meat, she felt herself grow slightly dizzy. And when the smell of the bloody animal flesh reached her nostrils, her stomach turned. Clenching her sides, she barely made it to the ravine behind the house before her stomach purged its meager contents. Dabbing her perspiring face with a little cool water, she sat down in a shady spot until the worst of her nausea passed.

She made a drink of wild ginger, but still felt queasy. The last thing she needed was for Jared to worry about her, so she'd just have to try to keep it a secret. She got back to work, but try as she might, Abish could *not* find a way to prepare the venison so it would appeal to her. She decided to replace it with some leftover squash and sliced goat cheese over the corn cakes to provide some extra substance.

Jared, finally returning, didn't seem to mind the lighter fare, eager instead to explain to her the latest news among the Council.

"Ammon has gone once again to confer with our new king, but it seems inevitable," he revealed. "The Amulonites and Amalekites are joining with the Lamanites in Jerusalem and some of the surrounding cities and are making preparations for war. Now that the high king is dead, they won't recognize Anti-Nephi-Lehi as their sovereign but seek to replace him with one of their own. But we've covenanted not to fight them."

"And we've buried all of our weapons," Abish added hesitantly. "We agreed that we would rather die than take up arms against our brethren."

Jared saw the concerned look on her face and quickly said, "Don't worry. I'll take care of you, and God will protect us. Perhaps the king will have some answers for us."

"The king is back in Nephi," she reminded him. "If they come against *us*, what should we do?"

"I don't know," Jared admitted. "But I know we will not fight."

* * *

By midyear, there was a tension in the city that was almost palpable. Yet Abish found herself nearly oblivious to it. She was too worried about her own situation. At first she could scarcely allow her mind to accept the reality of it—after all, how many times before had her body betrayed her? But then the days passed and the signs grew stronger until even she found it difficult to doubt.

She was with child.

She first told Teara. It had been surprisingly difficult for Abish to put into words what she had hoped for all these years. But she found she didn't have to; Teara understood.

She cupped Abish's hands in hers and said, "I knew it. Your prayers are finally being answered, my friend."

With tears clouding their eyes, the two women embraced. But Abish was reluctant to speak of it to anyone else and bade Teara to keep her secret. After all, they had no sure proof; only time would tell. But it was as if some superstitious cloud had returned because she was afraid to declare her state for fear her joy would bring immediate retribution. It was not until she felt the first stirrings within her that she dared tell Jared. After all, he had known disappointment as well.

She had waited until the remnants of their evening meal had been cleared away and then watched for a few moments as Jared sketched some new designs for the wooden lintels several patrons had ordered. His skill made her proud. The light from the lamp reflected off of his black hair as he was engrossed in his work. Her breath caught in her throat as she realized what this would mean to him. Especially if the child was a son. He could follow in his father's trade and be taught the words of the prophets at Jared's knee. Of course, a private part of her soul yearned for a daughter to raise. Abish imagined braiding her long hair and teaching her how to pick the most succulent wild roots for their supper. Hopefully Akah could help teach her to cook well. Surely her daughter would have every advantage that she herself had longed for: a caring mother, a proper upbringing. Her daughter would be taught how to be a good wife and mother. She would never feel as if she didn't belong.

"Jared?" she said casually as she picked up a basket she'd been weaving.
"Hmm?"

She smiled. "I know you're busy. But I have another project I thought perhaps you could work on."

Jared stopped and looked up at her before he spoke. "I know that you've been asking about a system that would bring water from the river to the house, but I don't think that's very practical right now. It makes much more sense to make use of water that collects in the barrel that I've made."

Abish restrained herself from responding to that line of conversation. "Actually that's not what I had in mind. Instead . . . well, I was thinking that you could take some of that leftover wood and put it to good use."

"Doing what?"

She gulped. "Making a cradle."

Abish watched as the realization of what she'd said dawned in his eyes. "Do you . . . are you saying . . . ?" Apparently speechlessness was contagious. He crawled across the floor to her and gently rested a hand on her stomach. "Are you with child?"

She nodded. "Teara confirmed it. It has been three moons now and so there is little cause for concern this time."

"A child!"

Abish could almost hear his unspoken hope. *A son!*

"He is growing strong," she prattled on. "I've hardly been sick at all anymore and last night, I felt him stirring within me."

Jared's hand pressed more firmly as if he longed to feel it as well. And then he jumped to his feet. "I'll start work on it right away. When I am done, no babe will ever rest his head more comfortably!"

Abish laughed. "You still have plenty of time. Come. Sit with me and let us give thanks for this miracle. Our lives are now complete."

But as they knelt in prayer, a howl echoed off in the distance. Abish trembled slightly, and as she thought of the life growing inside her, she found herself offering a silent prayer.

Please, Father. Let this child be born. Let us be happy.

* * *

It should have been the happiest time in Abish's life. As she watched her body change and grow and felt that she herself was growing stronger in both body and spirit than she had ever been, it should have comforted her. But she was far from feeling at peace.

After another meeting in Midian, Ammon eventually returned to them to report that, indeed, a vast army was being prepared to come against them. The Lamanites had been stirred up sufficiently to anger and would try to overthrow the existing government in Nephi, but it was inevitable that they would also target what had become its spiritual center: Ishmael. And because the summer had brought with it a drought instead of the cooling rains that would cause their crops to flourish, it made the Valley of Alma passable much earlier than usual—which meant that an attack could come at any time. But the people were standing firm; they would indeed stand by their vow and not take up arms again. Thinking that the only possible alternative would be to fortify the city against the invaders, Abish was somewhat dismayed to discover that no such defenses were being prepared. One night before bed, she shared her thoughts with Jared.

"What will happen if the army attacks the city and we are found defenseless?"

His brow furrowed as he responded. "Then we will be tested as we've never been tested before."

Abish lowered her head. "I'm not sure I have enough faith to stand by and watch that happen."

Jared took her in his arms. "You have more faith than you know. But we must remember our oath. Should we go to battle and save ourselves in this life, only to lose ourselves in the next?"

"But I want us to live, *together*. I want us to have the long, happy life I always imagined we would. I thought I had lost you once. I don't know if I can lose you again."

"You won't." He took her tightly in his arms. "The Lord will protect us. We have become a righteous people. We have nothing to fear."

Abish knew his words were meant to comfort him as much as her, because she could feel his arms trembling around her. She tried to return some of that comfort. "Then I will be by your side if they come."

Jared reached down and touched her stomach, now round and firm. "Now I'm not sure I have enough faith to watch that happen. I would rather know that you are safe somewhere and that, no matter what, part of me will always be with you. And yet you've already refused to go to your aunt and uncle's house in Middoni. It's far enough to the south that they may escape all of this."

Abish shook her head. "No. I won't leave Ishmael. It's my home, and my place is with you."

"Then the two of us will face this together."

"Not only the two of us," Abish prompted. When Jared smiled knowingly and placed his hand on her stomach, she added, "And God will be with us as well."

6

The days marched on, and Abish found that her faith, indeed, was being tested as never before. Though she should have been in confinement, the rules of protocol had grown slack as more news of the Lamanite army continued to filter in. Trying to find anything she could do to keep busy and pass the days more quickly, she eagerly accepted when Teara came to her one morning and suggested that they gather more healing plants and herbs. Scouring the hillside, Abish found it difficult, however, to fully enjoy the beautiful flowers that had seemed to grow overnight from the recent rain they had finally been blessed with, painting the land around them. The splendor of her surroundings did comfort her somewhat, though. It reminded her that God was all around them.

Her basket full, Abish went to join Teara. Sorting through the plants, separating the leaves and berries from the stems, she could almost imagine this was just another day of work. But every time she looked at her friend's eyes and saw the worry there, she was also reminded of what could soon be on their doorstep. Still she kept working, her hands moving in a rhythmic fashion while her heart and soul prayed to God. It was not the first prayer of its kind that had been offered.

The night before as she had lain awake yet again, unable to sleep even after Jared had found his escape, she had pled with her Maker. "Please, Father. Please protect us."

Even when the morning sun had burned through the heavy mist, sleep still had not found her. But somehow she had felt comforted as the new day began. Somehow, she knew that God had heard her prayers. Having collected sufficient cantharis, gelsenium, and other wound-treating herbs, Abish and Teara parted company. Because she promised Jared she would bring him lunch, Abish headed toward the marketplace. There she saw Ammon. He greeted her and, having seemed to develop the discernment of the late prophet, Alma, he looked at her with some concern.

With a frown he said, "Are you doing all right?"

She shrugged.

"I know this is testing us all to our limits," he offered, "but we must have faith."

"I'm trying. Each day I keep thinking that we'll hear better news. That by some miracle they'll grow tired of hating us and come around."

Ammon shook his head. "I don't think it will be that simple. But we cannot confront evil with more evil. That *used* to be the path we took." He grew more animated. "Just think what will happen when the cycle has been broken—when a group of people who have always been bent on murder and bloodshed suddenly steps back and offers only peace to their brothers! It could change the course of everything." Abish could feel Ammon's passion behind his words and tried to lean on his strength. "We made our covenant with God to *show* Him our faith. Perhaps now," he said and touched her gently on the arm, "God wants to know if we are willing to *act* upon it."

* * *

The harvesting was over and Ishmael's residents had been waiting and watching. As time passed, they were almost lulled into thinking that an attack would never occur. But then word came that the edge of the Lamanite phalanx had been seen from the valley ridge at Amulon, and by the time the messenger had been fortified with food and drink and sent ahead to warn the capital city of Nephi, the people of Ammon had begun to prepare themselves in the only way they could now—by offering humble prayers. Abish had been treating a supplicant on the far edge of the city when the news arrived, so she hurried home. But when she was just in view of the small hut, she thought of Jared waiting for her inside and she couldn't be strong anymore.

With a hand supporting her swollen belly, she hurried to a clearing in the forest and found herself at the familiar winding stream that had been their secret meeting place in those early days of newfound love. The water curved past the arching birch tree, and she wondered if it still held the many tears of joy that had run down her face back then. Now, she added silent tears of pain. Soon there was a noise behind her and she heard the familiar, uneven footsteps coming up the path.

"Abish?"

She wanted to hide as if that could delay the inevitable.

"I saw you running off." Jared said nothing else, but came and sat down on the rock next to her. After a moment he reached up high above her into the branches of the tree. When his hand came back down, he held a beautiful red bromeliad and began to put it in her hair. "This flower," he said, "has managed to survive clinging to the branches of this tree. It has only the air to give it what it needs to thrive and grow. But somehow it survives. We will survive this."

His words trailed off as she buried her head against his chest.

* * *

Somewhere in the distance, they heard the first sounds of the approaching army. The noise caused Abish's heart to beat with such ferocity that she could barely stand. Shaking the pounding of blood from her ears, she clung tightly to Jared's hand, afraid she was squeezing the life out of it. His own hand was trembling slightly, but the look in his eyes was solid and calm. Teara stood at her right. Akah and Laban joined them as well on this field along with the thousands of others who had come to show they had more faith in God than fear of man.

The sun was hot and beat down on the solemn gathering. A few of the younger children were whimpering—whether it was because of the temperature or from being made to stand still, she wasn't sure. Abish wiped away some sweat that threatened to drop into her eyes and blur her vision. As she did, she felt a cramp in her side. She had felt a few cramps earlier that morning, but they had not been as intense as this one. She ignored it, along with the occasional shouts that came echoing through the narrow gorge. She wished she had been as brave as those who had chosen to stand at the outlet of the pass, because they had the chance of being among the first to witness the miracle that might occur. When Abish had arrived in the clearing, however, her steps had slowed, though she could not blame that completely on the added weight she carried within her.

She had kept Jared's words of encouragement inside her all through the night. Now they came back to her full force as, to her amazement, she saw a literal wave sweep over the people as they began to prostrate themselves on the ground. In response, Jared helped her into a kneeling position, while he, himself, lay down and spread out his arms above his head. She could hear his muffled words of prayer, and she began to offer up her own with her hands raised to the heavens. Though a thousand voices spoke, the words of their hearts were the same, "Oh Father, be with us. Look down on us, Thy children. Soften the hearts of our brethren."

Her pleas echoed with those around her until their joined voices sounded like a rushing wind soaring up into the sky. Just then another pain caused her to grab her side. This time, she couldn't silence her cries and Jared looked up in dismay.

"Are you all right?"

She nodded her head. "I'm fine." It passed and she held out her hand to him. He took it and pressed his lips against her palm.

From her position, Abish could still see up ahead and she shielded her arms from the sun to get a better view. The trees were still so dense in that area; it was difficult to tell what was happening. Were they still coming? Where was the army? Her back ached from being on her knees and she was frustrated that her physical discomfort was distracting her so much from her praying. She closed her eyes again and began to pray more earnestly. Another spasm gripped her and her entire world was drawn into it. But she realized that it was not her cries that had been heard aloud. Instead, the sound came from up ahead.

Her eyes jerked open and she trembled at what she saw.

"Jared!" her voice shook. "The army is attacking! Our . . . our people are being killed."

He sat up quickly to confirm what she said. "Yes. I see the warriors. They . . . are here."

"What do we do? There are children here! They are showing us no mercy!" The realization of what was happening made it difficult for her to think.

"Abish." Jared took her by the shoulders. "I know this is selfish, but . . . I want you to run. Go hide yourself!"

"No!" she shrieked as the cries in the distance grew louder. "I won't leave you!" Almost as if her fears were being internalized, her pains increased to where she doubled over in agony.

She heard Teara's insistent voice at her side. "When did you start your laboring?"

"This morning . . . I believe," she panted before another pain could overtake her. "But I thought little of it because it's still early—"

Jared caught her before she fell to the ground. "Teara, Akah, please take her away from here. I beg of you."

As her friends tried to drag her away, Abish grabbed Jared's arm. "We must be together. I must be with you!"

Jared's face was so full of love that she felt her heart breaking. "But don't you see?" he said. "No matter what happens here today, we will always be together. And you . . . you will survive and our child will survive. In that way, I will always be with you."

"And if we don't meet again in this life?" she cried as they parted.

Jared smiled a bit sadly. "Then I will be waiting for you in the next."

She stopped fighting against the two women and allowed herself to be led back to the palace. But her heart was having to endure more pain than her body as she moved farther and farther away from the field. She felt like Lot's wife—wanting to look behind her, back toward what she was leaving. But she knew that would only make things harder, so she kept her focus on the path ahead. Teara helped her up a steep incline that led to the palace.

"There's so much jungle on this side of the palace. I wish we could take a clearer path," Teara said as she tried to clear away as much of the heavy growth as she could.

"I think we need to stay as out of sight as we can, Teara." Abish paused to breathe and then had to stop altogether as another pain coursed over her.

"Should we just stop here?" Akah said, worry in her eyes as she turned back to Abish.

"I'm fine. Just keep moving," Abish ground out, then gestured her friends forward as the pain subsided. She pushed forward and tried to follow the best she could. As Teara and Akah disappeared into the jungle, trying to clear an easier path, Abish struggled to keep up.

Suddenly a scream rent the air.

As terror coursed through her, Abish pushed aside the heavy palm fronds until she came to a clearing. There, she saw Teara lying on the ground with a bloody gash on her left temple, while a crimson-streaked warrior crouched over her. Akah was sitting nearby, as still as if she'd been turned to stone.

At first Abish thought that Teara was dead, and she cried out. The warrior looked in her direction, and she locked eyes with the man. Time seemed to stop as she thought back to that day when Lehonti had stared her down like a hunter eager to capture his prey. But as she continued to look at the man, she realized those memories and this present reality were not the same. This "hunter" trembled as he stood there, and his eyes betrayed something akin to fear. In fact, as Abish looked more closely, she realized this was hardly even a man. He was only a boy in warrior's clothing.

Teara stirred, and Abish hurried to her, ignoring the danger. Hovering over her friend like a protective mother bird, Abish examined the gash on her friend's head. Then she realized the warrior, who seemed taken aback by her actions and stood as if unsure what to do, would most likely regain his faculties soon and act. Though her body was trembling, she looked up and calmly addressed him.

"We are not your enemy, and we wish you no harm. Let us go in peace."

For a moment it actually appeared as if he was considering the thought. But then his face twisted into a look of both anger and confusion. The man-child lifted up his cimeter and let out a loud piercing cry. Abish shuddered and pulled Teara to her. As she imagined the weapon being lowered on their heads, she closed her eyes and began to pray. "Oh God, forgive them. They've been taught these wrongs by their fathers. They don't understand! Please help us."

Then she waited for the blow to come. But it never came.

Tentatively opening her eyes, she looked around her. They were alone. The warrior was gone, his cimeter left abandoned in the dirt before Abish's knees. The three women struggled to their feet and stood in awe at the mercy they'd been shown.

"Thank you . . ." Abish whispered in the release of the breath she'd been holding, then another wave of pain immediately washed over her. "Ah!"

"Come," Teara said. "Let us find shelter."

7

"Abish?"

The soft voice beckoned to her and drew her back from the pain that her world had been revolving around for hours.

"Here, drink this."

She felt cool water on her tongue and swallowed involuntarily, though much of it trickled down her neck. "Can you sit up a little more?" Teara tugged slightly on her arm, and Abish obeyed. She had no will to resist.

Abish looked around her old room at the palace, where she'd been forced to sleep after Princess Anrah had become jealous of her. It was so many years ago. The pain was making her delirious. She almost thought she could hear the princess's whining voice.

"She doesn't look very good." No. It was only Akah prattling on.

"She's doing fine," Teara said a little harshly.

Abish struggled to rise. "Your injuries. You should go and attend to them . . . I'll be fine."

"They're nothing," Teara protested. "It was just a flesh wound."

Abish collapsed against the bed again and said sadly, "Is there any news? Are Jared and Laban . . . ?" she asked hopefully.

"Everything is still chaos outside these walls," her friend said softly. "You must think of your baby now."

Abish felt as if there were things that Teara was reluctant to tell her. A sharp pain in her abdomen caused Abish to wrap her arms around herself and forget her questions once more. The baby! The intensity of the pain jerked her back to full consciousness. It subsided shortly, but she had scarcely taken a breath before it returned. She gasped, "I think . . . that the baby . . . is coming." Teara leapt into action. Enveloped by the contraction, Abish at least knew that she could leave herself in her friend's capable hands. Teara immediately ordered Akah to bring more water and look for more clean linens. Akah rushed from the room as quickly as her plump body could carry her. While she was gone, Teara helped Abish into a crouching position and continued to offer encouraging words.

"It won't be long now. You're doing fine. Just think—your baby will soon be in your arms. Now, try not to push until I tell you to. You're so close now. It won't be long."

Teara wiped Abish's brow with a wet cloth and dripped bitter liquid into her mouth to ease the pain. Time stood still yet seemed to be racing forward as Abish tried to make sense of Akah's senseless prattling and Teara's firm commands. In a moment of panic, she realized what was happening and tried to call out to Jared. But then Abish remembered he was not with her and she felt as if she were drowning in pain. The images of what may be happening outside the protection of the palace overcame her and she lurched to one side, luckily the one where Teara had placed a large jar. After it was discreetly emptied, Teara said, "That's a good sign. I think we're about ready."

Akah expertly knelt behind Abish, supporting her so she could focus all of her energy on the task at hand, because her body was indeed giving the message that it was soon. Up until this moment, she had only seen the miraculous process at work. And now, it was her own body fulfilling its ultimate design.

It seemed like forever before the squalling baby fell into Teara's outstretched hands. As Teara placed the tiny, mottled body on Abish's chest, she smiled. "You have a son."

"A son!"

Abish looked down at the perfect, squirming baby and released the sob she had been holding in.

A son! For Jared.

Whatever pain she had been feeling vanished away as Abish stared down into the tiny creature's face. The baby was alert yet still, and when his tiny lips began to move in a sucking motion, Abish placed him to her breast. She leaned back into Akah's strong motherly arms and let herself be carried away on the wave of contentment she felt. To think that on this day one little life had become dearer to her than almost any other was beyond her comprehension.

Thank you, Father.

Suddenly, Abish felt her body lurch upward again. She screamed once more. There was no time for thought as her body again tightened in rhythmic urgency.

"What . . . what's happening!" she gasped.

Teara smiled. "I had wondered . . . But I didn't want to give you hope and then find out I was wrong!"

"What . . . what?"

Soon another tiny cry filled the room, and the surprise on Akah's face added to Teara's own jubilant expression. Abish then saw what her friend held in her hands.

"You have another baby. A daughter."

Now they were all crying as Abish looked down into the precious face of her second child. Her arms and heart were now full, and for a moment, everything else that had happened that day was drowned out. Akah and Teara cleaned up the tiny space in silence while Abish looked down in amazement at the gifts in her arms. Her joy could not be more full, though she had one more thought before her weary body was allowed to rest.

A daughter.

For me.

* * *

When Abish awoke several hours later, though her belly longed for the plate of fruit resting on a nearby table, her eyes searched for her children, searched to know that they were here. And safe. As she tried to stand up, she found that her legs felt as if she hadn't used them for years, and she clung to the side of the table for support. Her body was exhausted, but she made her way over to where they were resting. They were so tiny! Of course, when she took them home, they would sleep in the cradle that Jared had made. If only she had known to have him make two! *Some healer I am*, she thought. To not have known that her own body was carrying twins. Perhaps that had seemed like too much of a miracle to ask for.

When Teara returned, she had finally managed to stop looking at her sleeping infants and start munching on a ripe mango. It had already begun to revive her body, and now she turned anxiously to her friend to have her spirit fortified as well. But when she saw her friend's blood-stained clothes, she wasn't sure that would even be possible.

"I should be by your side tending to the wounded," Abish said. "I feel as if I've abandoned my people."

Teara shook her head. "You're a mother now. You have a different set of priorities."

"Surely by now you know the outcome? Please tell me what is happening. I must know."

Teara took a deep breath. She looked so weary. "It appears that over a thousand of our own were taken from us, along with several Lamanites who were mistakenly cut down in the frenzy. But that is not all," she said as she grew animated. "After seeing how many of our righteous were falling under their swords, many of the warriors began to throw down their weapons and prostrated themselves on the ground. They have accepted the gospel and are, at this moment, at Ammon's side learning of God."

Abish tried to catch her breath and clasped her hands together as she thought of the young warrior boy who had attacked Teara. "Then our sacrifice has served a purpose. And surely those who we lost are with God." But she knew by the look on Teara's face that she had not told all she knew. The intense sorrow that was written there could only mean one thing. Her words caught in her throat. "W . . . where is he? Where is my husband?"

Teara reached out her hand and led her from the room and down the hall. Abish had to will herself to follow, and though each footstep hurt her body, they pierced her heart more.

Jared's body had been placed on a woven sleeping mat, a cloth of blue silk draped over him. Several women from her village stood at attention, and Abish realized that out of respect for her, they had chosen to ready her husband's body to be seen this way. Fighting back the tears, she slowly walked toward him. His black hair spilled out from beneath the covering—almost like a death shroud already had been placed upon him. Abish drew back the cloth until it rested upon his knees. With most of his body uncovered, she could see the numerous cuts he had sustained. She could also see where the sword had fatally pierced his side. A clean thrust. It would have been so easy to close—to where it would not even be seen. But it had been too deep. And there were some wounds even she could not heal.

As long as she lived, Abish knew she would never forget this moment. Stumbling back to her room, she collapsed on the bed and began to sob. Teara came and put her arm on her back, rubbing it soothingly. But Abish pushed her hand away. "I need to be alone. Please."

She heard the door shut behind her friend, and she wanted to let out a howl. There had to be something she could do to release some of this pain! But she would only awaken her children. Crawling across the floor, she touched her hands to each of their heads and realized that it no longer mattered that she was suffering. She was a mother now, and her pain would have to wait.

"I'm sorry, my dear little ones," she cooed softly. "You only have me now. But I promise you . . ." she lifted her eyes up to the heavens, ". . . and I promise You as well, that I will be strong. I will survive."

Land of Ishmael
82 BC

8

Abish could hear her children's voices outside, and she sighed.

Little Miriam's squeal cut above the raucous sound of Jarum's roars. She paused at her grinding and waited to see if her four-year-old daughter would rush into the house to announce that, once again, her doll was being held for ransom by the wicked "Nehor." When no such announcement was made, she returned to her work, but not without keeping a vigilant ear open for any more altercations. At least now the children were of an age to understand and give strict heed to her warning not to wander too close to the river or beyond the large ceiba tree that stood at the crossroads leading to the city square. Fortunately, the other mothers also took an active role in seeing that no child went beyond the boundaries of normal play. While they did not always agree on what those boundaries were, Abish found comfort in knowing she no longer had the responsibility of caring for the injured who crossed the boundries. Since the babies' births, she had given up healing. Abish smiled. Teara had done well over the years, becoming as indispensable a healer to the people of Ishmael as Abish had once been.

But much had changed these last few years.

Though Ishmael had enjoyed a few years of peace, news came almost daily about the struggles that were occurring in the land of Zarahemla. After apostate groups had arisen a few years ago, led by wicked men who sought for power and glory in their position, the land seemed to be under a curse. One named Nehor had been particularly aggressive and had persuaded many people that priestcraft was not a sin. Abish's heart had been broken when she heard that this wicked man had cut down her beloved one-time teacher, Gideon. Even though shortly thereafter Nehor had suffered an ignominious death, it did little to soften the blow, because, Abish knew, when one evil man died, another was soon to take his place. And a different man had sought to be king of Zarahemla and had drawn away many followers to him, causing the Nephite army to go to war against him. Even Alma had fought and been injured.

Standing to work out a stiff muscle in her back, Abish walked over to the doorway to see if the sudden silence that had ensued meant that her children were still present—but finally behaving themselves. She first saw Miriam just beyond the garden. The child was hunched over a tiny pile of what appeared to be discarded avocado pits. With a curved stick, she was carefully digging holes in the ground and dropping the pits in. Patting the dirt back into place and obviously pleased with herself, she looked in Abish's direction with a huge grin.

"Mama! Look! I'm planting 'cado trees. Can I have some for dinner?"

Abish stifled a laugh and walked toward her, trying to figure out how to explain her daughter's misconception without disappointing her too much. "Darling, I'm afraid that it takes a long time for a tree that size to grow. And even longer for it to produce fruit. But, if you are patient, then by the time *you* have children, you'll have all the avocados you can eat!"

Miriam looked down at her mother's stomach. "I'll have a baby inside me like when Jarum and me were there? How will it get there?"

With a groan, Abish realized that children had a way of keeping conversations going indefinitely, because one answer only spurred on another question. To distract her, Abish looked around. "Where *is* your brother? He didn't go near the river, did he?"

"No, Mama. He's with 'Ancum. They're finding more frogs."

Abish glanced in the direction of the community's central area where groups of women were beginning to waterproof tents in preparation for the season of rain that was to come. The hour was growing late, but the heat still made all but the early mornings and late evenings too uncomfortable to do such work. Noticing a group of children playing ball, she looked for Jarum's stocky frame among them, but could not make out his head among the crowd. She did see Teancum's mother, however and, grabbing Miriam by the hand, she hurried toward her.

"Zeta, have you seen Teancum and Jarum?" she asked, pushing down the tremor of nervousness in her voice.

"Hmm? Oh, I suppose they're off being boys."

Abish took a deep breath, reminded of the difference in "boundaries" she'd been thinking of earlier. "When was the last time you saw them?"

The other woman, probably sensing that Abish's sense of urgency might reflect upon her own lack of concern, now responded defensively, "Well, when I left, they *were* playing by *your* hut. I have just returned from the river with my washing and saw no sign of them there. How long have they been missing?"

"Well, just a little while," she responded sheepishly. The other woman's expression implied what she now felt.

It was then out of the corner of her eye that Abish saw a flash of bright green—just the color of the loincloth that she had dressed Jarum in that morning. As his familiar *whoop* echoed across the clearing to give proof that it was him, she let out the breath she found she'd been holding. With an apologetic smile, she bid Zeta farewell and led Jarum and Miriam back to the house. Only when they were out of earshot did Abish find that her emotions had not been completely resolved by Jarum's reappearance.

"Jarum! Where were you?" she demanded, crouching down to eye level. "Do you know how you worried me? If anything had happened to you . . ."

Jarum stood silent for a moment, and then his voice quivered. "I'm sorry, Mama. I was just playing."

A quick stab of guilt now joined her concern. "Please tell me where you are going. I know that some of the other mothers are not as . . . anxious as I am about where their children play. But I need to know where you are. Always. Do you understand?"

"Yes, but," Jarum squeaked, "you're squeezing me too tight."

Abish quickly released her grip on his shoulders. "I'm sorry."

It was then she noticed a trace of guilt on her son's chubby face as well. "Jarum? What *were* you doing with Teancum?"

Jarum's arms had been clasped behind his back and, up until now, Abish hadn't thought to ask why. Now, she reached around him and took the object he had been holding in his hands. As she stared down at the jeweled dagger, Abish hoped to control her emotions better this time.

"We had to have it, Mama!" Jarum explained, shuffling his bare feet in the dirt. "We were trying to get a big frog out of a tree stump and needed somethin' to cut a hole, so I 'membered this and I know you told me not to touch it. I was going to put it right back and—"

Abish cut off her son's last sentence. "In the house. Now!"

Jarum ran ahead, reaching the house well before the others.

As they walked sullenly back to the house, Miriam, who Abish had all but forgotten, tugged on the hem of her tunic and whispered, "Is Jarum in trouble?"

"Yes," Abish whispered back. "And we're going to have a little talk."

"Uh-oh."

She found her son curled up in his sleeping hammock and wondered if the gentle rocking motion was soothing his troubled mind. "Jarum, please get out and stand before me while I talk to you."

After a moment, two little legs swung over the edge of the hammock. Soon, two little feet were touching the floor. But two dark eyes were still cast to the ground, and Abish had to clear her throat before he would look up at her. "I am very disappointed in you," she found her voice coming out a little harsher than she'd intended and she knelt down in front of her son, hoping that she could calm the torrent of emotions that threatened to come out. "Not only could you have injured yourself, but you disobeyed me by taking it."

"I didn't take it out of the sh . . . sh . . ."

"Sheath? That doesn't matter." Exasperated, Abish stood and took the dagger over to the stone box where she had kept it, along with other items that held too many memories to be seen on a daily basis. "Because of your disobedience, there must be a consequence," she said in a low voice. Turning to look at him, she regretted what she must do next. "Due to your actions, you . . . you will not be allowed to go to the Planting Festival next week. Now, wash up for dinner."

Jarum's eyes were so wide with disbelief that she could almost see into their depths. It hurt her to see his pain, but she had to do it! Didn't she? Even at such a tender age, her son had learned not to question her judgment and so instead of protesting, he turned back toward his hammock, shoulders sagging. "I'm not hungry," he whimpered. "I'm just going to go to bed."

* * *

Mealtime was, needless to say, a somber affair. Miriam hadn't spoken much since the incident, and it had been difficult to ignore the quiet sobbing that came from the corner of the house. After clearing away the eating mats, Abish prepared her daughter for bed and then waited until silence left her alone with her tormented mind.

Perhaps I've been too hard on him, she agonized. *After all, this is the first festival we've had since . . .*

Quietly removing her work-stained tunic and setting it on the pile of other dirty clothes, Abish looked around at her humble hut.

At first she had felt guilty retrieving the money she had hidden from Jared over the years, but it had been enough that she hadn't had to return to her former trade and could stay at home with her children. For that she had been grateful, because in so many other ways, the years had not been easy. Aside from a few hammocks and a sleeping mat, there was little else in the way of furnishings in their dwelling. A pile of well-used pottery sat in one corner. Another held their meager supply of clothing and personal effects in a large rush basket. It was tightly woven to keep out most of the curious creatures of the land and which, Abish discovered, when lined with tea tree leaves, prevented the musty smell that damp days often caused. Her eyes then scanned past her children's sleeping forms to the final corner, where the carved stone box stood.

As if an invisible force were moving her, Abish went toward it. Opening the lid, she saw the wooden carving that Ammon had once made her, along with a bracelet from her childhood. Then, she took out the object that had caused them so much trouble that day: her father's dagger. Instantly memories flitted across her mind. First, of the day she had gone to Jared in his shop to ask for a present for her father and had been shown the beautiful jewel-encrusted dagger. Next, the horror she had felt when she had seen it strapped to Lehonti's side, learning that he had been responsible for her father's death. She had forgotten about it until several days after Jared's death and hoped God would forgive her for keeping it—but the dagger was one of the few reminders she had of her father, of Jared and how skilled he had been, and she could not bring herself to destroy it.

And she needed that link to the past, because sometimes there were days when she could barely remember her husband's face.

9

Abish's resolve almost broke several times over the course of the next week. Jarum refused to be cheered and moped around the house for days, even with Miriam offering to give him her piece of gooey honey *pah-lech*. Desperate for any advice, Abish paid a visit to Akah. With some extra reeds that she had gathered and dried the week before as a greeting gift, she found the older woman hard at work, as was usual.

"Ah, those will make a good, strong basket," Akah said approvingly, inviting her in. Using the company as an excuse to rest, Akah served up some fruit and cheese. They sat cross-legged on well-worn mats while Abish sought for a way to speak of her frustrations. Looking for an opening, Abish asked Akah how her own children were.

"Oh, fine. Fine. Just got word from Zaraph that she's birthed her fourth child. Mari shouldn't be far behind in number. The boys are doing well at their new trades. All of my . . . well, the children are doing well." Her voice choked up on the last words.

"How wonderful," Abish said as brightly as she could. "Of course, I keep thinking that, one day—" she broke off.

"Isabel might return? I keep hoping, but . . . she could be anywhere by now. If only Koram's family hadn't moved away so soon after the Day of Conversion, they might have heard something. Can't figure that girl out." Akah shrugged. "She was always so obedient, always did what she was told. Not like Abnor and Laman." The woman's eyes teared up as she recalled the sons who had been some of the robbers to die at the hands of Ammon. "But then, with no word, she up and walks out of here. Hmm."

"Yes. Children can be challenging at times." It was the perfect lead-in.

Akah listened intently to Abish's description of Jarum's disobedience, nodding her head at appropriate intervals. When finished, she said the words Abish longed to hear. "You did right. The boy needs discipline."

But now Abish played her own counter-advocate. "But he's so young and was very hurt when I punished him. Maybe I was too hard."

Akah harrumphed. "If you think it's hard now, wait until he's older and won't give in to the consequences. What then?" She pointed a plump finger at Abish. "Do you think I haven't thought about my two oldest boys—what I could have done different? They were always running around, getting into mischief. At first I just thought 'boys need to be boys.' Now I realize that boys are learning to be men." Her bottom lip began to quiver. "Maybe I gave in too many times when I should've stood firm."

Abish reached out to take Akah's trembling hand in her own. "I know you did the best you could." She sighed. "Hopefully our children will forgive our weaknesses and accept our intentions."

"Rightly said, rightly said. Of course, there were times when my boys were acting up and, well, all I wanted to do was to take them in my arms and tell them that I loved them. But," she lowered her voice, "Laban thought I was being too soft. Didn't want his boys being mother-coddled." With a grunt, Akah picked up their eating mats and hobbled over to the scraps bin for the animals, not noticing the change on Abish's countenance.

"Thank you, Akah."

"Ah, it was nothing," Akah shrugged. "Just some leftovers."

"No." Abish smiled. "Thank you for the advice."

* * *

Abish burst through the door of her home, startling Teara, who'd been watching her children for her. "Where's Jarum?" she cried out.

"He's fine," Teara replied, concerned. "He's just out back digging in the dirt with Miriam. I—"

Abish didn't wait for her to finish, but rushed to where her children were happily playing. When Jarum first looked up and saw her coming toward him, his little face puckered up as if he knew he must have done something to warrant being in trouble again. But, when she scooped him up and spun him around in her arms, his fear turned to delight and he whooped, "Again! Again!" Now Miriam was tugging on her shift. "Me too!" So she bent down and picked both of them up and they squealed with delight at the impromptu game.

Knowing some explanation was in order, Abish promised more after they talked.

"Jarum," she began, sitting down next to them in the dirt. "I want to talk to you about what happened the other day. I was very upset at what you had done."

Jarum's face began to sag again, so she added insistently, "but I want you to know that I love you. And I'm sorry for being angry at you, so angry that I punished you unjustly. I still want you to know that it was wrong what you did and that you are never to do it again, but, no matter what you do, I will always love you. And," she also hugged Miriam tight, "you as well. Nothing can ever change that. I want both of you to be obedient because it's what God wants you to do and what you must do to be happy. But I never want you to be afraid to tell me when you have been disobedient, because then I can help you find your way back to God again. Do you understand?"

Her answer was four tiny arms around her neck and a dozen kisses planted on her cheek.

"Does this mean I can go to Festival?" Jarum braved to ask.

"Yes." Abish laughed. "We will all go to Festival!"

After another exhausting spin, Abish shooed them off to prepare for bed.

"It was wonderful what you said." Teara smiled, having lingered in the doorway. "I hope . . . I hope to be as good a mother as you one day."

She put a reassuring arm on her friend's shoulder. Though Teara was now twenty and three years old, Abish had yet to see her even remotely become interested in anyone. Surely Koram had not ruined things for her that much. "Give it time," she offered. "It will happen."

"I know," Teara said. "I will try and be—"

"*Patient*," they both answered at the same time and then laughed.

* * *

So far the day of Festival had been everything Abish hoped it would be. All morning she had listened to her children laugh the unblemished laughter of children, and she wanted to capture the sound so she could hear it any time she wanted. All of her doubt about herself and her abilities as a mother vanished, if only for a moment, as she saw how happy they were. And it was all because she had stopped parenting with her mind and instead listened to her heart.

"Mama, come quick!"

Abish immediately shifted her attention to her son, who was frantically gesturing at the strange animals that had been brought in by traders who traveled beyond the borders of Shemlon to the south. She nodded and agreed that the shaggy sheeplike creatures were odd indeed. It reminded her so much of another time that she felt her mind and body shifting again to where she was a young child as well, enthralled by the wonders around her. They ran from stall to stall, sampling fresh melon and ripe avocadoes. There were corn cakes hot off the griddle, which they had to shift around in their hands to keep from being burned, and they ate while watching acrobats and jugglers, contortionists and magicians. The land was once again happy.

It was almost as if everything had returned to normal. Abish had once wondered if that would ever be possible. She was ashamed to admit that she'd had a hard time accepting the "newcomers" at first. For a while she couldn't meet their gaze without wondering if that was the one . . . the one who'd killed Jared. It had taken many hours on her knees to find a measure of peace. Even then, she still struggled to find a way to reconcile forgiving with forgetting.

Then she saw a welcome face in the crowd. Teara came over to them and was instantly assaulted by her children. Abish tried to pull them off of her to keep their hands, which were sticky from the melon, away from Teara's beautiful azure-colored dress. With her hair pulled back from her face in an embroidered headband, Teara's oval-shaped face was nicely outlined. Unlike many of the women around them, she had donned only a pair of small jade earrings with a single gold armband against her bronzed skin. And, in her usual fashion, the shadowing of her cheeks and eyes had been kept to a minimum. Abish smiled at how natural and young she looked.

Abish hoisted Miriam up onto her shoulders, much to the youth's delight. "I can see the whole world from up here!" They all laughed at her innocent perception. Then she shouted, "The king! I see the king!"

Indeed, King Lamoni was making his arrival. The noise of the crowd came to an abrupt halt as the drumbeats and flutes retreated in one last echoing declaration. On his canopied palanquin, their king looked regal indeed and deservedly so. The people had no thought to deprive him of this honor, even though his status over the years had been reduced to a mere figurehead. His bright-feathered headdress undulated in the slight breeze and matched perfectly the long crimson robe he wore, the length of which, Abish knew, was to disguise his missing limb—another reminder of what had been lost. Also noticeably missing was the queen who had once sat by his side at such events. Abish looked at Teara with a silent glance full of remembered days, knowing both of their hearts were heavy at the thought of all that had been lost over the years.

"Who are those men?" Jarum asked as he stood on one of the walls.

Abish strained to see. "Those are the king's guards. They are chosen from among the strongest and bravest men in the land. It is their job to protect the king and guard the palace."

"From what?"

Her son was too young to know of the dangers their city faced. Even though there had been little talk of war since that dreadful day, it was unlikely that peace would continue to be theirs much longer. But she didn't want to ruin the magic of the day with unpleasant thoughts. "Shall we take a closer look?"

Teara helped Jarum to the ground and with her holding tightly onto his hand, they inched forward into the throng. From their closer vantage point, they were able to see the king being lifted onto the steps of the temple court, where he could address his people.

"Good citizens of Ishmael and all who join us," he began. "I come before you this day, not as your king to rule over you, but as your servant, to add my prayers to yours that our land may prosper." A cheer went up from the crowd. When it dissipated, Lamoni continued, "I know that we have had many struggles over the years. But, for a while, we have also known peace. I pray that this peace will continue, so that we may continue to prosper, to grow, to be worthy of God's love and mindfulness of us. My people, you have made me proud. I have seen you comfort the sick and afflicted of this land." His eyes caught Abish's. "The orphans and the widows have been cared for, and the constant newcomers to our land have been welcomed with open arms. May it ever remain so, I pray, asking that God's bounty be continually upon us according to our righteousness." He ended with, "Go and enjoy this day. It is my only command."

With another cheer, the people dispersed to their choice of diversion. Abish had been both uplifted and distressed by the king's words, but again she shrugged off such troubling thoughts. She didn't want to be reminded of the past anymore. Not today. So she allowed herself to get caught up in her children's enthusiasm and challenged Teara to a race over to where the bonfires were being lit by flaming arrow. Skirting around the other anxious guests, they successfully found a viewing spot close to where the competitors stood. It was an exciting competition, and the gathered onlookers roared with approval both for those who missed and those who found success. Soon, all three stacks of cedar wood had been lit, and the crowd danced and frolicked in its flickering light.

"Abish?" came a deep voice behind her. "I thought that was you."

She turned around and saw who it was. "Captain Namon!" She offered her extended hand in greeting. "I must say I was quite impressed by your aim. None other found its mark with such certainty."

He gave her a slight bow. "I am humbled you would think so."

Miriam, wary of the stranger, had hid behind her mother.

"Sweetheart." Abish laughed. "Don't you remember Captain Namon? When we visited with the king? He is the king's protector. He keeps him safe."

"You do?" said a timid voice.

"Yes, little one." Namon knelt down and, removing one of the gold armbands from his massive right arm, handed it to her. "This would make a beautiful necklace for you. Would you like it?"

Miriam looked up eagerly at Abish. "May I?"

When approval was given, Miriam bravely let him fasten it around her. Jarum stood off to the side, frowning, with both hands on his hips. "And for you?" Namon smiled and dug deep into his pocket, pulling out an object. "I have little need of these anymore except for hunting, but this one was hand-carved from the finest obsidian." But then, adding in a whisper to Abish to allay her fears, "Do not worry. This one has been worn down and is no longer sharp."

"Mama! Look!" Her son beamed, holding up the prize. "A real arrowhead. Can I keep it? I'll be careful."

Taking a deep breath she said, "Yes, son. You may keep it."

Namon next addressed Teara. "I wish that I had a token remaining that would be worthy of you, my lady."

Abish cursed her lack of manners. "This is Teara. She has been a dear friend of mine for many years and now has become one of Ishmael's trusted healers."

"Ah," he smiled approvingly, "another healer. I am sure that in such company, you were trained well. Ahem." Namon crossed an arm over his chest. "I will not detain you any further from your celebrating. Perhaps we will meet again."

As he went to leave, Abish had a sudden thought. "Please! Stay. The night is growing dark and we are two women and children, alone. We would appreciate your company."

"Yes, yes!" Jarum clapped. "Stay!"

"I would be honored." He bowed again. "In fact, I should have offered to stay with you for just such a reason. Please forgive my lack of manners."

"There's nothing to forgive," Abish chided, watching as Namon hoisted *both* of her children up onto his shoulders. As they walked along, a very interesting thought crossed her mind.

Yes, she thought. *It just might work.*

10

Her plan to bring Teara and Namon together took precedence over many other responsibilities in the months that followed. Abish frequently arranged for her and Teara to walk past the palace when the king and his entourage were returning from neighboring cities. At other times, she would send an errand boy to the palace with a message for Namon to help her with some pressing job and find any excuse to discuss or include her friend. As the days progressed, Abish found that her usually mundane tasks could be stimulating when the motivation behind them had changed.

When the celebration of the fifth year of her children's birth finally came, it was the perfect opportunity for Abish to ask Namon to come and dine. She took extra care to make sure she chose the freshest fowl, that there were ample corn cakes cooking on the hearthstone, and that the honey and goat's milk congealed correctly in a ceramic bowl by the fire. And she'd even remembered to prick the skin of the squash! Though she was nervous at how it would turn out, Akah's patient instruction had served its purpose, and by nightfall, everything was going just as planned. Teara arrived first, carrying her own contribution: a bowl of corn pudding.

"Aunt Teara! You're here," Jarum yelled as he burst into the room, receiving a disapproving warning from his mother. "The Cap'n is coming tonight. Mama sent for him at the palace! Maybe he'll give me another arrowhead."

He raced around the room, giving his loudest imitation of a howler-monkey while Abish rolled her eyes, regretting her son's inability to keep a secret. She looked in Teara's direction, aware that her "surprise" had been ruined. When she saw Teara's face, however, she wondered if her surprise had been greater than she'd planned because her friend looked startled. Well, that wasn't going to deter her from her ultimate goal. She'd thought about it all day—Teara needed to know what it was like to be loved and cared for and, from what she'd seen so far, Namon was a good man who needed an even better woman. If the evening went anything like she'd imagined, he would find that woman in Teara.

"Miriam!" she called to her daughter. "It's almost time. Is your face washed?"

The little girl soon poked her head through the door. "I'm watching for him. Greetings, Aunt Teara. Someone's coming tonight. Someone handsmen!"

"That's *handsome*," Abish corrected. Even Teara couldn't help but smile at that.

Miriam's squeal alerted them to his arrival. When Namon came through the doorway holding the child in his arms, Abish felt a tug on her emotions that she hadn't felt in a while. But she pushed it down back where it belonged. This night was about Teara, though she found herself unavoidably taking a few looks at their guest. He wore a dark blue jerkin and leather tunic that had a tailored fit indicating a man of means, and which complemented his broad chest and muscular arms. His shoulder-length black hair was tied back with a leather cord, and there was just a hint of stubble on his squared chin. On his feet were sturdy sandals with a thick rubber sole that made Abish a little envious as she thought of the rains that were still plaguing them. And even though she herself was tall for a woman, he spanned a good three hands above her, which meant he towered above Teara.

Usually guests were served without the presence of children, but this was a special occasion, and Abish prayed that her children would not be too caught up in the excitement of it—especially when Namon chose to sit squarely between them! The women served him and then sat and watched as he helped himself to generous portions of the special food Abish had prepared. He praised the crisp flesh of the meat and how the squash had been cooked to perfection. He spread a generous portion of breadnut paste on *two* corn cakes and nodded in approval at the fresh-pressed guava nectar. Namon then spotted the pudding that Teara had brought and . . . completely ignored it!

Thinking that perhaps he considered it to be more of a dessert, Abish waited anxiously the entire meal, barely concentrating on the conversation she was supposed to be encouraging to see if he would sample it and likewise praise her friend's efforts.

"So, Abish," he asked, after finishing the last piece of turkey he had chosen, "it has been some time since you have visited with us in the palace. The king understands that you have new demands on your life but he frequently talks about you. Whenever an emissary from another land comes he always says, 'We have the best healer in all of the Lamanite Empire here in Ishmael.' And then he none-to-subtly probes until he uncovers all of their complaints and expresses his regrets that they do not receive the type of care he has at his disposal."

Embarrassed at receiving so much attention, Abish quickly added her own words of praise. "His Majesty is too kind. Of course, Ishmael is even more blessed to have one as skilled as Teara here. I am sure King Lamoni would be just as pleased with her care as he has been with mine."

"Yes, I am sure," Namon responded, looking at Teara as if noticing her in the room for the first time. "But the king has grown particular in his old age and habits can be hard to change. I should know."

Abish smiled, but she was finding it difficult to keep her mind focused on the dual goals that she had tonight. When her children shouted for their presents, she momentarily forgot about the apparent lack of connection she was sensing between the other two adults and instead retrieved the small packages she had prepared. She watched the faces of her young children as they excitedly opened their gifts. Miriam was delighted with the hair ribbons Abish had made, and Jarum seemed to approve of the tortoiseshell snake guards she had fashioned for him, even allowing her to fasten them around his shins to see if they fit. Teara then gave her offerings: a tiny book of ficus paper for when Jarum began his studies in the upcoming year—the thought of which caused him to wrinkle his nose—and a small rag doll which Miriam lovingly cuddled.

Relieved that something was going well, Abish watched as Namon reached beneath his cloak.

"Presents weren't necessary," she admonished.

"Don't deprive me of this honor," he said. "It has been a long time since I have had someone to buy a gift for."

The children were newly animated as their bounty grew.

"A hunter's belt!" Jarum cried, quickly tying the beaded strap around his waist. It hung down past his hips and Abish stifled a grin. "Look! There's a pouch for my arrowhead and a sh . . . sheath for my dagger." Seeing Abish's frown, he quickly said, "I mean, Grandfather's dagger. I won't use that part."

Miriam's own squeals diverted their attention, and they turned to see her holding up a pale yellow length of fabric. The small girl was delicately touching it with her fingers. "What is it, Mama?"

"That's silk, sweetheart."

"Silk? It's soft."

"Namon," Abish quietly directed her voice toward him, "this is too much. She's so young."

From his seated position, he leaned forward and whispered, "She won't be young forever. I . . . I once knew someone who liked beautiful things and so I hope it is to your liking. Well," he said, rising from his mat as if suddenly uncomfortable, "it is growing late and I should return to the palace. My time here this evening has been most enjoyable. Perhaps I may visit again?"

"Of course," Abish said, a little disheartened but not willing to give up yet. "Would you mind walking Teara home? She lives but a short distance from here and it is quite dark."

"Uh, yes. I mean, it would be to my honor to be her escort."

When the two of them had left, Abish pressed her hands up against her head to keep from screaming. Why were men so dense? She had invited Namon here tonight to see firsthand what a perfect match Teara would be for him. But he had hardly said one word to her, had not tasted her special dish, and then had seemed reluctant to be alone with her. What more could she have done? As for Teara—she cowered like a scared kitten in the corner of the house all night as if she hadn't an intelligent thought to put together!

Lying on her sleeping mat that night, Abish wondered how many more chances she would have to arrange for the two of them to be together. After all, Namon was a handsome and well-respected man and—guessing that he was not much older than she was—there must have been ample opportunity for him to have chosen a wife before now. Maybe he saw Teara as too young and immature. Maybe he was too deeply devoted to the king to consider matrimony. Maybe he had difficulty accepting Teara's profession as so many men did.

Maybe, she should just leave things in God's hands.

Groaning and flopping over onto her side, Abish listened to her children breathing heavily in the darkness. Miriam was still a little restless from the day's excitement, but Jarum was already fast asleep and making a slight "poofing" noise when he exhaled. She stifled a giggle. Jared had done the same thing when he slept.

A sudden spasm rose in her chest. It came out of nowhere and felt as if a vise had clamped down on her heart. Unstoppable tears poured from her eyes, and Abish put a hand to her mouth to keep from sobbing aloud. *Oh, Jared, I miss you so.* Why was it that the memories she could outrun during the day seemed to creep back with the shadows of night until she felt a loneliness as permanent as a piercing in her flesh or a marking on her skin? She felt branded—by solitude. The few hours that Namon had spent here tonight had been joyous, but now reminded her of what she and her children had lived without all these years.

A father. A husband.

Abish couldn't help but think back to the day she had buried Jared. Still sore from giving birth the day before, it had not stopped her from climbing up the rise to where her beloved's body would be interred forever. At first she had considered placing him conveniently next to her father's grave on the land near her childhood home. But then, considering Jared's opposition to living there, she thought better of it. When she had first seen him at the gravesite, she had had to bite the inside of her cheek until it bled to keep from crying out. The metallic taste in her mouth had soon mingled with salty tears as she knelt by his side. "Farewell, my love." She had turned away as his linen-wrapped form was slowly lowered into the ground. All of her friends and loved ones had been standing by her side, but she had felt all alone as she made the arduous walk back to where her tiny newborns waited for her.

Now fighting back the memory, Abish rolled over onto her side. Since then, many people had told her she should be looking for a man for herself. But she wasn't ready for that kind of love again—not yet. Instead, she wanted only to see her friend happy. To have their children play together.

She had to find a way to get Teara and Namon together.

11

The sun continued to rise and fall, and Abish sought every opportunity to gauge Namon's thoughts about the evening in her home. Under the guise of visits to the king, who continued to struggle with his missing appendage and overall health, she made sure his Captain at Arms was always in attendance. Afterwards, she would take Namon aside and make sure he understood her instructions for the latest tonic she had prescribed or seek his opinion on ways to make sure the king stayed busy. And then, while she was gathering her supplies out of earshot of the king, she would recall the "lovely evening" they had spent and how Teara had talked of little else. (A slight sin of commission, she decided, since Teara had to be prodded to discuss much of anything lately.)

"My children have been anxious to see you again," she hinted, "and I was thinking that perhaps you would join us for a picnic by the river. While hunting for herbs, Teara discovered a patch of ripe berries, which I'm sure will be gone soon without the rains."

"I would enjoy that. I will ask the king to give me leave again."

"If he doesn't," she said, "I will rebuke him for working you too hard. Surely he would not begrudge you a little freedom of your own to seek some kind of diversion—especially if there were a young lady here or near the palace?"

Namon cleared his throat, "I am afraid that I have been the one who has not allowed myself the time for such . . . diversions. Perhaps now," he said with a smile, "that will change."

Abish swung her satchel over her shoulder. "Then we will meet at the river the day after tomorrow?" Namon nodded his agreement. But as she reached the doorway, she gave a mischievous grin. "What should I have prepared? I noticed when you dined with us last month that you didn't care for pudding."

Namon flushed a deep red that was quite striking against his bronzed skin. "Uh, no. It carries too many memories," he said cryptically and then, turning on his heels, he left as well.

* * *

The morning of the picnic was a beautiful day, devoid of rain and mist and full of promise. Abish carefully packed the supplies they would need and reminded the children one more time to be on their best behavior. When they met Teara at the crossroads, she saw a flush of anticipation on her friend's face as well and it put to rest some of her fears that she was treading where one ought not to have trod.

Namon was dressed in less formal attire this time. His worn sandals, a linen tunic, and an unadorned leather jerkin suggested an air of familiarity that was encouraging. With his bow fastened to his side for protection from wild beasts, the only other hint to his former standing was his heavy leather shin-guards that had been sewn in a military fashion. Of course as he came closer, the many scars that ran across his arms and chest were another reminder that this had been a seasoned warrior once.

"Greetings," he announced.

The two women responded politely in turn, but the children abandoned all reserve and clamored up his legs. "Careful, you little monkeys!" He grabbed them around the waists and playfully asked, "Perhaps a dunking in the river would be just the thing for these wild ones?"

Miriam howled in protest, but Jarum pleaded, "Can we? Can we?"

"*After* we eat," Abish wagged her finger. "We brought no change of clothes and I won't have you dripping water all over the food. Teara and I have worked very hard," she reprimanded, gesturing to the baskets on their heads. "Now, let's be off."

They headed down the southward trail, past mahogany, ceiba, and cedar trees that would provide them some protection against the inevitable heat of the day. The morning sun, however, was still pleasant and it filtered down through the canopy into a kaleidoscope of emerald-toned hues. The scent of orchids and bromeliads mingled with the odor of decaying growth beneath their feet. All around them was the screeching of birds, the prattle of animals and the whining of so many insects that Abish was glad she'd taken the time to find the special leaves that, when crushed and rubbed on to the skin, acted as a repellant. All this reminded her that there was also a menacing undertone to the jungle around them, though the children laughed as if oblivious to these dangers. But they had been taught since youth to watch out for the rustling noise that the bush snake made as it crept through the underbrush, to look to the sky for sudden squalls that could change the ground beneath them into a rushing torrent of mud. They knew which frogs were poisonous and which plants were, too. Of course, she'd also taught them the medicinal value of the many plants that God had given them.

But the worst dangers of the jungle, she shivered, were the ones that couldn't be foreseen—or avoided.

It was hard to dwell on any of this for long when the air was so sweet and the company so pleasant. Abish finally saw Teara opening up as she picked delicate flowers to work into Miriam's hair. Namon was showing Jarum how to throw a small spear he had fashioned out of a stick—"For catching fish," her son quickly explained to her. It was so pleasant a scene. When they arrived at their designated spot, the two women set down their baskets and began to spread out the palm-frond mats which would protect them from most of the ground's dampness. Namon asked if he could take the children exploring, and Abish was happy to oblige. She wanted a few moments alone with Teara, to prepare her so that this outing would be an improvement over the other evening.

"It was very fortunate that Namon could join us," she prompted.

Was that a slight flush on her friend's face? If it was, Teara disguised it by taking out some banana leaves on which to lay out the corn cakes and dried fish. "Yes."

"He is good with the children, isn't he?" Abish added.

"Yes."

"What a good father he would make."

"I think I'll go scouting for some mushrooms," Teara said evenly. "There's a shady area over by the river that might have a good crop." Without another word or invitation for Abish to join her, she left.

What is going on here? Abish groaned. Why was Teara being so difficult? Did she know what Abish was trying to do and resented it? This was going too far. Abish rushed after her friend. "Teara, what's wrong?" she demanded.

When her friend didn't respond immediately, she asked softly, "Teara? Are you all right?"

Teara turned and looked at her with a tear-streaked face. "I am happy for you. I hope the two of you will find much joy."

What?

Abish stood dumb for a moment. "Teara? Whatever do you mean?"

"Namon and you . . ." a quiet sob ". . . should be very happy together."

Abish let her words sink in and then began to laugh. Teara, misunderstanding, began to cry harder, so Abish took her by the shoulders and spun her around. "No, you don't understand! It isn't like that between us."

"It . . . it isn't?" she gulped.

"No. That's not why I've been trying to spend so much time with him." She groaned and rubbed her forehead. "Are you trying to tell me that you *do* care for him?"

Teara wiped her eyes. "Of course I do! But, seeing you together, how he is with your children, I realized how much you needed a father for them. So I told myself that it was for the best if I forgot about him."

Abish smiled. "That was a noble sacrifice for you to make. But you forgot one thing."

"What?"

"You mentioned a father for my children, but not a *husband* for me. Though," she sighed, "if the truth be told, I'm not sure I am ready to open my heart again."

Teara blushed. "But if you were, Namon would be a good man to choose."

"Better than Koram?" Abish teased her about her childhood sweetheart.

"Koram seems like such a boy now compared to Namon. I'm glad that he chose another."

"It seems you are smitten," Abish beamed. "I think you ought to tell him."

Teara looked terrified. "I . . . I wouldn't know how to! Could you talk to him first for me, gauge his feelings? Perhaps then I can be brave."

"Gladly." Abish gave her friend a hug. "I'll do it now."

Hearing her children squealing off in the clearing, Abish went in the direction of the noise. She was not even within ten cubits of them when she heard Namon's voice, his back still turned to her. "Coming to check on your children? I have not thrown them in the river yet," he chuckled.

"How did you know it was me?" she asked.

"I could tell by your footfall."

Of course. "I used to be able to do the same," she said as once again memories of Jared unfolded. "But everything is different now."

"I understand. So much has changed over the years. Take me! I am a captain without an army. A warrior without any weapons. As useless as . . . as . . ."

"A goat with a fifth leg?" she chuckled.

"Exactly!"

Abish seized the moment. "And if there were something that could change that?"

Namon looked at her quizzically. "Like what?"

She glanced over at the children, who had been put to the task of picking berries but were eating as many as they stored away, then led Namon a little further down the river. "Like a wife and a family to take care of?" she finally revealed. The shock that registered across his face made her wonder if she had spoken too boldly. "I know that feelings cannot be forced, but—"

"Abish," he stuttered. "I think you are an amazing woman. In fact, you are unlike any that I have ever known. But, I do not know that I could care for you that way. And it is not because of the children, they are wonderful, too—"

He couldn't finish his sentence because of how loud Abish was laughing. "Oh, Namon, I'm so sorry. It never occurred to me that I was misleading you like that as well." She gulped in air between laughs. "I seem to be bungling things right and left. It is not for me that I have been asking these questions. It's for Teara."

"Teara? I had no idea she was even aware I existed! I have to admit," he added sheepishly, "that was one of the reasons I kept accepting your invitations. Little good that it has done me. That first night at your house she hardly said a word to me. In fact, she seemed a little withdrawn, as if I had offended her. And she's hardly spoken to me since."

Abish sighed. "That might have had something to do with the fact that you didn't partake of the pudding she had brought."

"That was hers?" He slapped a hand to his forehead. "You must understand that it was not an intentional affront. As a soldier, growing up, I am afraid that corn pudding was one of the staples of our existence. I grew tired of it after so many meals."

How simple some misunderstandings are.

"So she *does* have feelings for me?" he questioned.

"Yes." But it was her friend's place to reveal how much. "Teara is somewhat timid when it comes to men. Her heart was broken once and I think she's afraid to open herself up again."

"Of course. I understand that only too well." Abish's silence encouraged him to explain. "I told you I once knew someone who liked pretty things. Well, I was in love with her. I thought that she would wait for me while I finished my soldier's training. But instead, she married another. My brother."

"It must have been difficult for you."

"Especially because it was my brother who betrayed me."

Abish sighed, knowing what it was like to feel betrayed. She explained some of her own past. "It was all very painful to me, and I struggled to move on. But I have learned that living in the past can keep you from having the future you deserve."

Namon took a deep breath. "Then I will not let that happen," he said determinedly. "So what must I do next?"

"Well, at this point, I think the best answer I could give you would be to ask her to be yours before someone less timid does!"

Laughing, they returned to the thicket to look for the children. Miriam was still gathering berries, but Jarum was nowhere to be seen. "Would you mind taking Miriam back while I look for Jarum? I'm going to have to give him a lecture again about wandering off," Abish said with a frown.

She watched the two head back toward their picnic area and then stomped angrily through the trees. "Jarum! Where are you?" she said loudly. "It's time to eat and we're not going to wait all day for you." Dried leaves crunched beneath her feet. "*Jarum!*" she shouted. "Fine. I'll have to eat all of the sweets myself then!"

There was no answer.

A sick feeling began in the pit of her stomach.

12

"Jarum?" her voice barely came out as a whisper. There was an eerie stillness as if even the wind sensed her fear. Her breath came out in ragged gasps as she now stumbled through the jungle, searching for something, anything to show her where her son had gone. A bird's hiding spot was disturbed, and the bird fluttered away in a crimson blur, squawking furiously at her. An old, dead log blocked her path, and she scrambled over it, ignoring the scratches that stung her legs.

Abish stopped.

The canopy was so thick that she stood in near darkness, the colors blending together into a wall of green. But something seemed out of place. A section of palms curved unnaturally, smoothed down into a bowl shape. She went to it and picked up the basket Jarum had been gathering berries in.

"Jarum!" she half-screamed, half-sobbed.

Throwing the basket to the ground, she ran like one of the creatures of the forest. *Where could he be? Why did he wander off? Why did I leave him alone?*

Her self-recriminations threatened to slow her down, so she thrust them away. She had to focus. Stumbling over a nearly dry creek bed, she wondered if he could have come this far. Perhaps he'd become disoriented and believed he was moving back to their spot, when, in reality, he was moving farther away from safety. Once again, she found herself paralyzed by her emotions and had to force herself to think. She looked to her right. From here, the ground rose sharply. Surely this would have stopped his progress. She looked back the way from whence she came. Had she missed something? Should go run back and ask for help?

A loud cry echoed through the jungle. It was inhuman, she knew, but it nearly stopped her heart. She began to retrace her steps, combing through the deep underbrush like a small animal hunting for insects. It felt that hopeless.

Please, God, help me find him! Help me find my son!

Her heart and the jungle around her stilled like the calming of a storm. It was then she was able to hear a faint moaning. Pushing all other distractions aside, she ran toward the sound and discovered its source. A cry leapt into her throat and she felt as if years of life had been stripped from her. Now she had to force each step and fight back the vertigo that sought to overcome her. Her son's small, unconscious body was almost hidden by the tall grass that surrounded it. The wound in his side still released a trickle of fresh blood. Abish's whole body trembled as she looked down at the wound in her son's side.

Jared. Just like Jared.

But then something ripped her from her paralysis and she reached down and snatched him up in her arms.

When Abish burst through the trees carrying Jarum in her arms, she immediately saw Teara and Namon sitting with Miriam on the ground. "What happened?" Teara cried out as she jumped up to help.

"I found him," Abish gasped as she ran toward them, "off in the trees. It must have been a peccary. A small one, or he would be—" She began to sob again.

"Abish?" Teara grabbed her by the shoulders. "Look at me. It's going to be all right! Together, we will not let Jarum die. But you must be strong for him."

Strong. I have to be strong.

"Keep as much pressure on his side as possible," Abish ordered, snapping out of her state of shock. "Teara, find some wild garlic, the kind with the purple stems. Mash it up into a paste—"

Teara touched her hand. "I know what to do."

She rushed off into the bushes while Abish continued to assess the situation and determine what was needed. So near the river, there would be no agave for a needle. Frantically looking around, she wondered what else she could use. Namon, sensing her frustration asked, "What can I do?"

"I need something with which to sew up his side. He's losing blood so quickly that—"

Then it occurred to her. Rushing to where their forgotten picnic stood, Abish dumped out a bowl of beans. Spying a nearby dead tree stump, she ran to it, digging into the decaying pulp with her hands. Deep in the recesses she found what she was looking for. When her bowl was full, she hurried back to Jarum's side.

"Mama?" came Miriam's scared voice. "Is Jarum going to be all right?"

She went and knelt beside her daughter. "Of course, my precious. Do not fear."

Teara had returned with the needed supplies and knelt down by the frightened girl as well. Cradling Miriam in her arms, Teara kept the girl's gaze averted by telling her stories about prophets of old. As her words sought to distract and calm the little girl, Abish began to work.

The bleeding was not great but Jarum was small and would not tolerate much more blood loss. Cleaning away as much of the blood as she could, she instructed Namon to hold the wound closed the best he could. Taking one of the squirming giant ants that had been placed in the bowl, she avoided the sharp pinchers that struggled to find their mark. Abish held her breath, knowing that she was not ready for them to clamp down . . . not yet. Glad for her son's unconscious state, she expertly angled the insect on top of the wound. It would be easier the further down she worked. As soon as the small hairs on the ant's legs registered contact with the torn flesh, they clamped down unmercifully. Satisfied in their placement, Abish gave a quick twist to the creature's torso. It came off with a loud snapping noise. Though the insect was now dead, the muscles which contracted the pinchers would not release, holding the flesh firmly in place. She took another, then another. After placing more than a dozen, she glanced in Teara's direction, nodding that she was confident that the blood flow had been staunched.

Abish did not realize until now that tears were streaming down her cheeks. She buried her face in Jarum's hair and praised God for sparing her son's life.

"We should get him back home," Teara said at her side, applying a pungent salve she had made to the sutured wound.

"I'll carry him." Namon knelt across from Teara with Jarum's small body between them. The look that passed between them was not lost on Abish.

Finally home, she laid her son on her own sleeping mat. On the way back, his eyes had fluttered open momentarily and he had whispered, "Hungry, Mama," before he fell back asleep. Now, he groaned slightly and Abish checked to make sure she had some extra willow bark to make a tea for the pain if necessary. Miriam was an angel, bravely letting Abish tuck her into her hammock for a nap with a promise that her brother would be fine.

Abish walked to the doorway, the reality of what had happened beginning to sink in. A short ways off, she saw Teara and Namon talking together. It seemed casual at first. Namon spoke some words, and Teara blushed and lowered her head. He reached to take her hand in his and placed something in it. Though Abish couldn't discern exactly what it was from her distance, she knew what it meant.

A token!

Abish marveled that such happiness could come from near tragedy. Life was strange, she thought. As she leaned up against the frame of the doorway, she found herself fingering the pendant around her neck that had once been Jared's token. She had rubbed it so many times that the intricate carving had all but vanished. Perhaps, she thought, that was why tangible gifts were given—often they outlived the giver.

* * *

Jarum healed quickly over the ensuing weeks as children were apt to do, leaving Abish to wish that her guilty conscience at allowing him to be hurt was as easily mended. Though a slight fever had developed the second day, by the third, he was hungry for his favorite foods and asking if Teancum could play. During that time there were many well-wishers who stopped by the house, offering prayers and portions of food so Abish could stay by his side as much as possible. But as her son grew more restless, she knew she could not keep him in bed forever. Though not having him by her side terrified her, she had finally let Teara and Namon take her children down to the market so she could have a break.

Left alone to finish tasks that had been ignored for too long, she noticed a shadow in the doorway.

"Greetings, Abish."

She looked up and smiled. "And you, Ammon. It has been some time."

"Yes. I'm sorry I did not come sooner, but I have just now returned from Zarahemla. The Lamanites have not relented, and there have been even more attacks as of late." His voice grew weary. "Of course, you have been dealing with your own concerns. I was sorry to hear of Jarum's accident, but I'm sure he could not have been in better hands."

"I was not quite as sure at first." She bent over her weaving. "My hands have been unpracticed for too long."

"Yes. You must miss it."

Abish smiled sadly as she stood and went to check on the dye pots. "That's not all I miss."

"Abish, about Jared—"

She held up a hand to stop him. "There are many of us who have lost loved ones. In that respect I am not alone."

"Yes. But my father died peacefully at home surrounded by loved ones. You had none of that to give you comfort."

Abish looked up from the pot and stopped stirring. "Then I suppose my comfort had to come from somewhere else: the faces of my children, from my devotion to God. And from the assurance that Jared is in a better place, waiting for me."

"And that," Ammon nodded solemnly, "is the greatest source of comfort we have."

* * *

Not since the day of her baptism had Abish's friend looked happier.

Though Teara had insisted on a simple affair, Abish knew that there would be so many in attendance and that the preparations for her wedding were becoming a bit overwhelming. Helping all she could, Abish had to admit that, in a different way, it was becoming difficult for her as well. Watching Teara being fitted for her bridal attire or hearing the heartfelt vows that were being prepared brought her back to a time when it was her waiting in Akah's house, listening for the approach of *her* bridegroom.

Her friend soon returned from another outing with Jarum and Miriam and they stood together, talking of plans while the children played. But Teara, even amid all of her own concerns, sensed that something was on Abish's mind. "Are you thinking of Jared?" Teara asked.

Abish shrugged, "I find it difficult not to at times like these. But this is your day!" She clasped Teara's hands in hers and tried to stifle the tears that threatened to come. "This is about you and Namon and your lifetime of happiness together."

"But I want you, as my dearest friend, to be happy as well. I want to see you find love again."

Abish sighed. There was no one more excited about love than someone who was *in* love. "My day will come. I'm not that old! There's still time." Abish decided it would be best to change the subject. "I should be asking you how you are doing. Not only have you been thinking about your wedding day, but I know you have been called for in your duties day and night."

"Yes," Teara said, suppressing her yawn with a smile. "Ever since the influx of even more converts to our land, I've barely had a moment to think. But I have wanted to ask you something for a while."

"What? Is it about the ceremony or," she winked mischievously, "the wedding *night*?"

Teara playfully slapped her on the arm. "Actually, I've been trying to make a decision." Abish waited silently until she explained further. "Once I am married, should I continue my healing?"

The question surprised her and she shrugged. "I don't know."

"How did you decide?"

"I suppose circumstances decided for me," Abish admitted. "Jared was never happy with it to begin with and in that final year before he died, I was so content that we were finally coming to know each other again that I grew not to miss it as much. It helped knowing that you were competent and that our people were being well cared for. And then, when Jared died," her voice caught, "I wanted only to think of caring for our children."

"And you've never considered returning?"

Abish inhaled sharply. She thought back to that horrible day when Jarum had been injured. Something had awakened inside of her when she had struggled to save her child—a satisfaction and intense sense of belonging that reminded her of why she had become a healer in the first place—and it made her wonder why she had abandoned it all those years ago. The natural answer was that her children had needed her. But then she started to think that was only an excuse that she had used from the beginning to convince herself that history would not be repeated. She would never abandon her children in order to put her own needs first.

She would never make the same mistakes her mother had made.

But these feelings were too raw, so instead she answered, "At first Jarum and Miriam took up so much of my time that I would never have imagined returning. Of course, my resources aren't what they once were and though I dread the thought of accepting charity when I have the capacity to work with my own hands, I hate the thought of leaving them. I suppose I will have to face that possibility some day. What does Namon think?"

"Namon isn't much help. He says he wants me to be happy. And I am happy to care for our home, but I'm happy when I am healing people as well. How can I be happy doing both?"

This honestly baffled Abish. "I'm afraid I don't have an answer for you."

Teara sighed. "Then I will just have to keep praying about what my future should hold so I can be ready for it."

Abish nodded in agreement. But even though this was such a happy time, she couldn't help but wonder if any of them could truly be ready for what lay in their future.

13

"Mama, more milk, more milk!"

Miriam's voice pulled Abish out of her stupor. She hadn't been sleeping well this past month. Thoughts of Teara's impending wedding should have been foremost in her mind, but after the news that the Nephite city of Ammonihah had been utterly destroyed by the Lamanite army, she wondered if any of her people were sleeping well.

"Mama!" Miriam shouted, impatient at the delay.

"You need to say please!" Abish countered before pouring the tiny cup full again. Too full. As Miriam raised it to her mouth, it sloshed over the sides and down her freshly washed tunic. "Be careful, Miriam! I have more than enough to do around here without you dirtying every piece of clothing you own!"

"Abish, is everything all right?" Akah asked, appearing in the doorway.

"We're fine," Abish said, embarrassed that her short-tempered moment had been witnessed. "I was just trying to get Miriam to be a little more careful." She then rushed over to the small girl whose lower lip was trembling from the reprimand. "I'm sorry." She dabbed at her face with a cloth. "You did nothing wrong. Mama's just tired. We'll have you cleaned up in no time."

"It sounds like you could use a trip to the market," Akah said, giving her a knowing smile. "Why don't you go and take advantage of the latest arrivals from Lemuel."

Abish looked at the messy scene around her—the dirty eating mats, piles of laundry and other untended chores—and then bit down her guilt and agreed. She strapped on her sandals, grabbed a woven pouch and thanked Akah again for always knowing when she needed her.

"Every mother reaches her limits now and then," Akah clucked. "You aren't the first to raise your voice to your children, you know."

"I know. I shouldn't have gotten so impatient with her, though."

"You're too hard on yourself. We all make mistakes."

Abish shrugged, thinking about how many she'd made over the years.

In the marketplace she took a deep breath, reveling in the sights and sounds around her. Vendors were newly thriving, thanks to the unseasonably warm weather that had brought with it an early planting season. Voices shouting that they had the freshest fish, ripest mangoes, or newest imports from neighboring communities competed with each other above the chattering of shoppers. The sun beat down on her shoulders and head as she walked along, returning greetings of friends old and new. Abish stayed on the Street of Vendors, though she should have faced the inevitable memories that would come by going into the market of the artisans because for weeks she had struggled with what to give Teara and Namon as a wedding gift. Glad that at least Teara had found success with something for Namon during a recent trip, she knew that she wanted her own offering to represent both the love she had for her friends and the happiness she felt knowing they had found each other. But what?

Teara had the same problem Abish herself had had in the early stages of marriage. Over the years she had received such a supply of mats, baskets, rugs, and blankets as payment from supplicants that there was little else that she really was in need of. In fact, Abish often laughed as she visited her in her small home that Teara would have to return to live in the palace or make her new husband sleep out back for lack of room.

Lack of room . . .

At first she rejected the idea that came into her mind. It was too much, and yet somehow Abish knew there had to be a way to make them accept her offer. Rejuvenated by her scheme, she impulsively purchased some costly white fish in celebration of her continued meddling and then headed home.

Once again Akah had served her well. Abish saw Miriam's dirty shift cleaned and drying on the thatched roof as she approached the house. Her daughter was off playing in a clean new one. Fresh bread was baking near the fire pit, and Jarum was busy whittling away at a new fishing spear. *How did she do it and make it all look so easy?* Abish sighed.

"Mama!" Jarum jumped up, showing her his work. "Look! I'll catch a bunch of fish for us for dinner tonight!"

Abish patted his hand with one of hers, using the other to slip the parcel of fish she had purchased behind a pile of baskets. "Wonderful! I can't wait to taste fish again."

He proudly skipped off while she went to thank Akah. The old woman waved off her compliments and, shuffling away, reminded Abish to call for her when she needed to "take a walk" again.

Hoping the smile she gave her daughter would be enough to tell her all was forgiven, Abish put Miriam to task picking out the tares that inevitably ended up in each of their wheat purchases. Each day when Abish examined their dwindling funds, she found that no longer could she afford the finest cuts of meat or the prepared breads that had once been taken for granted. So now their wheat was full of chaff, their meat, mostly fat. Her children hadn't noticed these substitutions, but Abish had felt the reality of it: the chasm that constantly split what they *had* and what she *wanted* for her children.

"Mama!" Jarum came yelling into the house.

"Jarum," Abish gently scolded. "Remember your manners."

"Sorry. Can I go fishing with Teancum now? He has a new spear, too, and we're gonna have a contest and see who catches the biggest fish! I think it will be me because my spear is really sharp. But his father made his and so I don't think that's fair." He took a deep breath. "Can I go?"

Abish stifled her laugh. Though it still worried her every time he was out of sight, she realized that holding on too tight could be just as harmful. "Of course. As long as Teancum's older brother goes along."

"He will."

She smiled and said another silent prayer as she watched him run off.

* * *

The gathering in the square for Teara and Namon's wedding was greater than even they could have imagined. It appeared everyone, young and old, wanted to join in the festivities. Even King Anti-Nephi-Lehi, wanting to wish Namon well, had come from the capital city to join them. Abish accepted the explanation that the king had known Namon's father when they were both young, but as she watched their rotund ruler she still had to wonder if it wasn't really the succulent food that had drawn him there.

Abish reassured Teara as she waited anxiously for her future husband to appear that everything would be taken care of. As shouts went out from the crowd, they watched as a group appeared on the horizon: friends and family who had joined in the procession of the bridegroom and would soon arrive at their door. Then the bridegroom would knock, and Teara could choose to ignore or let him in. Since the conversion of their people, it was common to carry out what had once been only a Nephite ritual, but Teara surprised them by also asking if they could continue with her own people's practice of the tying of the knots. Ammon could find no reason for this tradition not to continue, and Abish was glad, because she had always found it poignant that the couple would tie together the hems of their cloaks, symbolically representing that their lives were now tied together as well. The guests could then laugh at the couple as they tried to move throughout the celebration attached in such a way. Occasionally, the knot would come loose and old women could cluck through toothless gums that they knew it would not last!

Teara looked beautiful. Small flowers had been braided into her dark hair and her delicate frame seemed engulfed by Namon's towering one. As the couple was led before Ammon to receive his blessing, Abish caught Ammon looking at her and found her eyes welling up with tears. But quickly regaining her composure, she turned to her friend and waited until Ammon pronounced them wed before the eyes of God. The crowd cheered and the ceremony completed, Abish was no longer compelled to stand her ground.

"I am so happy," she cried, throwing her arms around Teara. "For both of you." Then addressing Namon, "Do you realize the treasure you've found?"

"There is nothing that could compare," he solemnly responded.

She looked at the glistening bejeweled comb in Teara's hair that had been Namon's gift. It was exquisite, but could never compare to the light in Teara's eyes. This reminded her of something. "Did Teara give you her gifts?"

Namon flushed a deep red. "Yes. Both of them." He laughed. "And of the first, she made me eat the whole thing!"

Abish laughed as well. "Well then, you had better develop a taste for corn pudding again."

"I realized afterward," Teara said as she joined in their laughter, "that it was a silly joke and that the feathered belt should have sufficed."

Namon took his new wife's face between his large hands. "There was nothing more you could have given me this day than your love."

Now a voice shouted off in the distance. "To the new couple!" Everyone cheered their approval and waited for volunteers to fill their cups and plates with food and drink.

"Mama! Mama!" Akah had brought the children forward on the rise, and Abish knelt down to welcome their sweet embraces. "Isn't Aunt Teara beautiful?" Miriam asked.

"Almost as beautiful as you!" She smiled as her daughter twirled around in her yellow silk gown. Abish stood and held both her children at her side as a pair of jugglers came onto the scene.

Namon groaned. "I am afraid Lamoni . . ." he motioned to where the king sat regally on his canopied palanquin ". . . is treating this like a royal event. Hopefully there are not too many more surprises."

"Mama." Jarum tugged at her shift. "Come dance with us!"

"In a moment. There's something I have to give to the happy couple."

"Don't you worry," Akah said, "I'll keep an eye on them."

Abish thanked her and waited until they walked away. "Now, for my gift."

"You didn't have to get us anything," Teara protested. "Bringing us together was enough."

"But this gift is something I've had for a long time and realized that not only was it mine to give now, but that I had to give it to you and Namon. I know that your home is too small for the two of you to live in and that you've had quite the discussion on living again in the palace."

"Hopefully it will be for a short time," Namon said, "until I can make other arrangements. Teara is being more than patient."

"Then I have the perfect solution. My gift," Abish said as she took Teara's hands in hers, "is for you and Namon to live in my childhood home." Ignoring the look of shock on both their faces she continued, "I won't accept 'no' for an answer. You believed in my plan once to have the worst patients kept in one place," Abish reminded her friend. "There is nothing of charity to this—think of the time this will save you each day. Please do what I was not able to do."

"We will think upon it," Namon said finally.

Teara threw her arms around Abish in an embrace. "I'm so glad!"

"How can I say 'no' to that," Namon chuckled, signaling for a cup of sweet nectar to be handed to both women.

As Abish watched the couple rejoin the gathering, she felt that familiar combination of happiness and longing that chose to resurface at such moments, and once again she tried to combat it with patience and faith. But as her own life stretched ahead of her into the unknown, she began to wonder if her meager supply would suffice.

14

Abish stood outside her hut and hoped for a slight breeze to give her some relief from the stifling heat that had been so prevalent for the last two years, regardless of the season. The forest was particularly noisy this evening as resident groups of primates and birds echoed their mating calls across the jungle canopy. Abish lingered in the doorway, wondering if the creatures knew anything of the agony or joys of parenthood or if theirs was merely the fulfillment of an instinctual need to survive and procreate. As for her own offspring, she could still hear her seven-year-old children inside whispering to each other, trying to settle down for the night. Just then she heard a nearby rustling. Her senses alert, she waited to see what form emerged from the thick foliage: the tall image of a person or the slinking shadow of a more frightening foe. When a voice accompanied a familiar shape, she relaxed.

"Teara!" She quickly retrieved a lamp from inside the house to add more light to her friend's way. "You aren't alone, are you?"

"No. Namon walked me as far as the crossroads. He had some news to give the council and will come for me shortly."

Abish couldn't help but glance into the swaddling pack on Teara's back. At nearly a year old, it was unusual for a child to still want to be confined in such a way, but Benjamin always seemed content. "Well, I'm glad you stopped by. You've been so busy settling in to your new home that I've barely seen you. Are things still going as planned?"

Teara nodded, explaining how the bulk of the rooms of Abish's childhood home had indeed been turned into a sick ward, with the smallest of the living quarters comfortably made up for the three of them. Abish knew better than to argue with Teara about that, instead reveling in the fact that they had at last accepted her gift.

"I'm so happy to know it is being put to good use." Abish cocked an eyebrow, surmising there might be another reason why her friend had stopped to visit.

"So everything really is well then?" They stood just behind the glowing embers of the fire pit to keep their conversation from giving her children yet another excuse to stay awake.

Teara sighed. "We were just visited by travelers passing through from Shimnilon. They mentioned that there is an outbreak of strange fevers in the neighboring land of Siron. It is bad enough that their governor has restricted all travel to and from the city."

Abish shook her head. "That's awful." Though the height of the rainy season was approaching, there had only been a few cases of the usual seasonal illnesses in Ishmael. "How are they faring?"

"Not very well. Many of the young and able-bodied have been afflicted. Their physicians have been pushed to their limits and have had little success. I fear that many cling too much to the old ways and still try to disperse 'evil spirits' with chants and diagnose illness with floating grains of wheat." This was something Abish knew only too well. It took a long time before some people accepted her prescriptions of herbs and tonics, and practical advice of rest and nourishing food. "The people, I fear, need help," Teara said compassionately. "And you know how quickly these illnesses can spread as well. It would help if we could understand it before it finds its way to Ishmael."

"Siron is a good three days' walk, and who knows how long you'll be abroad." Abish frowned. "Even though Benjamin is old enough to be weaned, I can't imagine that Namon would be agreeable to your leaving."

Teara pursed her lips. "He's not. But that's not why I'm hesitant to go. You see. Well," Teara said demurely, "I believe I am with child again."

"Oh Teara!" Abish squealed, then hushed herself. "Are you sure?"

"I think so. But I wanted to wait a few more weeks to be sure."

"Perhaps this time you'll have a daughter and we can spend our days together—" she broke off to catch her breath as Teara laughed.

"I think the only person more excited than you will be Namon!"

"There is no question of you leaving," she said, wagging a finger at Teara. "Especially with some unknown illness in the land."

"But the people need help," Teara said with a searching stare.

Walking a few paces away, Abish sought to formulate a coherent thought in her mind. All of the questions she'd been struggling with the past few months were being forced to a head. She would have to choose. But what would everyone think? How would this affect her children? She remembered something her father had once said when she asked how he decided what was best for his patients. He responded that at some point it was no longer about *what* decision you made, just that you had the courage to make one.

Abish took a deep breath and smiled at the look of relief on Teara's face as she said, "I will go in your place."

"Oh, thank you! I was hoping you would say that. I know it's much to ask and I wouldn't if I didn't think it was so important that someone go and help them. Your children are welcome to stay with us while you're gone."

"All right. I'll come by with them in the morning."

As Abish went back inside and watched her children sleep, she said a silent prayer. It was for them, not for herself, so she felt as if it might be heard.

Watch over them. Protect them.

Then she went to prepare for her journey.

* * *

It had been a long time since Abish had traveled this far. Though she hardly lived a sedentary lifestyle, childbirth and age had taken their toll and she began to wonder if she were up to the task. But she accepted the challenge and set off on the arduous hike across the mountains to the east, comforted when she saw the valley floor on the morning of the third day.

She approached the city gates of Siron by dusk, and a rough-looking guard instantly commanded her to halt. "I can't let you in," he huffed. "We have a sickness among the people and enough trouble as it is without foreigners pestering us."

"I know," she tried to explain. "That's why I am here. I am a healer from the Land of Ishmael and have come to lend my services in whatever capacity you need."

She knew that he would be incredulous to her request and could almost hear his thoughts: A *woman* healer? But Abish stood her ground and waited. Perhaps he realized she wouldn't budge or perhaps there was such a sense of desperation surrounding the city that at last he unbarred the heavy gate and allowed her to enter.

The streets were all but deserted.

Every now and then a dark shadow would scurry around the corner of a building. Dim lights flickered behind shuttered windows, and there was an eerie stillness in the air that made Abish uneasy. She would have to find a place to take refuge for the night. But she knew no one and felt reluctant to attempt to locate an inn this late in the evening. Finally, she found a secluded area just behind the communal well. Drawing out her cloak from her pack, Abish crouched in the corner and propped herself up against a crumbling wall and slept.

When morning came, she examined the scene around her while working out a crick in her neck and found that she could not help looking—as she often did in a new land—for a particular face in the crowd. But then again, Abish remembered cynically, her mother had rarely awakened before noon. Some early-risers, however, were coming to the well to draw their daily water. By their appearance, they were lesser servants and most likely to have the information she needed. She approached an old woman with stringy black hair and a pronounced hump on her back. Ignoring the suspicion in her eyes, Abish revealed her quest and asked who was in charge of the city. At first the woman refused to answer, but then must have decided that her loyalties would be for naught if they were all dead.

"Lord Ahimelek is the man you want to see. You can't miss his house—it's across the riverbank where the crossroads begin. Just follow the sounds of merriment and feasting," she sniffed, hobbling off with a water jug on her head.

After having breakfast and washing her face and hands, Abish felt better prepared for what might lie ahead. Contemplating the possible rejection she would receive, Abish then followed the woman's instructions, pausing only to ask briefly if she were on the right path. Soon the smell of incense-laden fires filled her nostrils, and she let it lead her until she could finally see the outer patio leading to the governor's house. Two rough-looking guards stood at the borders of the pillared square, and she took a deep breath as she approached them.

"Stop!" one of them ordered. "No beggars allowed here."

Though indignant at the insult, she tried to respond calmly again "I'm not here to ask for anything. Instead, I would like to be allowed to practice my healing in your city. If I could speak to your Master—"

"He can't be disturbed," one of them interrupted brusquely.

"But if I could just—"

The two guards stepped closer together, bridging the slight gap that had allowed her to catch a momentary glimpse into the inner confines of the compound. The old woman had been correct in that the occupants appeared to hold little concern for the sickness that existed outside their walls. Disgusted, Abish walked away. Now she had no choice but to limit her work to the poorer villages on the outskirts of the city—where the law of the land would have less interest, and where perhaps she could do some good in whatever time she had here.

15

Wiping her sweat-stained brow, Abish regretted the confidence that she'd had several days ago when she first arrived in Siron. More than ever, she wished Teara were here. She took a moment to step away from the latest casualty and assess the situation.

The shaking, sweating and nausea were all symptoms she had become familiar with during her years of treating this seasonal illness, and yet what she had been seeing here had confounded her—and her remedies were providing just the slightest relief from the fevers and intense pain that her patients were experiencing. During the last outbreak her people had dealt with, she had realized that it was more important to merely keep them resting and nourished with a little broth than to fight against the numerous other symptoms for which she had no answers. In doing so, recovery was expected within several days. But as she wandered throughout one particular village, she found this was a different type of foe: one that struck unmercifully and with unchecked agony.

Her latest casualty had suffered from the headaches, vomiting, and skin fever that she had expected, so she employed the usual treatment. He had sickened a fortnight ago, she was told. One day he was working in the fields and the next he was being carried back to his tent by other workers. Prayers were offered and the stars consulted; the small idol left at the foot of his bed left Abish to wonder if the spreading of the gospel had even reached this far corner of the land. When she first saw him, the man was unconscious and unresponsive. The family was desperate, not caring what steps she took as long as she saved him. But it was not until last night that she had noticed that his skin had taken on an unusual pallor. Thinking it was just an illusion from the murky light that the cheap oil lamp cast, Abish waited until morning to see if her suspicions were correct. As dawn came, she pushed back the flap of the tent to let the first light in and realized that not only had the man's skin turned a sickly yellow but that he was also lying in a pool of his own blood. His mouth still hung slightly open from his last raspy breath. Suddenly needing air, Abish turned back around and exited the tent.

What was happening here?

Abish took a deep breath and looked back toward the tent. In a moment of courage, she returned to the scene of devastation, trying to push past the hysterical family members that now crowded around the corpse; she realized that she had not even had time to discover his name. His wife had become hysterical and had to be carried off, while the man's mother ripped at her clothes and hair. Abish could only stand there in silence, baffled by what she saw around her and hoping that the intense emotions that were building would not be directed toward a stranger who had only come to help and was finding that she could offer nothing.

What of the others who are sickening? she thought numbly. *Are they to suffer the same fate?*

The old, the young, the men and women that she assumed had been robust before being struck down—would she find them in a few days drowning in their own blood? She felt helpless and found herself wandering away from the sight to the river. Washing her face and arms brusquely with the tepid water that had formed in a shallow pool, she ignored the incessant buzzing of insects around her and wondered if it would just be best to leave for home. Her remedies were for naught. Those who would live would live and those who were fated to die were dying.

The rest of the day was so discouraging that Abish had all but decided to leave Siron and return for home. Hoping to replenish her supplies, she was wandering around the nearly deserted marketplace when a nervous, young girl approached her.

"Are you the healer?" she whispered.

Abish looked at the girl who wore the attire of a rich man's servant. "Yes," she responded warily.

"My mistress asks for you to come. Her child has become sick and she heard that you might be one to help."

Abish agreed, wondering how news of her slight successes had overshadowed the failures. "Who is your mistress?"

"Lady Yak-tuk. She is wife to Lord Ahimelek."

"So Lord Ahimelek now wishes to see me?" *How ironic*, she thought.

"No," the servant bowed. "His wife sends for you. For her child's sake. The master must not know you are present."

The situation becoming clear, Abish nodded and followed her guide through the streets of the city where only a few brave citizens, desperate like her to stock up on meager rations or retrieve what they hoped would not be tainted water, dared venture. As she watched them, Abish wished she had more answers to give, explanations as to why they were stricken so. But as the servant led her through a palm-laden pavilion to the inner sanctum of the women's quarters, Abish realized that she had better find some reserve of confidence or this might not go well.

She was brought to a room that was cloaked in darkness. All of the windows were covered and hung with chuchum blossoms to prevent evil spirits from entering. A young boy lay on a nearby bed, while a woman knelt beside him. Abish waited while the servant made the announcement of their arrival, and only then did the woman turn to look at her. Sorrow was written so plainly upon her face that Abish wondered if the mother already knew what was to be her child's fate. As Abish approached, she briefly appraised the child's situation: a yellowish tinge was just beginning around his eyes, and she watched as his limbs quivered slightly. Just as she neared the bedside, he lurched to one side, vomiting a stream of blood-tinged bile. Abish leapt back just in time as one of the servants ran to hastily clean up the mess.

"He has been like this for days," the mother whispered. "I don't know what more to do for him. Our healers have come and gone, shaking their heads. Our priests' prayers have been for naught. Do you have any answers?"

Abish dreaded her question. "I'm not sure I do. This is unlike any illness I have seen before, even during the wettest years. Some symptoms are the same, but this coloring," she brushed back a lock of the boy's dark hair, "is unfamiliar. What does it mean?" For too long Abish had had Teara at her side and had grown used to speaking her thoughts aloud.

"I . . . I don't know," the woman stammered.

"I'm sorry," Abish gestured for one of the servants to bring cool water. "I didn't mean to ask you such a question. Try and get as much liquid down him as possible. Keep him comfortable and cool his brow with a wet cloth, perhaps fanning him as well. There's little more I can offer. It's in God's hands now."

At first the woman looked as if she had been slapped. "You're one of *them*? A believer! I should have known. Next you'll be telling me that this is your God's will and that I should just accept our fate. But I won't! This is my only son and I won't let him die!" The mother flung herself across her son's body, eliciting a slight groan from the unconscious boy.

The servant who had brought Abish there now stepped behind her. "You'd better leave. If she becomes agitated, her husband could discover you here. Depart through the east gate." She pulled her over to the doorway. "That's down this corridor and to the left. Go quickly and quietly so you won't be discovered."

Dejected, Abish realized she had no choice but to leave. She moved as stealthily as she could, trying to avoid the boisterous laughter that seemed to come from every corner of the house, making a mockery of the pain she had just witnessed. But in her attempt to remain unseen she became lost and, in a panic, she realized she'd gone too far and had reached the great room where the feasting was occurring. The conversations of those present were muted, but the aura of it reminded her of the gatherings that had occurred in her own home when she was a child, so she knew the gist of the words that were being spoken.

A large, rotund man draped in a costly blue tunic was reclined on several silken pillows. He had a trained jaguar at his feet, and Abish recognized that such a man must be the master of the house. Aside from the numerous servants who attended to a myriad of his needs, there were a few well-dressed women who were stroking his brow and feet and seductively walking between the other male guests. It took only a moment for Abish to assess their duties, especially when one received a playful squeeze on a particularly ample section of her body. She squealed in mock protest while the others vied for similar attention. Abish flattened herself back against the wall, sickened by the vulgar display and the callousness of the man whose son lay dying in the other room. Her fists clenched and she found herself taking one more look, half-tempted to confront him.

Instead, her attention was stolen by one of the young women who flirted and laughed at his side. She was beautiful in a way that defied description. Her hair was arranged in intricate coils that glistened like stars amid blackest night. The gold that graced her from her arms to her ankles should have weighed her down, but she merely floated like the smoke from the nearby lamps—slow and languid—between the other guests that were arranged on silken pillows around the room. Though veiled, there was something familiar about her face, and Abish found herself blinking twice to convince herself she was being deceived.

No. It couldn't be. Unless her mother had found a way to reverse time, the raven-haired beauty was not her mother, and yet still she could not shake the feeling that she had seen this countenance before. Abish wanted to creep closer and solve the mystery, but before she could, the woman led one of the male guests through an opposite door.

Her efforts frustrated, she left the compound and waited in nervous anticipation, wondering when, if ever, the evening would end for those inside. As she sat huddled within her cloak, Abish noticed a few shadowy forms exiting the premises, and she watched anxiously to see if the attractive woman would be among them. At first it appeared that she was not going to be one of those leaving. But then, as the moon rose to hover above the city like a giant silver pendant, the woman at last appeared, wrapped in a green cloak, her head now brazenly bare.

The woman passed quickly as if unaware of Abish's presence, leaving the scent of some exotic flowered perfume as an easy trail to follow. She moved through the darkness with a precision that revealed she knew her destination well while Abish continually stumbled over unseen obstacles. Forced to concentrate on her every step, Abish soon realized that her prey was no longer in sight. Standing with her hands on her hips, she was considering her next move when she felt the cold steel of a dagger against her throat.

16

A voice hissed in Abish's ear. "Who are you and why are you following me?"

Abish didn't dare move.

"I . . . I only wanted to . . ." she gasped. "I mean you no harm. I'm not armed."

At first she couldn't discern if the woman believed her, but the dagger was lowered and Abish was set free. She turned to face her attacker.

There was an emptiness in her eyes that Abish knew would haunt her for a while. But it was more than the hollowness of the woman's stare that kept her attention. Beneath the heavy make-up and satin veil, Abish recognized that this creature of the night was Akah's daughter who had run away all those years ago.

"Isabel? Is it you?"

At first there was no response to Abish's question. Then the woman said, "Come with me. It's dangerous to be out alone this late at night."

Abish followed until they came into a courtyard. There was an impressive brick dwelling lit from within by a number of lanterns, and they went to it. The woman rapped thrice, and the door opened. She gestured for Abish to step inside. Isabel then motioned to a servant woman to come and take her cloak, asking, "Is he asleep?"

"Yes, mistress. Some time ago."

"Good." Then turning to face Abish, she asked, "How did you find me?"

At first Abish didn't know how to answer. "I, well, I wasn't looking for you. I came here hoping to help with the illness that has afflicted your people and was sent for at the governor's house this evening. I was just leaving when I came upon your . . . gathering."

"So you saw who I am, what I do?"

"Isabel." Abish's words stuck in her throat. "Why?"

Sitting tiredly in a nearby chair, Isabel played with one of the gold bangles around her wrist. "It's work, and as you can see, I'm paid handsomely."

"I still don't understand. Your family misses you. Why did you leave?"

Her countenance hardened into a look that Abish remembered so clearly from her own mother's face. When Isabel spoke, her voice seemed an echo of itself. "When that prophet-man came—Ammon, wasn't it?—he told us that we had to forgive those who had wronged us. It was the only way or we would be held accountable. I tried not to think about it because I couldn't bear the thought of what it meant. It meant that I was in the wrong and they . . . they were now blameless!"

"Who, Isabel? Who was blameless?"

But Isabel continued as if not hearing. "I was good; I didn't tell. No matter what they did, I never told. Mama and Papa never knew because I kept my secrets."

A sick feeling welled up inside her. "Isabel? Who are you talking about?"

Isabel looked at her as if remembering she were there. "Does it matter anymore? They're dead now. Ironically, I suppose I have Ammon and your god to thank for that. But they weren't merciful enough to allow me my hatred of them for everything they'd done to me."

Abish almost pushed away the thoughts that were formulating in her mind. Could it be? Her elder brothers had died years ago: one at the hands of Ammon, when he tried to attack the flock the missionary was protecting, and the other when he tried to strike down Ammon when he had been overcome by the Spirit in the throne room of King Lamoni. Abish remembered her own disgust over the two boys at their callousness and disregard to others. Were they who Isabel was referring to? And if so, what could they possibly have done to her to deserve such animosity?

Oh no!

Abish rushed to Isabel's side, but her ministrations were pushed away. "It doesn't matter anymore," the girl repeated. "They're gone and I'm here. Though, I thought that leaving my home would mean leaving the memories behind. But it doesn't."

Abish knew that only too well herself. "I'm sorry for you, Isabel," Abish soothed. "If only I had known. What your brothers did to you wasn't your fault, but you can't continue to live this way. You learned enough before you left home to know it is wrong!"

"I won't forgive them. I can't!" Isabel's eyes bored into her. "So you think it's easy to forgive someone who hurts you? Well, do you remember that day years ago when Teara was attacked?"

Abish remembered only too well. It had been during one of the city's celebrations. The two of them had parted ways and Abish was on her way to meet Teara when she'd come upon her friend and the two attackers. Later, she'd discovered they had been Akah and Laban's two wicked sons—but surely Isabel didn't know this because even Teara didn't know.

Isabel's eyes narrowed into black slits as she said mockingly, "How sad it was that my brothers came upon her all alone in the jungle."

"What are you saying?"

Isabel shrugged casually. "I was jealous of your friendship. When I saw her, I decided that perhaps I could do something about that."

Abish felt sick inside.

"Well?" Isabel demanded. "Would you forgive?"

Abish knew what she had to say to get Isabel to come with her, but as she went to speak the words, they caught in her throat. It was too much information to process. Had Isabel really been so cruel? Her brothers had almost violated her dearest friend that day. How could Isabel have done that? It reminded Abish so much of her mother's selfishness that Abish felt a familiar flash of anger spark up inside her—a feeling she thought she had finally come to control.

"Teara had done nothing to you except try to be your friend, Isabel! And I had tried to be your friend as well. I can't understand how you—"

"If you don't understand, then you can't help me." Isabel's eyes now held a combination of despair and anger.

"No, Isabel. I won't leave it at that. You must let me try to help you. In time you'll come to see things differently. And perhaps I will as well—"

"There would not be enough time for me to change the way I feel. Go. There's nothing you can do to help. I've accepted my fate, and if your god condemns me, then you condemn me as well."

"But I don't condemn you!"

"Get out! Leave!" Isabel screamed. "I don't want you here."

* * *

How could she have failed so miserably?

Abish stumbled into the city square in a daze, beating herself mentally until she could barely stand. Isabel had needed her to speak with faith and compassion. Instead, she allowed her own anger and self-doubt to creep forward and ruin what may have been her one chance to save the girl! *Oh, Father!* She stumbled, blinded by her tears. *Forgive me!* Once again she was being torn in many directions. She had barely helped the people here even though she had stayed much longer than planned. And her children surely needed her back in Ishmael. Yet if she left, would Isabel continue to be trapped in a life of misery and sin?

She slept fitfully in her pitiful corner behind the well, leaving her thoughts as bruised as her body the next morning. As she wakened and stumbled toward the city gates, Abish felt sickness everywhere: sickness of the body and of the spirit. Then, up on the rise behind the city's main temple, she saw a grove of trees. Staggering toward it, she fell upon her knees, pleading as she had not pled for many years.

"Oh, my Father, I am so sorry. How could I have been such an unworthy servant? I come before Thee as low as the dust and beg thy forgiveness. Please don't desert me as I have deserted Thee."

Abish was drained. Depleted. There was nothing more she had to give, and she collapsed to the ground and slept.

* * *

A quiet breeze brushed across her body as the call of a macaw echoed somewhere off in the distance. Abish raised her eyes to heaven and watched as a single beam of sunlight broke through the morning's haze, and she felt strengthened. This was no time to fail. She knew what she had to do. Rushing back to Isabel's house, she nearly pounded the door down with her fist. Ignoring the stares of neighbors, Abish waited until the servant-woman from the night before opened the door.

"Is Isabel home?" she asked anxiously.

The older woman tried to close the door again. "No."

"I must speak to her. Please. It's of utmost importance."

The woman snorted. "Why would I get her? She sent you away last night."

Abish ignored the servant's protestations and pushed past her into the house. But its rooms were empty, though it looked like Isabel did not live here alone. It didn't matter who she entertained within the confines of this house—Abish was past judging her. She wanted only to save the young girl.

Unwilling to be defeated, Abish returned to the governor's house. If she had to sit all day by the wall waiting for Isabel to make an appearance, she would do it! Though the sun beat down on her and she soon grew faint with hunger, still she waited. Finally one of the gates opened and she jumped up and saw Lady Yak-tuk, dressed in mourning white and with her entourage of women and guards.

"I know her!" the grief-stricken woman shrieked as she saw Abish loitering by the doorway. "She is here under false pretenses and is a threat to our city. My husband has ordered her thrown out."

The guards did not question the truthfulness of that statement but grabbed her roughly by the arms. Abish protested and demanded to speak to the governor and explain, but to no avail. By the time they were at the city gates, she was bruised and hopeless. "If you're caught within the city walls again," one of the guards explained, "you'll be cast into prison."

This made no sense! After her prayer, she'd had such a feeling of peace that everything would be all right. Why was this happening? Didn't God want her to help Isabel? Looking longingly back at the city walls, Abish realized there was little she could do now but return home.

17

Fortunately, the worst stretch of Abish's trip was crossing the brief mountain range that had signaled the end of her original journey. Now there were only a few flat valley gorges to pass through. If Abish stopped for nothing but food and water, she might be with her family again soon. This thought spurred her on until finally she descended the last hill just as the sun had broken through the clouds and rimmed the valley in muted light. As she looked down at the mist in the valley below, she wanted nothing more than to find a soft bed of grass on which to lie down.

Abish dabbed at her dripping brow and ignored the sound of thunder overhead. The return trip had taken more of a toll than she'd thought and her legs now felt like rubber beneath her. But she had to surge onward. *Think of Miriam and Jarum.* How happy a reunion it will be. This was, she realized as she trudged along, the longest she had ever been away from them. And yet she had carried a part of them with her. No longer feeling alone, she cast a silent prayer heavenward that everything had gone well in her absence. As the muscles in her legs began to burn, Abish kept herself distracted with pleasant thoughts, like the time Jarum had caught a frog and tried to hide it under a bowl. It had been quite a surprise when she'd gone to prepare dinner that evening! Or there was the time that Miriam had found Abish's wedding gown and put it on, dragging it across the dirty floor of the house before Abish discovered her. As she came upon the young girl humming while she pranced around, instead of angry thoughts entering her mind, Abish realized sadly that it wouldn't be long before her daughter fit in the dress.

Such thoughts helped to pass the time, and soon the borders of Shilom came into view. But Abish stopped only long enough to replenish her water supply at the local well. Any fatigue was surpassed by the knowledge that night would soon be upon her and she was still far from home. So she continued onward. There was nothing else to do.

When she at last saw Ishmael's temples rising in the distance, Abish nearly wept from relief. There were moments when she feared she would not make it. The few hours of sleep she'd had over the last several days were no longer sustaining her and she had never been more exhausted in her life. Splashing the remaining water from her goatskin pouch on her face, she felt revived enough to continue down the now well-trod path toward the city center. Crossing the rope bridge that spanned the deep ravine, she looked down momentarily. Suddenly her line of vision crossed and dual images swayed beneath her. Abish gripped the side ropes more tightly and felt her way across the expanse. There was little traffic along the well-worn trail, and she quickened her pace, finally coming to the small village. In the distance, she could see Akah's hut.

But as neared the small dwelling, her strength finally gave way. She tried to shake off the dizziness that rushed over her and ignore the pounding in her head. Somewhere in the distance, she heard the sound of a voice calling her. As darkness enveloped her, she reached out.

She was falling, falling.

* * *

Abish fought against the gentle swaying of the ground beneath her and tried to sit up. It was too much effort. Her tongue felt as if it had grown three sizes in her mouth. Her head, two sizes too small for the grey matter inside. She managed to crack her eyes open a little and was instantly punished by the light from above. Clamping them shut again, she shielded her eyes with a shaky hand and tried again. Was she moving? The light now flickered in such a rhythmic fashion that it called her back into unconsciousness again. Resisting was futile and she sank back into the confines of the rocking prison in which she was being held.

And then, the rocking stopped and the dreams began.

She was a child again and she felt the stone walls around her pressing in and the voices of her mother and father in the distance. With a sob she cried out to them that she was sorry. So sorry. Only, she couldn't remember why. The air was so heavy she couldn't breathe. She had to get the weight off her chest.

The light returned and she felt herself released from the crushing pressure. She was floating on a cloud and wrapped in mist. An image materialized off in the distance and she tried to fly to it . . . *Jared! Wait for me!* But he soared faster and faster, like a giant eagle, and she couldn't keep up. She felt alone, abandoned. Once again, voices swirled around her. But the voices were kind and gentle this time, and she cried out in her mind when she saw two figures coming toward her.

Sarah! Jacob!

They looked so happy. Abish tried to go to them—the loving couple who were her friends so many years ago. She wanted to fly—fly away to the heavens where she knew she would be free! She wanted to embrace them and tell them that she now had children of her own—but they shook their heads. They would not take her with them! And somehow, she knew she didn't want to go. She fell like a rock to the ground and felt a thousand arms trying to hold her to the earth.

When next she regained consciousness, Abish had the sense that she was not alone. But she only had energy to half-open her eyes and when she did, she saw through a milky haze Akah's face hovering a few feet above the hammock she was in. Unable to differentiate between dreaming and reality anymore, Abish groaned. This time the voice that responded made sense.

"You're awake now? Good. Everyone will be relieved." The old woman gestured frantically, and soon there were two faces above hers.

"Abish? Praise to God, our prayers have been answered."

"Teara?" her voice cracked as if it hadn't been used for years.

"Rest, there's no need to exert any energy. Would you like food, water?"

She managed a brief nod, unable to verbalize which. Both were brought and she grunted slightly when the water was introduced. "Just a little," Akah ordered as the tepid liquid was poured into her mouth. Most of it trickled down the side of her neck, but enough moistened her mouth that she was able to ask, "Children?"

Teara explained, "We've been caring for them."

"How . . . long have I been ill?"

"Long enough," Akah huffed.

"For seven days and nights, you have hovered between life and death, Abish," Teara elaborated. "I thought it best to bring you to your—I mean, our home," she added, "to care for you and so the children would not be afraid."

Abish cast her eyes around her and recognized the familiar walls of her childhood home, though which room she was in she could no longer tell. Giving a sincere smile, she managed a weak, "Thank you."

"A few days ago your skin started taking on an awful color like spoiled milk." Akah's eyes widened. "Never saw anything like it before in my life."

"It was . . . the illness I saw in Siron," she managed.

Teara frowned. "If I'd known that something so horrific awaited you, my guilt would have been two-fold at letting you go there."

Abish protested as much as she was able. "After what I saw, it's a miracle that I survived."

"Ammon gave you a blessing. That was what did it," Akah said matter-of-factly.

"And now you're back with us." Teara squeezed her hands tightly.

She groaned slightly as she adjusted her legs, which felt as heavy as bricks. "Are there any here that have been afflicted with this illness?" she suddenly thought to ask.

Teara shook her head. "Not that I know of."

It was then Abish noticed the protective silk netting hanging around her bed, another reminder of her privileged past. But she was no longer comfortable being pampered. "I should try and get up—"

"Oh no, you don't," Akah ordered, forcing her off shaky legs and back into the soft bed. "You'll stay as long as you need to. Your children can be with me a little while longer until you're set right again. There's certainly enough room now that I'm all alone. Now, we'll leave you to rest. Call out if you need anything."

Abish was too weak to argue with anybody and she lay back, trying to take it all in. She knew how close she had come to death, having witnessed the merciless course the illness could take. God must not be finished with her yet.

"May I come in?"

Abish turned toward the familiar voice and saw Ammon standing shyly in the doorway. "Akah said you were resting and threatened to run me off if I wore you out."

She managed a small grin. "I believe her."

"You had me worried. I thought you might not recover."

"Now who needs to have more faith?" She laughed softly.

The mood lightened, and she raised a trembling hand to keep him silent while she spoke. She found herself telling him about Isabel and the life was she living. They both agreed that this was not the kind of news to tell Akah and her family, especially if their daughter eventually made the choice to come back to them—at which point it would be her story to tell.

"Oh, Ammon!" Abish suddenly broke into tears. "It was all my fault! If I hadn't faltered, she may have come back with me!"

"Abish, you can't take responsibility for this. Isabel has made her own choices." He knelt beside her. "It is up to God to soften her heart. Hopefully she will remember that she is still His daughter and there is always a way back. That is the power of the Atonement, Abish. It is the gift that Christ gives to us."

Abish smiled. "Promise me you will always be my friend."

Ammon replied, his green eyes sparkling, "Yes. Friends always."

Land of Ishmael
77 BC

18

The new year had arrived and the citizens of Ishmael were leaving their tents and homes and gathering in eager anticipation for the celebration. Even the brothers of Ammon and King Anti-Nephi-Lehi had come to share this day with them. Abish and Teara's families joined in the pilgrimage as well and listened as the morning air began to reverberate with the sound of leather drums and conch-shell trumpets.

Abish smiled as she led her children to the festivities. Jarum was growing so tall and handsome, and Miriam carried herself like the young woman she was becoming. But after the king's procession was finished, her children reverted back to the children they still were, squabbling over their differing desires of the how the day would be spent. Jarum wanted to watch the wrestling match in the main square while Miriam longed to see the dancers from Shimnilon. Abish tossed up her hands in defeat, but the matter was resolved after Namon agreed to take Jarum and Benjamin with him and Miriam found a friend whose family of five girls shared her interests.

Left alone with Teara and Ruth, who was anxious to toddle off with the others but still too young, Abish was a little worried that her friend could not endure the excitement of the day. Little newborn Rebekah was asleep and swaddled contentedly against Teara's back, but Abish knew that her companion must be tired, so she led them over to a nearby wall.

"Is it just my imagination," Abish laughed, "or has she grown since yesterday?"

Teara sat next to her with a grunt. "I long for the day when she can walk."

"They will be grown before you know it. My own are growing up before my eyes."

"Nine years of age is an independent time. When I passed by your house yesterday, I saw Miriam hard at work."

"She seems to thrive on the very tasks that drive me mad. I've never known a girl who was so organized and capable. In the course of a morning, she'll have all the pots mended, the water drawn, a batch of bread drying on the rack and at least two skeins of yarn rolled!"

"Tell her that if she ever struggles to find things to do," Teara said, "she is more than welcome to come to my house! I don't know how I would be able to keep up with it all if you hadn't agreed to practice your healing again."

With Teara still living in Abish's childhood home, it made sense for her to continue to care for the worst of their patients. Abish, however, had been in charge of traveling about the countryside ever since she returned from Shilom and had fully recovered. Hers was the more demanding responsibility, but with Teara's children so young it was the only way they could tend to the healing needs of the people.

"I don't know what I'll do without Miriam when she's gone."

"She still has many years before a handsome young man will catch her eye . . . and snare the most beautiful and capable wife in Ishmael."

Abish sighed. "Miriam is beautiful, isn't she?" It was inevitable that she would be. At times, she saw a bit of herself in her daughter, and during disturbing moments, she saw her own mother staring back at her. But Miriam had a spirit of goodness and selflessness that Saranhi had never known. This inward quality and outward appearance would make for a powerful combination as her daughter matured. If only Jared were here to chase the unwelcome suitors off!

"Now I know how you have felt," Teara said, stroking the set of tiny fingers that had appeared on her shoulder, "wanting to keep your children close to you. Already I'm afraid for them. What will the future bring? What trials will they face that I can't protect them from?"

Abish looked into the infant's dark eyes. "I don't know. The only thing we can do is try to prepare them the best we can."

When she saw Ammon walking toward them, Abish found that a smile had quickly replaced the worry on her face.

"Greetings." He held up a hand in friendship, and they returned the gesture.

"Well," Teara said with a sigh, "I had better see how Namon is faring."

Ammon sat down at the vacated spot on the wall. "What a righteous example of motherhood," he said as they watched Teara walk away. Abish nodded silently. "Of course," Ammon flushed as if realizing his omission, "you are also an admirable example."

"That's all right. I'm not entirely sure she's the standard I want to be held to!" she said with a small laugh. "But I also admire her."

Ammon cleared his throat. "Jarum will be beginning his apprenticeship soon, won't he?"

Abish nodded. "Yes."

"Has he chosen a field?"

It was on her tongue to say that her son's path would have already been decided for him—if things had been different. But she had vowed to keep the past in its place, so instead she answered, "We've not decided yet. I suppose there's time. For now, if he continues to learn to read and write it will be enough."

"If he needs any suggestions, I know of several men who are eager for a hardworking boy. So let me know."

Just then Ammon's brothers came walking past. They gave Abish a greeting, which she returned, adding that it was always an honor when they all came to visit. "The privilege has been ours," one brother said. "We are always amazed when we come among this people and see their faithfulness."

"It's true," Ammon said with much seriousness. "And yet do you remember when those at home nearly laughed us to scorn for coming to this land!"

Omner smiled. "I do not recall it being that bad." But the other brothers seemed to share Ammon's sentiment.

"And yet how great is our reason for rejoicing," Ammon continued. "Who could have supposed when we started from Zarahemla that God would have granted unto us such great blessings?" His voice became more animated. "Again, I ask you, what great blessings He has bestowed upon us? Our brethren were in darkness and now they've been brought to see the wondrous light of God. Thousands of them now rejoice and have been brought into the fold."

Abish had known Ammon long enough that she recognized when the Spirit had begun to fill his soul. He continued to expound on the wonders of their mission here, comparing their work to the work of a farmer—who would thrust in his sickle and reap with all of his might. But when he finished, Abish was surprised when Aaron rebuked him.

"I fear you are being swept away by your own pride, my brother."

Ammon flushed and looked down. "I don't boast of my own strength, nor in my own wisdom; but I confess that my joy is full and my heart is brimming with joy. Still, I rejoice only in my God."

With a hearty slap on his back, Aaron accepted his explanation and then directed their attention to the arrival of the king.

Left alone again, Abish couldn't contain her own reaction to his words. "You care about this people as if they are your own children. I've never witnessed such . . . love like that." Then she spotted her own children playing in the distance.

"I think you understand that love very well, Abish." He reached over and touched her hand gently with his. It sent an unexpected tremor through her which he must have felt as well because he immediately withdrew it.

At first she was afraid he would say he had some important matter to attend to. But he remained, and she was glad for the company.

She was about to ask Ammon if his brothers were going to stay for a while when she heard a shout. A stranger suddenly burst through the wall of trees into the clearing, stumbling and fighting for breath. He was Lamanite, but since he was not attired as a warrior she instantly relaxed. That is, until he began to frantically wave like a man possessed.

"An army . . . they are coming. You must be warned!" he panted.

Ammon jumped up and ran toward him, followed closely by Abish.

"Who has amassed an army?" he demanded.

"It is the Lamanite army once again," the stranger gasped. "I come from Midian. When we heard the news, we began to flee. I was sent to give warning to those who may not have heard. But my foot was injured and so I've been delayed; they could be on the outskirts of your land even now."

Ammon and Abish stared at each other in horror at what this meant. They pushed their way through the crowd with the messenger until they found the king. The reality of their situation was written plainly upon every face, but Ammon somehow managed to stay in control.

"God will be with us," he said as he saw the fear on Abish's face.

"Take this man to the palace," King Anti-Nephi-Lehi instructed one of the councilmen. "Give him food and drink and whatever else he needs." Then he turned to Abish. "Would you come and tend to his injury?"

Abish tried to keep down the bile that threatened to rise in her throat as she nodded.

Ammon now addressed the crowd with a loud voice. "Have the weavers' and potters' guilds take the children to the palace and hide them there. The rest of us will do as before and plead that the Lord will soften our attackers' hearts once again."

Abish's head was spinning. *Not again! I can't think about it. I can't do this!*

Ammon looked down for a moment then raised his voice once more. "I'd give anything to stop this from happening again." Ammon groaned. "At least we can protect what is most precious to us this time."

Abish now knew beyond any doubt how much Ammon had suffered all these years. These were his people as well and she had to be strong for him. "God will be with us." She repeated his words.

He took a deep breath and looked at her, unashamed of his tear-streaked face. "Yes. He will be with us. I wanted to believe that something so horrible could never happen again—that evil would eventually have its fill and we would be left alone. I was wrong, and now even more of my people will suffer." Ammon reached up and rent the collar of his tunic, symbolically expressing his grief. "Yet I will not cease to do everything I can to protect them." He then strode off into the anxious crowd.

Abish kissed her children, trying to hide her fear from them, and sent them off with Akah. And then, standing there for one more precious moment, Abish left as well to do what she knew she had to do.

19

Hours passed until Abish was so weary that she could barely support herself. The wounded kept coming, and she had to remind herself that it was not for Jared that she now feared. He would not be brought to her again, battered and broken. She would not have to say good-bye to him again. Instead, she had to face the multitude of those she called friends and tend to their wounds while their loved ones stood by and prayed. Even when she began to stagger from person to person and the world slurred around her, she kept on—mending bones, closing wounds, wiping away blood and agony from their pleading lips.

At the end of the day, the only difference was that there was no glorious wave of repentant souls stepping forward to take the place of those they had slain. Pure evil had come against them in the form of their own brethren, spurred on once again by the Nephite apostates. Only the sun sinking below the horizon had frustrated their bloodlust, thus saving the remaining Anti-Nephi-Lehies. Sheer willpower propelled her forward as Abish moved through the crowd, giving final instructions for the remaining wounded. She had kept her feelings in check for so long that she almost collapsed in tears; however, when she saw Teara coming toward her, her own tunic stained with dark patches of blood, she knew she must go on.

"You should have let Namon take you home," Abish said guiltily.

Teara protested. "I want to stay as long as I'm needed."

"The worst seems to be over . . . for now. You look as if you haven't the strength to stand. Your children need you. Go home and convince your husband to go with you if you can."

Teara wearily agreed.

Wanting to reassure herself that the worst of the threat really was past, Abish went to find Ammon. Perhaps he'd already given the order for the children's return. All Abish wanted now was to hold Jarum and Miriam in her arms. Of course, she had better clean herself up first—and then she would take them home. Since the fighting had been mostly to the north, at least they would not have to witness the carnage on their trek back. They might even be able to find some peace tonight.

All she had to do was look at Ammon standing next to his brothers by the palace wall, however, to know that it would be a while before he felt any semblance of peace. *This bloodbath has aged him*, she thought as she went to his side, desperate to comfort him.

He barely registered the touch of her hand on his arm. "Abish," his voice croaked. "Have all been attended to?"

"Nearly," she said. "There are only a few waiting who were not so severely wounded. What do we do now?"

He spoke as if it took great effort. "We need to speak with the king."

"Now? It's grown very late and you're exhausted."

"This can't wait."

Though he had not asked her to accompany them, Ammon did not protest when she fell into step behind them. Soon they passed through the outer gate into the inner courtyard, along the path that had become familiar to both of them over the years, until they came to a dimly lit corridor that was sparsely guarded. There was none of the fanfare or protocol to announce their arrival. When they entered the throne room, they saw King Anti-Nephi-Lehi next to his brother, King Lamoni, who was slumped forward on his throne with the matters of the day weighing heavily on him as well. If not for the color of his tunic, one would never assume that this was the ruler of what had once been a prosperous land. Instead, he was faced with the realization that outside the walls of his sanctuary there was only death while he sat here helpless to do anything about it.

"Your Majesty," Abish said first.

King Lamoni raised his head and a slight smile crossed his face. He flicked a few fingers on his hand to motion them both forward. "Then it is over?"

Ammon now spoke, "For the most part. Who knows if they will come again on the morrow."

"I have sent spies to assess the situation," King Lamoni explained. "They will remain on the outskirts of the city, prepared to send a messenger should they again attack. At least we may have sufficient time to protect our children once more." His head dropped into his lap as silent sobs racked his body. "These attackers have already attempted to dethrone my brother. It will not be enough that all who believe suffer. They wish to exterminate us!"

"That is why," Ammon said solemnly, "we are left with no choice. We must leave this land."

Aaron, Himni and Omner nodded their agreement. Their clothes were also stained in blood, and it was then Abish noticed that Himni had a large gash on his left arm. She rushed to him but he waved her off. "Thank you, Abish, but we have more important matters to attend to." Then he added, "After what we saw today, we agree that you are left with little choice. But where shall the people go?"

"I will inquire of the Lord and if he says to us, go down unto our brethren, will ye go?"

"But . . . but . . ." sputtered King Lamoni, "the Nephites will kill us! They know of our many murders and sins." The king had risen from his throne and tried to stand, but the day had robbed him of his strength and his one leg was not sufficient support.

His brother helped him back into his seat. "Calm yourself. Ammon would never do anything unless he was directed of God."

"Yes," Ammon agreed. "I will go and inquire of the Lord what we should do."

King Lamoni's face softened. "Yes, inquire of the Lord. If He says for this people to go down, then so be it. And if that means we will be their slaves, then perhaps that will repair some of our sins against them."

"No." Ammon shook his head. "It's against the law of our brethren, which was established by my father, that there should be any slaves among them. Instead, let us go down and rely upon the mercies of our brethren."

King Anti-Nephi-Lehi agreed. "Yes. Inquire of the Lord, and if he saith unto us go, we will go; otherwise we will perish in this land."

But King Lamoni nodded wearily. "You have served me and this people well since you came. I am forever in your debt and I know that you will continue to serve this people, even if it is without me." Ignoring the shocked looks around him, he said, "If God commands our departure, I am not sure I can leave the remainder of my people who have not accepted the gospel of our Lord and who will undoubtedly choose to stay. They will need further guidance and perhaps time before they accept His words and ask for forgiveness of their sins. Besides," he tapped the stump of his leg. "I will not be carried like a babe from the only home I know."

Abish felt tears welling up in her eyes. They would miss him, but she understood how he felt. The thought of leaving Ishmael was more than she could conceive as well. There had been a time when she had never wanted to return here, but she had since allowed Ishmael a place in her heart. It was where she had received the gospel, where she had been reunited with Jared, and where her children were born. She thought she would die here as well and join her father and Jared up on the hill.

"So go," King Lamoni pleaded. "Ask God and save yourselves."

After Ammon left, minutes seemed to pass like hours as they all eagerly waited for his return. The night was quiet but heavy with their fears. To think that this morning all she had thought about was celebrating with her people and now they had been torn apart again.

When will this end?

* * *

By the amount of light filtering through the trees outside, morning had come some time ago. Abish looked at her children sleeping on blankets in the throne room and then sat up. Lying awake most of the night praying about the situation had helped calm her fears but left her physically exhausted. Teara and Namon had joined them as well to try to rest, though Namon had left a few hours ago to join the two kings in the council chambers. When she saw Teara stir, she went to her.

"Did you sleep much?" Abish asked.

Teara shook her head. "No, and it appears you didn't either. There was a lot Namon and I had to discuss last night," she added. "Abish, I must talk to you—"

They were interrupted by the sound of trumpets. The throne room doors opened, and a throng of people who had been anxiously awaiting word outside began to filter in. As the room filled, Ammon and his brethren returned from the council chambers, followed by the kings and the other council members. They stood in front of the gathering, at which point Ammon stepped forward, raising both of his hands to quiet the crowd.

"My people," he began. "The Lord has answered our prayers. He said unto me, 'Get this people out of this land, that they perish not; for Satan has great hold on the hearts of the Amalekites, who do stir up the Lamanites to anger against their brethren to slay them; therefore get thee out of this land; and blessed are this people in this generation, for I will preserve them' from the wrath of their enemy as they do so."

Ammon's face had taken on a glow as he spoke. Now he slumped as if the power had gone from his body, leaving Aaron and Omner to support him on either side. A collective sigh of relief was released throughout the room.

The meeting dispersed. There was much to do now that God had revealed His will. Ammon began to send out orders for the people to gather their flocks and herds and organize themselves into various camps over which a common leader would preside. After yesterday, their numbers were even less than before, but the magnitude of moving those who had survived and wished to leave was going to be a monumental task. God had kept His promise to preserve them as word arrived from the king's spies that the Lamanite army had been stricken with a strange illness in the night. Now they would have ample time to gather themselves and their belongings and leave.

Abish walked to where Ammon stood, sure that he had been given the knowledge to complete the move. "We will be like the children of Israel as they fled Pharaoh's army," she encouraged.

"A strange analogy," he sighed, "because I do not see myself as a Moses."

Ammon smiled weakly and told her to go and organize her family, but faced with the prospect of what lay ahead, Abish found it difficult to act. She looked around her. Everyone was scurrying about. The king sat distraught with his head in his hands. Namon and Teara were clinging to each other, and she went to them for commiseration.

"It's so hard to believe that we have to leave our homes," she lamented. "We have so much to do in such little time." It was then she noticed that the couple had shared an agonizing look between themselves. "What? Has something happened?"

The sorrow in her friend's eyes should have prepared her for what she said next.

"Please try to understand," Teara said. "This has been a difficult decision for us. But we're not going with you, Abish."

20

Abish was stunned. She knew she must have misinterpreted her friend's words. "Do you mean," she sought to clarify, "that you've been assigned to a different group than I will be in?"

Namon shook his head. "No. My duty is to stay with the king."

Abish felt a wave of emotions overcome her. "Your duty is the safety of your wife and children!" she blurted out, instantly regretting it. "I'm sorry. My weariness makes me speak out of turn. But do you know what this means?"

"We spent all night discussing it," Teara said. "Namon is a man of loyalty and he has pledged his life to the king."

Abish drew near and in a whisper tried to reason with them. "The king could release you, if only you asked."

Teara shook her head. "Do not make this any harder than it already is. We are sorry and will never forget you. Perhaps we will meet again . . . someday."

Abish knew that they were empty words with no real promise behind them. This was most likely the last time they would see each other. Her head was spinning as she thought about a future without her best friend. But she couldn't make Teara feel any worse than she already felt. "I will miss you and pray for your happiness every day," Abish said. The two women threw their arms around each other, letting their tears freely flow.

"Making Teara happy will be my life's ambition," Namon added.

Abish nodded and grasped his forearm in a friend's farewell. "You'd better take good care of her," she tried to say lightheartedly, "or I'll walk back across the wilderness to find you."

Back in the village, Abish found that Akah had already begun to pack her meager supplies. The thought that much of this would have to be carried in packs or baskets on the heads and backs of the travelers made it a little easier to decide what to take and what had to be left behind. Abish watched as Akah stared forlornly at the one prized possession that she did own: a large stationery loom that had been handed down from generations of mothers.

"I suppose this is too big to take," she said with a frown.

"Perhaps," Abish suggested, "Laban could help dismantle it, and we could divide it into sections among some of the travelers. I would be happy to carry my share."

Akah huffed. "You'll have enough to carry as it is, what with you being alone and all. Best to accept things as they are. I'll leave it behind."

That said, Abish gathered up her children, who were waiting for her outside. "Come, we've much to do."

"Where are we going, Mama?" Miriam asked.

"To a new land, sweetness, and we will start a new life there."

"Is everyone coming?" Jarum asked.

Not wanting to add to the stress of the moment, Abish felt it was best to keep Teara and Namon's decision from them. "Almost, my son. Now, let's go home and gather our most important things."

Frivolous clothing and trinkets were cast aside. Standing in the middle of their humble house, Abish tried not to think of the months of work Jared had put into building it and that she'd invested in sustaining it. *No. Don't think about it.* Gathering a few pots and extra water bags, she knew that food would be the most important supply: corn and hard tack, dried meat, and fish. Mentally checking off the list in her mind, she felt the air growing hot and stifling in the tiny dwelling, so she threw open the door for some fresher air. There was no point in locking up, she thought wryly. Let beggars or thieves take what they wanted after they left.

A warning trumpet sounded from off in the distance, and Abish knew that there was little time left. She took one last look at the carved box in the corner. It would be too heavy to carry, but she couldn't resist removing the precious items she'd kept stored there and fastening them securely to her body beneath her shift. And then, hoisting one of the baskets on her head, she signaled for Jarum and Miriam to finish. As she watched them tying their belongings into a pack, Abish nearly cried as she saw that Miriam had taken her at her word and left her rag doll lying in its usual place in her hammock. Setting down the basket, Abish went and picked up the doll.

"No, Mama. You said only what was most important! Besides, I'm too old now."

"Your friend will be the most important thing that we could take with us," Abish soothingly explained as she tucked it into Miriam's belt. "You will not feel the weight of her at all. Now we must go."

They went to join Akah back at her house. The reality that in a few hours this would all be a memory was evident on the older woman's face as well. But the adults were trying to be strong for the children.

"Could you watch the children for me?" Abish whispered. "There's something I must do. I'll hurry as fast as I can and catch up if needed."

Akah eyed her nervously, then shooed her on her way.

Across the village she ran, up the grassy incline toward the Old City. As her childhood home came into view, she tried not to think about Teara again, because she had only the briefest moment to pay homage at her father's grave. Though Abish had tried over the years to keep it cleared of brush and foliage, the inevitable growth would always return to where her memory had to serve as to its location. With her gone, there would be none who would stop and tend it.

"Father," she said as she quickly knelt. "I'm leaving. This time, I fear it will be forever. And where I'm going, I may never find Mother. Please help her if you can. I don't know what lies ahead, but whatever it is, I will be strong. Watch over us, I pray." She stood and wiped the tears from her face before heading to her next destination.

By now her muscles were screaming from the frantic exertion. As she reached Jared's grave, she was practically limping. The flowers she had placed there just days before had shriveled up in the heat, and she brushed away their wilted corpses. Her hand pressed into the ground as if trying to create one last connection with her beloved. The soil was warm and damp. "I will always remember you and will see that our children always remember you as well. Your spirit will go with us to this new land. We will make you proud of us." In one final gesture, she took off the pendant from him she always wore around her neck and placed it on the grave. "You gave this to me along with your heart. Now, I leave my heart with you."

* * *

The people of Ammon followed the main trade route at first, walking by day and making camp at night. They brought with them their animals, food, and makeshift tents. Even the children carried water gourds and light sacks of grain because they didn't know how long they would be forced to camp. Somehow the great mass of people had been organized into camps, and the connection they felt as they walked along as a displaced people was powerful. The strong men carried the weak and elderly in hammocks between them. The mothers of few assisted the mothers of many. It was as if they were one giant family.

Almost.

Though she was surrounded by thousands, Abish felt alone again. She thought of Teara back in Ishmael with her husband and King Lamoni. Even King Anti-Nephi-Lehi had delayed his departure in order to organize willing groups of followers in nearby lands. (And once he left for good, the land of Nephi would be completely left to the mercy of their new king.) And lastly, she thought of Jared and her father lying abandoned in the ground. She thought of everything she had left behind.

They came across abandoned campsites along the way. Had others been forced to flee as they had been? But the fires were long cold and there was little evidence of recent habitation. And then, on the second day of their journey, a great storm arose and the group scrambled for shelter in outcroppings of rocks and shallow caves. For hours they huddled together, pelted by the wind and rain. Abish clasped her children tightly underneath a large oiled cloth. In the morning, they looked up into a clear blue sky without a single cloud to remind them of last night's fury. Much of the vegetation had been washed away by the temporary rivers that had been formed in the deluge. A few animals had been sucked into the flood, but thankfully none of the people had been injured. As the group sought to recover what they could, Abish knelt to scoop up some grain that had spilled from a nearby bag—but it was sodden and trampled and looked unsalvageable. She called to the children to make sure they were once again safely at her side.

Gradually the landscape around them changed. Gone were the lush jungles and rugged mountains of their homeland. They had come upon the rolling hills and valleys of Zarahemla, and Abish could see the River Sidon floodplain off in the distance. "We will reach Hill Manti in a few days," Ammon explained to her that night as they gathered around one of the campfires. "After a fortnight of traveling, everyone will be glad to rest while we learn of our fate."

She smiled weakly, knowing that for a few of their group, fate had already stretched its hand. Two had died of snake bites the day before, both men. One woman had passed a few days earlier in childbirth. And there was a child who had wandered off.

She shook off the memory. "Will this soon be over?"

"Hopefully. My brethren and I are going down to speak with the judges to try to soften their hearts toward us. Hopefully we will find some sympathetic ears to hear us." He paused, "Would you like to come with us—you and the children? You could stay in my father's house. I know my mother would love to see you again."

Abish felt a moment of guilt at leaving her people, but then gratefully accepted. Perhaps, if only for a short time, she might be reminded what it was to rest.

21

The large and small temples that lined the River Sidon soon gave way to the great paved road that signaled the main entrance into the walled city of Zarahemla. Their tiny group heading into the city had received enough stares as they passed through the various collections of towns and villages that dotted the broad floodplain. But it wasn't the travel-worn Lamanite woman with two children by her side that made the residents gawk *or* the sons of Mosiah reunited again—it was a certain man who accompanied them. The inhabitants had recognized the sons of their late king, but many took a second glance when they saw who stood at their head. It was Alma, the former chief judge over all their land and son of their late prophet, who led the weary travelers closer to the city gates!

As they had left the main group behind the day before and followed the central trade route toward the valley, they were blessed with a wonderful surprise. As Abish made camp and started a small fire for her children, she saw another traveler, who was making his way in a similar direction. He came upon them at the bank of the River Sidon, and Abish immediately recognized him as Alma. Another man named Amulek accompanied him. Though she had been surprised, her emotions could not match those of Ammon. Ammon had been so overcome by their appearance that he had collapsed to the ground! Abish later teased him that it must have been the "strenuous" hike of the day, to which he playfully admitted, "The last time we entered Zarahemla, I recall I was carrying your pack as well! I suppose I have grown weak in my *old* age."

"If you are old, then what does that make me?" Abish returned his jest and cherished the camaraderie that had developed between them.

All that evening the long-time friends sat around the fire, sharing stories of their travels, rejoicing in each other's successes. Ammon became so enthusiastic at one point that his brothers accused him of boasting again. But she knew how he felt: this overwhelming feeling of God's love for them. Then they began to share each other's sorrows. Ammon told of the recent attack on Ishmael, his heart reliving the tragedy along with his words. But when Alma spoke of the faithful in the city of Ammonihah who had been cast into a pit of fire for believing his words, and of his own imprisonment, Abish wept. Again, so many innocent lost. Abish continued to listen well into the night, but then found herself drifting off into a surprisingly deep sleep, awakening only when her children pounced on her the next morning. A bit ashamed, she quickly gathered up her things because she saw that the men were already set to go.

The city of Zarahemla was just as she remembered, and she felt as if she were being reunited with an old friend. By the time they reached the stately residence that was Alma's home, she felt that perhaps she was growing older as well! At least a score of steps confronted them at the end of the palm-lined walkway, where a beautifully carved portico marked the entrance into a spacious courtyard. After Alma greeted his wife and instructions were given for the unexpected guests, Abish introduced her children and asked about Hannah's own sons.

"They are at their studies, but we will have them prepared to meet with us at this evening's meal," came the welcome reply. "Dinner will be arranged along with a room where you can freshen up and the children can rest."

As they all entered the main doors, Abish saw that Alma's home was decorated with the same green-hued stone that King Mosiah's home had been, but the layout was in the latest tradition of multiple rooms built around a central courtyard. A beautiful fountain graced the center, surrounded by flowering plants of all kinds. Miriam and Jarum were, for the first time in days, speechless. They all followed a young servant to their temporary accommodations, which were two adjoining rooms in the east corner of the house. A choked sob almost escaped her lips as she saw the luxuries around her. Miriam was already gingerly touching the silken curtains that hung from the window while Jarum initiated one of the soft feather beds in the corner.

"Children!" she reprimanded. "We must clean ourselves first. We are guests here, and I won't have you forgetting your manners." They obeyed and allowed their faces and hands to be scrubbed in the nearby bowl of fresh water. As soon as she had finished cleaning, they heard a rap on the door. Abish opened it and saw a servant carrying a small pile of clothes in her hands.

"My mistress hoped that these would fit you and your children," the young girl said. "Let me know if there's anything else you need. The evening meal will be served in the main dining room shortly."

"This will be wonderful. Thank you."

She helped Jarum and Miriam out of their travel-stained clothing, though seeing them in such beautiful attire created mixed feelings within her. She thought of the disparity between what they had and what she'd grown up with, but then she reminded herself that her children were growing up with love and that was the most important thing she could give them. Satisfied with their appearance, Abish tucked them into their beds for a brief rest while she attended to her own grooming.

Letting out a small sigh as the door of her room closed behind her, Abish tried to reconcile herself to everything that had happened in the past few weeks but found that it was still too much to fully grasp. Instead, she faced what seemed like an even more formidable task of making herself look presentable. A large ceramic bowl sat on a nearby table, a soft towel by its side. Abish looked inside at its foamy contents and realized it had been ages since she had taken a milk-bath. There were also several bottles of fragrant oils and a cedar wood comb, which made the job of untangling her hair a less painful experience. She ignored the paint pots. Such decoration had never appealed to her before, so why begin now? Far from elegant, she hoped she at least should no longer look like a wild-woman and sought affirmation from the small pyrite mirror on the table.

She was pleased with what she saw. Even though she was now in her third decade of life, she still had the lustrous, thick hair of a young woman. Turning her face so that her scar did not show, she admired the still smooth texture of her skin and was glad that high cheeks and full lips were still considered attractive. Thankfully her people had adopted many of the Nephites customs regarding beauty, so extremes, such as elaborate piercings and other physical deformations she had always disliked, were being done away with.

But then, realizing that she was crossing the line into vanity, Abish put down the mirror and went to awaken her children.

* * *

Her family found their way into the dining area, where Abish saw that Ammon, his brethren, and Alma and his wife were already present, along with Amulek and a few other dignitaries she did not recognize. Three handsome young men were also in attendance, and Abish realized that these were Alma's sons! The two oldest were mere children when she last saw them but now she could see that, even amid a few boyish grins, these young men were already taking after their father. Helaman was the oldest and tallest, with sandy brown hair and a seriousness that belied his youth. Next to him stood Shiblon, she reasoned, stationed in order of age and with the same brown hair and confident stare. It must be Corianton who stood beside him. She stifled a smile at the thought that his hair reminded her of the color and texture of a howler monkey's fur. She watched as he shifted slightly on his feet, and Abish sensed a measure of impatience as he waited for them all to arrive and be seated.

The food was excellent, and yet Abish wondered if the rest, like her, felt a little guilty knowing that their people most likely dined on dried fish and corn gruel tonight.

At first the conversation was joyful as the brothers and friends retold their many trials and successes. Again Abish noticed the obvious interest of Alma's two older sons while the third let his attention wander. And then Alma addressed Ammon. "I have arranged to speak to the council tomorrow regarding your people's plight. I can only hope that they will be mindful that many of their own fathers once asked for refuge in this land and were granted it graciously."

"We will accept the council's judgment," Ammon said. "Though I know that this night will be spent on my knees."

The others nodded their similar intentions.

After they finished their meal, Ammon suggested that Abish and her family stay with him at his father's house during their time in Zarahemla. His mother, he said, would never forgive him if he didn't persuade them to.

The late king's residence was just as she remembered, but as Queen Rebekah shuffled forward to embrace Abish as if she were a long-lost daughter, it was obvious that time had exacted its toll on this once vibrant queen of Zarahemla. Her hair was stark white and her face well-lined with time, but something of her grace and stateliness remained. With tears in both their eyes, they let unspoken words remind them of their losses and impart strength to one another for the trials that must surely lie ahead for them all. The queen smiled as Jarum and Miriam came forward to be introduced.

"We shall have to spoil them while they are here," Rebekah beamed, clapping her hands together with delight. "In fact, I may not let you go!"

This seemed a real possibility when, after they were shown to their rooms, the former queen begged to tell them a bedtime story. "It has been so long since I sat at the bedside of my own children," she sighed. "And as the years pass, the thought of my own grandchildren seems to be a fading dream."

Abish patted her hand sympathetically.

Free to attend to her own needs, Abish left her children to their surrogate grandmother's care. Standing in the middle of her expansive room, she was once again struck by the difference between what her children had grown up with and what she herself had known. Abish had always accepted that she could never provide them with the luxuries she had been surrounded with, but at least hoped that with Jared at her side they would have everything they needed. Now, as they faced an uncertain future, what would she have to offer them? A mud and dirt hut that leaked in the rain? A cave in some hillside that was always dirty and damp?

She knew that wealth could not ensure a happy life, but, for the moment, it did not seem to hurt.

Glad her children couldn't see her, Abish ignored her own rules and suddenly leapt onto the bed, flinging her arms out wide as she sighed in blissful comfort. She must have dozed off because she was momentarily disoriented when there was a knock on the door.

"Greetings, Abish," Ammon said when she opened the door. "My mother wanted you to know that your children are in bed and that she may not let you take them away from her."

Abish laughed. "There are days when she would be welcome to them! I'm glad they came with us. I couldn't bear to be parted again."

"Could you endure a *brief* parting and walk with me through the city?" he asked. "There are still a few hours of daylight left, and I thought you might enjoy seeing it again."

"I would love to," she said enthusiastically.

Abish and Ammon left the house and walked down the score of steps that would lead them toward the main square. A small river lay to the west, nestled between gently rolling hills. They took one of the many pedestrian esplanades that funneled like tiny rivulets into the "river" that was the Street of the Temple. While many smaller temples lined the main thoroughfare, the most impressive was the Great Temple. Its base covered at least seven acres of the main sacred precinct. It rose above the city and allowed the priests in the highest prayer chamber to cast their eyes on the whole of the populace below. The setting sun added to the splendor by casting upon it a crimson glow.

Ammon must have noticed her looking at it. "Even though there are more unbelievers in the city now, it is still considered to be the focal point of Zarahemla."

"Have things changed that much?" she asked. "We've scarcely been here, but it appears to be the same beautiful city that you brought me to all those years ago."

"Perhaps it's not with the outward eye that all the changes can be seen," he sighed.

Though it was late in the day, the marketplace bustled with thousands of people from the surrounding towns and villages. Abish was still full from dinner and turned down the many appeals of food vendors trying to rid themselves of their remaining wares. Ammon, however, accepted a rosy mango and munched on it as they walked along, leaving Abish free to focus on the scene around her. She sought to uncover the hidden faults that were around them because for now, everything appeared normal. Though the people had also been plagued by wars over the last few years, the market still appeared to thrive, drawing in merchants and traders from the land southward to the land Bountiful. She remembered that it was divided into separate sections in order to accommodate the still-differing Mulekite and Nephite customs. But surely these differences weren't at the root of the problem.

They passed through the marketplace and turned the corner at the public baths. Decorated lintels marked the separate entrances for the men and women who would use the naturally-heated vestibules for both enjoyment and various rituals.

"Alma tried to explain to us earlier," Ammon said, wiping his mouth with the back of his hand, "that already the tenants of the law of Moses are being selectively obeyed, even by believers. New customs and traditions are being established that, though not in defiance of the Law, are perverting the heart of them." When Abish looked confused he continued. "Consider the blessing of infants. Apparently some groups have begun to include a water purification ritual when the babe is but eight days old."

"Do you mean like baptism?" she was shocked.

"Not exactly," he said, "so the leaders of the Church do not yet condemn it. But while the letter of the law is still obeyed, the spirit is being tampered with."

Abish felt disturbed at what Ammon was saying and began to see the city with new eyes: from the well-dressed procession of priests that went by on their way to the temple to the overly ornate and excessive adornments of the upper-class women. Was prosperity turning to greed? Merriment to sloth? There was a fine line, she realized, between the two. And what of the beggars who sat unsuccored in the streets? Zarahemla had always cared for its poor, for the widowed, the fatherless. Maybe Zarahemla *was* losing its former greatness. Just then they turned down the Street of the Artisans. Though enough time had passed to temper most of her own loss, she still felt the familiar longing whenever a blacksmith's shop came into view. Ammon must have sensed this because he reached out and took her hand, gently squeezing it before dropping it back at her side. Abish looked up at him to give him a grateful smile, but he turned away quickly. Not quickly enough.

She had seen the look in his eyes.

Suddenly Abish was catapulted back in time. It was as if she had just left her adopted land of Melek again to go back with him to the land of Nephi to preach to her people—but first they had stopped here in Zarahemla to receive permission from his father. It was then Ammon had told her that she wouldn't be going with him because he had begun to have feelings for her. Abish had been upset, of course, but at the same time, she had known what it was like to hope again. To believe that she might not be alone forever.

And now, one brief glance had shook her foundation and left her wondering if her life was going to be unbalanced yet again.

"We should return," he said huskily.

She didn't protest.

He escorted her back to her room, where she lingered for a moment in the doorway as he walked away. Finally alone, she checked briefly on her children, smiling as she heard their deep, heavy breathing and the looks of contentment on their faces. Her own must have appeared equally satisfied. As she snuggled down between the soft, warm covers of her bed, she found herself contemplating not only her people's future—but her own as well.

22

Abish hurriedly ate the hearty breakfast the servant had brought her. After discovering that the others had gone to the house of Alma, she made arrangements for the children and went to join them. As she entered the great room, they all turned to greet her. Everyone, that is, except Ammon, who seemed distracted.

"Has there been any news?" she asked Aaron, who was closest to her.

"In a way." He smiled at her impatience. "The council has just barely dispersed. Alma pleaded our case, but it was decided that the people should be given a say in the matter. We must wait until the various provinces report back."

Knowing that patience was still a quality she lacked, Abish headed for the gardens. She had hoped that walking along the rows of delicate hyacinth and fragrant hibiscus flowers would take her mind off of things, especially what had happened the night before. Tired and discouraged, she plopped down on a nearby stone bench and placed her head between her hands.

"Greetings."

She looked up to see Alma coming toward her. Back in his home once again, he seemed to be slightly lost. A section of dark auburn hair tinged slightly with grey had fallen loose from its tie, and he fidgeted with the ornate sash at his waist.

"It seems," she said with a grin, "you've grown unaccustomed to a few things since you've been away."

He smiled as he sat beside her. "I almost could not sleep last night because of the softness of the bed. This bench would have sufficed because I have definitely known worse."

She nodded in agreement. "I was touched by the account of your travels. Tell me," she asked eagerly, "did you happen to meet the family of Jacob the farmer and Sarah when you were in Melek?" After all these years, she couldn't help thinking of her Nephite foster family.

He furrowed his brow. "I cannot recall the name. But then I was not there long, though I had great success during my brief stay."

"I'm not surprised. There were many good people when I lived there."

"With so many faithful already among them, it took little time before others joined the fold. I wish I could say the same about the following city. When I heard that Ammonihah had been destroyed, I felt great sadness, but was not surprised. There was such great wickedness in the city that to this day I can barely stand to think of it. Of course," he added, "if I hadn't gone there, I would not have met Amulek. His friendship was worth all of the trials that I suffered there."

"Before that you were in Gideon, correct? And afterwards, Sidom?"

"Yes. We had just left there and traveled down the River Sidon when we ran into your party. You were a welcome sight, indeed."

"I'm sure you were a welcome sight for your family as well," she said. "Your sons are nearly grown men! They must have missed you."

"Yes," he sighed. "Though I am not sure that all three understand equally why I had to be gone so much."

Knowing to whom he referred, she said softly, "Corianton does seem like a . . . challenge."

"That was a delicate way to describe him, Abish." After an uncomfortable pause he said, "Ammon tells me that you saw something of our city last night. I hope you were not completely discouraged by what you saw."

"It was a little disheartening," she admitted. "But change is inevitable. If only more of your people could see the error of their ways and come back to the truth."

"I pray so as well. But it can be hard, especially when some will not even accept that they are doing wrong. Why can they not realize that this life is a probationary state and we have only been granted a brief time to prove ourselves worthy?" Alma suddenly smiled. "Enough of this gloomy talk. We should think of something more pleasant to discuss. Ahh . . . I know."

"What?"

"I will tell you of something that has transpired since last night. Perhaps it is not my place to do so, but I feel compelled to share the good news. For a while now, someone's heart has been divided between the work among your people and a beautiful girl who caught his eye a few years ago. At first his brothers chastised him, but I explained that it was not wrong to exchange one type of mission for another. A wedding is just what we need to cheer ourselves up right now."

Abish hoped that she'd disguised the surprise on her face quickly enough. Of course, the sudden heat she was feeling might indicate otherwise. Her heart began to beat faster as Alma continued speaking.

"So regardless of the council's decision, it appears Himni knows what his future holds. We are glad for him, of course, and are sure that he will be as dedicated a husband as he was a missionary. I know his mother is overjoyed." Alma paused slightly as if waiting for her to respond, but she was unable. "Well," he said, appearing a little confused at her silence. "I will leave you to the peace and stillness of this beautiful place. Someone will let you know when a decision has been made for your people." He bowed slightly and then made his exit.

It was a good thing he had left because the tears flowing down her cheeks would surely have given her heart away. Would she ever stop jumping to conclusions? Why had she allowed herself to consider that it was Ammon he had been talking about?

A glance was not a commitment.

***

Jershon.

Abish tested the name on her tongue but it still sounded foreign to her. And yet, it was to be the land of her children's inheritance. The council had come back with word that morning, and Abish tried to listen patiently as Ammon explained that they were not to stay in the valley of Zarahemla, but were to take their trek to the east to a land yet uninhabited that bordered the sea. Jershon. Ammon explained that in the language of his forefathers it meant "land of the expelled." She thought it appropriate. Not sure how the rest of her people would take the news, she herself was weary enough to accept any land they were given.

Her children must have sensed the tension that was in the air because even before they had left Zarahemla, their excitement quickly mellowed to nervous anticipation. Forcing a broad smile onto her face, Abish knelt down and asked, "Are you ready for an adventure? We are about to see many new and wondrous things, so we must be strong and brave."

"I'll be brave, Mama!" Jarum puffed out his chest.

"Me, too," Miriam agreed, though not as eagerly.

Abish accepted Rebekah's offer to take the children to see the newborn colts once again while she finished packing. It was then that Hannah found her to say her final farewell.

"It is so far," Hannah said. "I will pray for you every day."

"We will need it."

"Oh, Abish," her companion cried, "how I wish you could stay. It would be nice to have a true woman-friend here."

Abish sighed, knowing how it felt to lose a friend. "I wish I could stay as well. But surely we will meet again."

"Then we will not say farewell, but instead—until we meet again."

Left alone in her room, it was then that Abish noticed three pairs of shoes on the bed. She didn't recall seeing them there before. She walked closer and realized that they were three new pairs of rubber-soled sandals. Not sure who had been responsible for this act of generosity, she gratefully scooped them up and added them to their meager belongings.

Blinded by the tears that again threatened to well up in her eyes, she rounded the corner of the nearest hallway and ran straight into Alma.

"I'm sorry!" she gasped, reminded of a similar mishap once with his father.

He laughed. "No harm was done. Are you prepared to leave?"

"As much as we can be. But I am anxious to see how the people react to the decision."

Abish watched as a mixture of emotions played out across the leader's face. "I have decided to journey back with you to your camp. It might help if your people hear from my own lips that God will be with you and that, though by this decision it may not appear so, the people of Zarahemla are concerned for your well-being."

"At least Ammon will still travel on with us," she said. "The people have come to depend upon him so much that they would be lost without him."

"Yes," Alma smiled. "You *all* would be lost without him. I think I realize that now." He paused briefly and then spoke so deliberately that Abish knew there was something more to be discerned within his words. "Yesterday we spoke of change, how it can be difficult for some. You must give some people time to change, Abish. Be patient."

Abish scrunched up her brow. Was he speaking of their journey? Of her people? Still not understanding his words, she excused herself and went to find her children.

***

The group spent the remainder of the day making their way back to the outskirts of the city where the people waited for them up on the rise.

The glow of a thousand campfires looked like stars in the oncoming dusk. The travelers had been mostly silent as they walked; they were all trying to decide how to prepare the others for the new, longer journey that lay ahead.

Their arrival back at camp was heralded by many joyous shouts. As if they were arriving dignitaries, they stopped short as several people rushed forward to retrieve their packs and offer them food and drink. Even Akah had been waiting anxiously for them, hopping from foot to foot like a parrot. Abish grew uneasy. "What is it? Is everything all right?"

"Come," Akah said, grabbing her by the arm and leading Abish back to her tent. As the flap was pushed aside, Abish realized they were not alone.

"Teara!" Abish shouted as her eyes adjusted to the dark. "Namon! What . . . what are you doing here?"

Her friend rushed forward and embraced her, too overcome for words.

"I'm afraid that I have had to repent of my selfishness," Namon explained. "I should have known better than to break the tender heart of my wife by separating her from her truest friend. I spoke with the king and he granted my boon. So we came as quickly as we could. Can you forgive me my pride?"

"There is nothing to forgive," Abish sobbed, "now that we are together again. All of us."

They went and joined the others on the bluff as Alma stood to address them from an outcropping of rocks.

"People of Ammon," he began. "For that is what you will be called from this day forth. I bring you greetings from the great city of Zarahemla and from my people. But I deign to call them *my* people, because now we are all one people in God. We have been humbled by your zeal for all that is good and for your honesty and uprightness in all things. Because of this, we welcome you to our land." A cheer went up among the gathering. Abish hoped they would still feel that way when they heard the terms of the welcome. But Alma had a way of speaking that was very pleasing, and she could already sense the people accepting the plan. "After much consideration, we have decided that it is best that you have a land of your own. A land that will belong to you and to your posterity if God is willing." He then went on to explain regarding the location of Jershon and how the Nephite armies would protect them.

Abish noticed a few frowns on the faces of those who listened, but most seemed ready to leave at once and possess the land, even if it meant another fortnight's travel. Would they still feel that way after they had wandered for days as strangers in a strange land?

But for now, the people's concerns were pushed aside as they enjoyed feasting on the extra supplies that had been brought to celebrate Himni's betrothment. With Teara back at her side, Abish found herself enjoying the remainder of the evening with the others. She caught Ammon looking at her several times throughout the night and smiled tentatively in return; having him there made her feel as if everything would be all right. As the campfires burned out, they were all content. It had been a long time since they had been able to celebrate without fear and it bolstered everyone's spirits and confidence in what lay ahead. Abish hoped that feeling would continue.

Hopefully, in this new land that held such promise, they would at last find peace.

Land of Jershon
74 BC

23

Abish stood and walked away from the pot of boiling fat where the animal hides were soaking. She had finally mastered the skill of knowing how long to submerge the skins so they would repel the rain but not so long that they would become too soft to work with. But she still dreaded the task. The smell that permeated the village on such days was repugnant. The heat, barely tolerable. She looked longingly at the half-finished structure off to her side. She had hoped to finish the stable roof this year before the rains began again, but Namon had been so involved with the addition onto his own home—which his growing family desperately needed. Ammon had offered to help her, but his responsibilities in the continued establishment of the city along with his duties as high priest gave him little time to spare. She would have to relent and spend some of their precious senines of silver to employ help from the city. The idea *had* crossed her mind in the meantime to make a covering that was large enough to give the animals some shelter from above.

Quickly, Abish repented of her ingratitude and returned to work. After all, she had a residence to call her own, while others still lived in damp caves. She had a small field of newly sown manioc this year—more than enough to give her share to the army's stipend—while others still toiled for a mouthful of bread. And her family was safe, while so many of the Nephites still wept over loved ones lost during the previous year's battle with the Lamanites to protect the exiles.

She wiped the sweat from her brow. There was so much to do, and she was already behind on several of the visits to supplicants she had promised to make. Exhausted, Abish decided instead to go into the city and talk with Ammon about "borrowing" the council courtyard so that those who lived on the outskirts of the city could be seen at a scheduled day and time in place of her always traveling to them. Since Miriam was still at Teara's and Jarum was at his studies, it was a good enough excuse to do it now.

Though I shouldn't need an excuse to visit Ammon, she protested inwardly.

Their leader was sitting at his usual place in the council chambers, but remained motionless as she entered. With his head propped on his hands, she realized that he wasn't merely deep in thought but was asleep! A laugh escaped, causing Ammon to look up and blink rapidly. He gave her a welcome smile as he began to roll up some leather scrolls that lay on the table.

"Hard at work I see," she teased.

"Even my dreams are filled with unfinished tasks," he said as he gestured her in.

"The council depends heavily upon you."

Ammon shrugged. "When it comes to matters of war, I think they would do better depending upon one of those chattering monkeys out there." Abish frowned, wondering now if she should add her problems to his. "But the job seems to have fallen to me, so I need to deliver these maps to the captain of the Nephite army," he said then continued. "I shouldn't have to go too far past the city borders. Would you like to come? I haven't even asked you what you wanted to see me for, so it will give us time to talk."

She agreed and helped him carry some of the awkward scrolls. They walked in silence for a while, except for the many greetings Ammon had to return. Everyone was glad to see him, and Abish hoped their friendliness would remind him that he was appreciated as well as needed. He was like a father to them all and she said so.

"A father," he chuckled. "As if I would know anything about being that."

"There are many ways to be a parent. The people look up to you and depend upon you," she explained. "A parent's job is to guide and direct. You do all that—and more."

His voice softened. "And you have had to be both mother *and* father all these years."

"Which explains all of the mistakes I have made." She frowned. She explained briefly about the struggles she'd been having with Jarum and his studies. Ammon listened in patient silence until Abish realized that she'd been rambling on for a considerable amount of time. Embarrassed, she stopped and waited for what she knew would be his practical advice.

Instead, he led her over to a nearby stream. Kneeling down, he let his hand drag in the water. There was a large rock near his foot that he suddenly picked up and threw near the bank of the river. Abish jumped back, laughing as water splashed on her. Flashing her a smile, Ammon said, "No matter how big the rock, the water will always find a way around it. The important thing is that the water is already on the course intended for it."

"In other words," Abish said, kneeling down beside him, "I should accept that Jarum will be whatever he wants to be: whether it is a scholar, a merchant, a beekeeper . . . or a farmer."

"You should accept that you have given your son the foundation that he needs to make these decisions for himself. He has faith in God, believes in the Christ who is to come. Everything else is inconsequential."

Abish frowned. "But what if it isn't enough? What if he . . ."

"Goes astray?" His voice drifted off, and Abish could still hear the pain of remembrance in his voice. "Then he will need your strength more than ever to help him find his way back. You are doing a good job raising your children, something so many of our women have been forced to do alone. If only it were not so. If only I could have done something."

"You still blame yourself too much," she said, seeking to comfort him.

"With everything that has happened to this people, perhaps not enough." He scowled.

He cupped up some water to drink and Abish did as well, savoring the coolness on her tongue. A gentle breeze brought with it the smell of warming ground and verdant life, and she breathed deeply, wishing she knew what else to say to comfort him.

Ammon wiped his mouth with the back of his hand. "I could talk to Jarum some time—if you would like."

"Yes!" Abish said. "I would like that very much. Perhaps he needs to hear this from a man's point of view. Let me know when would be a good time."

"I will."

As they knelt there, she gazed at their dual reflections in the water. At times she felt as if there were no one else she had ever been as close to— except Jared. But then she would sense the part of Ammon that she knew he still kept hidden away deep inside, and she wondered if he would ever let her in.

He shifted as if to stand and she went to do so as well, but found herself a little off balance from having knelt for so long. Ammon reached out to steady her. His grip on her arm was steady and warm, and when she could not resist looking up at him, she found that his eyes were already intently on her, as if taking in every aspect of her face. Abish should have felt embarrassed to be under such scrutiny, but it had been the first time in a long while since she had felt as if someone were truly looking at her. She held his gaze. Now they were so near each other that she could feel his warm breath on her face. She breathed him in as well.

He was so close. So close.

But then Ammon released her and, stumbling away, he stammered, "We should go. Captain Moroni will be waiting for me."

Now her mind was off balance as well, but Abish silently gathered her portion of the scrolls and followed numbly after him down the path.

She had a difficult time organizing her thoughts after that. Though amazed at first at how young the Nephite captain was, she scarcely said a few words to him, letting Ammon regale him with her story and praise her abilities as if nothing had happened between them back at the stream.

"Your people are lucky to have Abish," Moroni agreed.

At the mention of her name, she politely smiled and focused her attention back on the pair of men. Moroni was a hand-span shorter than Ammon, with a darker and stockier build, leaving her to wonder whether his heritage was that of Nephite or Mulekite. There was a carved tortoise shell amulet around his neck, the significance of which was unknown to her. And, of course, there were the weapons which hung at the captain's side: a compact dagger in its sheath and a larger wooden sword with several obsidian heads protruding from the shaft. Weaponry had changed much in the last several years, especially since many skills like metalworking were slowly being lost as so many of those who had employed them had died from the Lamanite attacks on their land. Their deaths had been so sudden that they had not had time to pass their trade on to future generations. Just like Jarum had never been trained under his father's hand.

Abish fought back a shudder, and the captain must have thought she was unsettled by his appearance, so he tucked his blood-stained implements behind his back. But while his outward appearance was meant to strike fear into his opponents, she could see integrity in his eyes, and the dedication he had to his men was obvious. And, more importantly, she sensed that he fought not out of anger toward his enemies, but out of a desire to protect all that they held precious.

The captain and Ammon now began discussing the latest tally of grain that the Anti-Nephi-Lehies were to deliver to support the army. Abish let her attention wander again and she looked down into the valley toward the main part of the army's camp. Tents spread out like hills of new-sown hay, and the soldiers scurried about like mere ants from where Abish stood. A group of soldiers was training in a nearby clearing, and she could hear echoes of orders being shouted. Her people appreciated these men who were willing to give their lives to protect them. But at the same time, surrounded by them, it was also akin to being prisoners within the land.

It was then she realized that Ammon was at her side. "Moroni and I have much more to discuss. Perhaps you would like one of his men to accompany you back to the city."

Abish looked into his eyes, hoping for some small sign of the tenderness she had seen before, but saw only the competent leader concerned for his people. She shook her head. "I can manage on my own." She would talk to him later about the council courtyard.

24

Abish's frustration over Ammon's behavior was forgotten in the months to come by a few moments of joy. At last the final wall on her house was finished and the roof had been set in place just as the season of rain began. Miriam had already sewn beautiful curtains for the windows, and it set the finishing touch as they hung them. And Jarum had surprised her by announcing that he was to receive an award from his teacher for the most improved transcription. She hoped her face had not exhibited too much surprise and that she had conveyed only the pride she felt. Part of the honor included being able to inscribe his favorite scripture on a commemorative metal plate for his graduating class. She knew she had Ammon to thank for her son's change in attitude and was grateful for the extra time he had been spending with Jarum lately.

These were the happy moments of their lives. And as the rainy season lengthened its hold to where sun and fresh air became distant memories, Abish stored those moments away and drank them in from time to time when she needed a reminder of what she was doing it all for.

Finally, there was a break in the weather, and it was as if they were all being born again. Even Abish felt her inhibitions leaving as she abandoned the work that had piled up during their internment and insisted that her children accompany her on an impromptu excursion to the seashore. They did not refuse. Now her only task was trying to keep Jarum from running too far ahead and balancing their necessities on her head while Miriam walked by her side. Supporting the basket with one hand, she looked down and smiled at her daughter, who looked adoringly back at her.

The tang of the sea air reached them first and Jarum immediately jumped in while Miriam bravely dipped her toes in the water's edge. Abish was content to find a shady spot beneath a nearby palm and watch. But she was not allowed to rest for long. Though she had instantly recognized the smirk on Jarum's face, she wasn't able to avoid being doused with the water he had scooped up in a broken coconut shell.

"You'd better run!" She laughed, chasing after him with a handful of sand.

Soon, they were all three covered in sand and seawater. It wasn't until she held up her hands in mock defeat that they realized how hungry their play had made them. Calling an extended truce, they abandoned all manners and delved ravenously into the manioc cakes, corn pudding, and fruit that had been brought. Sticky, sandy, soaked, and satiated, they then lay back on a large woven mat Abish had spread out and sighed contently.

"Mama?" Jarum asked.

"Yes, son?" Abish said groggily as the lull of the ocean's waves and a full belly made her sleepy. She turned on her side to face him.

"Tell us about Father."

"Yes, please," Miriam joined in, eager to listen as well.

She smiled, knowing this wasn't the first time they had been told and aware of what questions they would ask. "Your father was a good man. Kind and hardworking. He was a blacksmith and had been trained well in his craft since an early age."

"But then our people buried their weapons," Jarum interrupted.

"Yes. They buried their weapons and so your father did what honest work he could and continued to be a respected member of Ishmael's council."

"You're moving too far ahead!" protested Miriam. "Start at the beginning."

Of course, Abish laughed inwardly. Her daughter wanted to hear how they had met. The *romantic* details surrounding their courtship. She replayed the story in her mind and then carefully chose the one she shared with her children. She had come upon Jared in his shop and been impressed by his strength and skill. But her mother had forbidden them to meet, instead arranging for her to marry the wicked Lamanite commander, Lehonti. She held them enthralled as she rehearsed the part where, after her father had died, she had escaped from her home, only to be taken captive by Lehonti. Miriam's eyes widened when Abish reminded them of how she had received the scar across her face by trying to help Jared, who had come to her rescue and was struggling with Lehonti. But in the end they had prevailed and fled to her uncle's home in Middoni for temporary refuge before traveling on to the coast, their identities hidden. After making arrangements for a boat, they tried to sail southward.

"But instead, God made a storm come so that you would sail northward to the land of the Nephites!" Miriam interjected. "But then Father went overboard to save the boatman and was lost, and you washed up ashore in Melek, and it took years before you found each other again!" she ended triumphantly and a little short of breath.

Jarum pouted. "Let Mama tell the story. It's hers to tell!"

"Son," Abish reprimanded. "You both know the story well enough to tell it. But yes, all of that happened. And then your father and I found each other again and were happy for a time."

Now frowns were on all three of their faces; no one was anxious to continue the story from this point on. So instead, Abish told them of their birth—of how surprised she was that there had been *two* babies in her womb. "I knew then that God was mindful of me, by blessing me with a son *and* a daughter—my joy was complete."

Jarum traced a finger through the sand in front of him. "Do we make you think of his death, Mama?"

Abish felt tears welling up in her eyes and she fought them back. "No!" she said, fighting even harder. "You both make me think of his life." But then, she lost the battle. Her children scurried across to her, threw their arms around her, and soon three sets of teary eyes were blinking in the blinding sunlight.

Abish looked up at the sun overhead. "It's later than I thought. I suppose we should get some work done today while the good weather holds."

They made their way back reluctantly, but the smiles held and everyone went happily about their work. A good part of the day had passed before something occurred that dampened her spirit more than the rain had.

Abish was just hauling out the sleeping mats to freshen in the sun when a figure approached them from the east. Even at that distance, Abish recognized Namon's tall frame. She went to meet him and greeted him when they were within speaking distance. "I see you couldn't resist being outdoors as well. Teara and the children must be ecstatic to be free again. But, where are they? Is something wrong?" she frantically added.

"There is a problem that has developed in the city. I am headed there now to meet with the other council members."

"It's not . . ." she broke off, lowering her voice. "We're not being attacked, are we?"

"Not by the Lamanite army," Namon nervously rubbed his brow. "A man has come among us. A stranger to Jershon and the surrounding areas. Rumor has it he may be from Zarahemla and, for all intents and purposes, a member of the faith. But, well . . . perhaps it is nothing. I have been sent to gather some of the others leaders to see what this is all about."

Abish looked back at the house where her chores still waited, but her curiosity won over work. "May I go with you?"

Namon had known her long enough to know she hated waiting for news. "Of course."

Since she didn't know how long she would be gone, Jarum and Miriam were told to stay with Teara, at which point she followed after Namon. By the time they reached the city, they had met many other leaders along the trail. Abish was not unmindful that she was the only woman among them, but the others must have grown used to her unconventional presence because she was politely ignored as she entered the council grounds as well. To her surprise, she saw that there was a fair-skinned man who had been bound in strong cords and placed in the center of the open courtyard. Obviously this was so they could accommodate more than the indoor setting allowed, because their numbers continued to swell until they were standing arm to arm. Namon had left her to take his place in one of the twelve elevated council seats that were situated on the rise so as to see the proceedings below. Ammon was seated among the twelve, and he rose and stepped forward when all were gathered. A hush fell over the crowd as he spoke.

"Brethren of the council, I am pleased that you have hastened here today in response to my request. I see that many others have also joined us." He briefly caught her gaze. "You are welcome, as this concerns all who desire peace and are concerned for the well-being of our land." He paused and walked forward slightly toward the man who stood bound. "You have been brought before me," Ammon addressed him personally, "as a disrupter of that peace and as a hindrance to that well-being. But I will not pass any judgment until you have been allowed to speak for yourself. State your name . . . and your business."

Abish scrambled to some nearby steps for a better view. From here she could examine the man a little more. He had a fair complexion, against which his black hair made a startling contrast. She couldn't see any discerning marks or talisman that distinguished him among the people, other than his manner of dress, which was attractive and suggested he was in station above those of the lower-class. He seemed harmless enough. She listened as the man responded to Ammon's words.

"I recognize you, son of Mosiah, and am honored to be in your presence. Naturally I would that our meeting could have been under more fortunate circumstances." He raised his tied wrists up to display them and shrugged as if it were a mere inconvenience. Then he stood as proudly as was possible and said, "I am called Korihor."

25

Suddenly, Abish felt as though what little peace she'd been feeling had shattered. But why? What was it about this man that made her feel as though her life were to change yet again?

"I mean you no harm," he continued, "having come only to be among you and perhaps share a thought or two. After all, there is no law in this land regarding a man's beliefs. It is not as if I have come to kill you or rob you of your sustenance, but to bring enlightenment where there may be despair and misery."

Ammon furrowed his brow. "There is no misery here except that which God allows to test us and which His Son will be sent to relieve us of. Speak more plainly about your intent."

Korihor again shrugged harmlessly. "I see that you have yoked yourselves as your brethren have in Zarahemla. What a shame that you should put such hope and faith in something you cannot even be sure of." Abish watched as murmuring began throughout the courtyard. *Who was this man? What did he really want?* Amid the commotion, the stranger's voice now carried like a dagger. "Surely," he continued mockingly, "you do not hold to the antiquated belief that there is a Christ that is to come? How can you know this? For hundreds of years the so-called prophets have told stories about His coming, and He has not come. Has He? Well, has He?" He turned in a circle and held out his wrists again. "No, I say that He has not nor will He. And so you go throughout your lives bound by foolish ordinances laid out by ancient priests who know nothing about the demands of your lives. They would have you shackled in ignorance while I," now his words dripped honey, "would offer you freedom. Life!"

Abish could not comprehend what she was hearing. How could someone have so little regard for all they held precious? From the look on Ammon's face, he was as close to rage as she had ever seen him, but his words were spoken in his usual controlled fashion. "From the little that you have shared, I beg to differ that you have anything to offer us. This manner of freedom that you suggest is not freedom at all, but would lead to bondage. It is you who have been deceived, and we know by whom."

Korihor laughed. "And now you would have your people believe that there is a devil as well? What sort of deranged minds are leading you?" He turned his back to Ammon as if speaking only to those who had gathered. "Would you listen to this man, whose obvious intent is to deprive you of all that this life has to offer by saying that you will be damned if you experience a little delight or joy? There are unending pleasures to be had, experiences that will open your horizons to what this life is really for—"

"Enough!" Ammon shouted above the man's diatribe. "I have heard more than I ever would have needed to make a judgment regarding you. I know you as well. You are what our fathers have warned us against since they left Jerusalem: a deceiver, a flatterer, an anti-Christ. You will not be allowed to utter one more word designed to lead this people astray." He turned and addressed the other members of the council in tones that were too soft for anyone else to hear. When he rejoined them, his expression was both pleased and disappointed.

"You were correct about one thing," Ammon continued. "There is no law that we have by which we can prevent you from speaking." He made a slight gesture with his right hand and suddenly two guards appeared. "But my duty is to protect this people, and from now on, only the monkeys and lizards will be your audience because we do have the right to *expel* you from our land. And may God have mercy on your soul and protect those who may be subjected to your lies in the future."

Ammon fell wearily into his seat. Korihor was escorted, none too gently, from the proceedings to what Abish hoped was far away from their land's borders. Though they could not end this man's treachery, Abish knew from experience that one day righteousness would eventually triumph over all evil.

But she was more concerned about the effect this trial had taken on Ammon. He looked so weary lately. When she made her way inside to the council chambers, she saw him sitting at his table alone. He was not moving. He did not appear to be looking at anything. And then suddenly, his shoulders slumped and he rested his head against his hands as if it could no longer bear some unseen weight.

Unsure what to do, she turned and left.

* * *

Abish glanced at the sky. Jarum should be home soon. Ever since she had let him decrease his workload at school and focus more on his farming he had been so much happier. She had not relented in regards to his reading, but realized that subjects such as dialect translation and astronomy could be expendable if it meant he would gladly pursue the rest. If only both of her children could be happy right now. Miriam had been so moody lately. Abish tried to recall her own temperament when she was nearly twelve years of age, but then realized that their situations were vastly different. While she had been living in a palace, surrounded by servants who catered to her every whim, Miriam had always faced a life of responsibility and sacrifice. Though her daughter never complained, it sometimes occurred to Abish that she was less than happy. Perhaps, when they had a moment, she would talk to Miriam.

And as far as Ammon was concerned, she hadn't seen him much since the trial. In public, he appeared to be every bit the strong, confident leader that they all depended upon. In private, she wondered if it was a different story.

Just then she heard a whistling and looked up to see Jarum strolling toward her.

"Alma's visiting the city," he said excitedly.

Abish smiled. "He is?" It had been nearly three years since they'd last seen the prophet and heard the words that had led them to this new land. "Why has he come? Is he staying with Ammon?"

Jarum shrugged.

A slave to curiosity, Abish knew she had to find out. Not sure she could trust Miriam yet to finish the tricky preparation of the manioc on her own, she set her to repairing a few of their fishing nets while Jarum finished his homework. Though the sky was starting to look ominous, she took her chances and brought along her thickest oiled cloak and wore her rubber-soled sandals as she rushed toward the city.

A crash of thunder had just set her teeth to chattering when Abish arrived at Ammon's home. After an insistent rap on the door, it opened and she was ushered in.

"Abish!" Ammon said, surprised.

"I heard," she explained, shaking off some of the rain, "that Alma was visiting."

As if in response to his name, the prophet entered the room. "Greetings, Abish. It has been a long time."

"Yes," she said self-consciously as she was ushered in, now dripping water all over the floor. After a brief gesture from Ammon, a serving-woman appeared to mop up around her. Abish was embarrassed, but the woman only smiled at her as she worked before Ammon dismissed her for the day.

"Come." He gestured to her. "Sit down and dry yourself."

She took the proffered cloth and began to dry her hair as Ammon arranged another chair across from the table. "Jarum told me you were visiting," she said. "I wanted to make sure I had a chance to see you. How are you doing?"

"Well enough to do the work," Alma said with a smile. "I arrived yesterday, but you were on my list of those I wanted to see as well."

Abish smiled. "I'm honored. Of course, I would have understood if you didn't. I know that you're very busy and that your visit must be of the utmost importance."

Alma agreed solemnly. "That it is. I am afraid that Zarahemla has seen more than its share of disturbances recently. In fact, the most recent is one that we have had in common." At Abish's confused stare, Alma explained, "That man, Korihor, who caused trouble among your own people not so long ago made an appearance in the capitol as well."

"He did?"

"Yes," Alma continued. "He was sent to us from the land of Gideon and was brought before me and the chief judge. He proceeded to revile us for our teachings." He then went on to reveal how Korihor had justified his wickedness by saying that he was only expressing his beliefs and that there was no law against that. And when he asked for a sign, he was struck dumb and could only confess to his deception in writing. After that, he was cast out and forced to beg for his sustenance, traveling about until he was eventually killed in a neighboring land.

"Is that why you're here?" Abish asked. "To tell us that he won't bother us anymore?"

"In a way," Ammon answered. "Alma thought it was important to bring to our remembrance that just as the preaching of falseness has the ability to do much harm, so does the preaching of the word have the tendency to do much good."

"Korihor was killed," Alma explained, "by your neighbors, the Zoramites." Abish listened to his words carefully, still not sure she understood their meaning. What did the Zoramites have to do with them? Alma went on, "It has been brought to our attention that they have been perverting the ways of the Lord and are being led into wickedness. They are significant in number, and we fear that they might enter into a correspondence with the Lamanites if given the chance."

Ammon leaned across the table toward her. "Alma has suggested that a group of us should try to share the word of God with them. He has brought two of his sons with him and a few others from Zarahemla as well. It would only be for a short while, but could help us maintain the peace that we have known recently. Not to mention," he grinned, "that it will feel like old times again."

As the essence of what he said sank in, Abish frowned, realizing that this meant that Alma had only come here to leave again . . . and take Ammon with him!

"I know this must remind you of when we first went among your people," Ammon said gently. "I was none too sure of it myself. Somehow I found the courage once and I must find it again! Perhaps this, too, can save more of our people and bring them to the truth."

Abish nodded grimly. She didn't want Ammon to go, but there was nothing she could do or say that wouldn't reveal why she wanted him to stay. And though she wondered if he was using this as an excuse to run away from something, she had to admit she hadn't seen him this happy for awhile. "Then I will pray for you until your return."

Ammon smiled, his green eyes sparkling. "I knew I would have your support. Thank you." He reached briefly across the table and touched her hand, quickly pulling back as if remembering that Alma also sat there.

Unsettled, she blurted out, "The land of the Zoramites is close to the border of Siron, is it not?" Ammon nodded. "Then I have a favor to ask." She brought to Ammon's remembrance her encounter with Isabel and how she had been cast out of the city before she could help her. Both men nodded in agreement that they would make every effort to find her. Relieved, Abish also made them promise to say good-bye before they left. Then she quickly retreated before the lump in her throat became any larger.

26

The missionaries had not even been gone a month, but it felt like years. Only work seemed to bridge the long gap between sunrise and sunset for Abish lately.

"I'm finished with the milking, Mama." Miriam's soft voice came from behind her.

Abish turned. "Good. Do you have time to help with the mending before you go to Aunt Teara's?"

Obedient as always, Miriam nodded in the affirmative and went back to her work. Her daughter had agreed to help Ruth tend Teara's three younger children while Benjamin was taken on an errand. He had been promised a dog for his sixth birthday and wanted to choose from a recent litter they had heard about in a neighboring village. When Jarum heard, he'd tried to convince his mother that he would need one for his upcoming birthday. She wasn't persuaded.

Abish looked at the sky and realized that she had better finish and head into the market. Lately, if one did not begin at the break of dawn there would be no more meat and even less fresh produce. Of course, she could always send Jarum fishing again, but living so close to the sea now, she had had enough fish to last her a lifetime. Also, if she left now she might catch Jarum at the crossroads and keep him from running off before he finished his studying.

She moved toward the house to leave word with Miriam. As she approached, she heard issuing from the doorway the clear, melodic tones of her daughter's voice:

> *"My God hath been my support;*
> *He hath led me through mine afflictions*

in the wilderness;
[Rejoice, O my heart.]
And he hath preserved me
upon the waters of the great deep.
He hath filled me with his love,
even unto the consuming of my flesh.
No longer droop in sin, [o soul].
He hath confounded mine enemies,
unto the causing of them to quake before me.
Behold, he hath heard my cry by day,
and he hath given me knowledge by
visions in the nighttime.
Rejoice, O my soul."

It was one of the more popular hymns that had been circulating through the land lately—taken, she believed, from the first Nephi's words. She could not remember who the composer was, but if he could have heard Miriam singing, he would undoubtedly have been pleased. Abish sighed. Every day she could see her daughter turning into an even more beautiful young woman. She was growing slim and strong, with dark, searching eyes and glossy black hair. Even though her opinion was the subjective one of a mother, it was obvious that her daughter would soon outshine all around her.

"Miriam?" she stepped into the house, not sure if she should praise her singing and reveal, in the process, that she had been eavesdropping. "I'm going into the market. Don't lose track of time or you will keep Aunt Teara waiting."

Her daughter nodded as Abish grabbed her goatskin pouch and headed into the city.

She smiled at the other villagers that she encountered on her way. A group of potters were making rain jars, and as she passed, the women waved cheerfully. Another group of young girls were braiding ropes—a task that she especially did not envy as the coarse yucca fibers nearly wore the skin off her hands by the end of the day. Men were either hunting or in the fields. Children were gathering sticks for fires. Sometimes the work seemed endless; how welcome the upcoming planting festival would be.

"Jarum!" she shouted as her son at last came into view. He was walking beside his classmate, Teancum, and she didn't miss the slight frown that crossed his face as he noticed her and then whispered something into his friend's ear. They parted, and he came over to her. She sighed as she noticed that the hem on his blue tunic would have to be lengthened yet again. Convinced that he often grew overnight, Abish was also proud of the handsome young man that he was becoming.

"Mama, can I go fishing with Teancum and Ka-lel?" were the first words out of his mouth.

Abish took a deep breath. "You promised to work on your transcribing for at least an hour each day."

"But, Mama! They're going now and may not wait for me."

"A true friend would understand that you had commitments to keep and support you. I know this is difficult, but you made a promise to your teacher."

"But my friends always get to do what they want. Teancum says—" When he broke off abruptly, Abish cocked an eyebrow at him. "Well, he says you treat me like a baby."

"Jarum," she said more firmly. "You may be dressed in a man's clothing, but you are still my son and must do as you are told. One day you will thank me for pushing you so."

"But I want to be a farmer, like Namon." he protested. "So why should I take the time to learn something that I'll probably never use?"

Abish was not going to fall back into that argument once again. Long ago she had decided that someone in their family would know how to read and write, regardless of their vocation. As for being a farmer, she knew that Namon's current profession was out of necessity in order to support his family. "A man is only as wise as he is learned," she quoted, not remembering who had actually said it.

Jarum smiled. "The Lord despises the learned who are puffed up."

Abish widened her eyes in disbelief. "Why, you—! Well then, it will be your job to continue to learn and mine to see that you do not become 'puffed up.'"

With a playful swat on his rump, she sent him along the path back to the house. *If only Ammon were back home*, she thought sadly. *He'd have some advice for me.* But she realized that it wasn't only for her children that she wanted him home. After the group had left, she was startled at first by how much she missed his companionship. But it shouldn't have surprised her. As far as adult conversation went, Teara was so busy now and Akah had seemed even more confused and forgetful than usual lately. But Ammon had always been someone she could turn to with her thoughts and concerns, and these past few weeks had reminded Abish how important it was to have that kind of connection with someone your own age.

Their time apart had also given her time to try to discern whether the last words he had spoken to her had been intended to give her the hope she'd carried with her since.

She thought back to the day of the missionaries' departure. Abish had found Ammon in his home packing for his journey. She'd waited for him outside, as was proper, and held out a freshly-baked batch of corn cakes when he came to greet her.

"Thank you," he said with a smile. It was only then she saw the great mound of food behind him. "The people have been most kind."

She had laughed. "Well, at least I won't have to worry about you starving. But I will worry."

"It won't be for long," he assured her. "Then I will be back and . . ."

"And?" Abish prompted. *Then what?*

He had said gently, "Perhaps things will be different."

But now as she continued on her way toward the market, the practical side of her returned. He was gone. For now. And as usual, she had to find a way to carry on alone.

* * *

The situation with Jarum improved for a little while. Soon the only battles Abish had with him were the usual ones, like reminding him to wear his snake-guards when he went off into the woods to fish or finish all of his greens—even when she could only find bitter ones. But some days she wondered why she couldn't have been blessed with cooperative children. Sometimes her son wore her out, and there had been so much to do lately.

Abish couldn't remember the last night she'd slept well—and it wasn't just because of the unbearable heat that had been plaguing them. Alma and Amulek had returned days ago with no knowledge of Ammon, other than that Corianton had joined him in his journey to Siron, while the others continued on to preach in the outskirts of Antionum. Even though Alma felt reassured that everyone was safe, she was far from calm. Combined with Miriam's continued moodiness, she was at her wit's end.

"Miriam!" she said forcefully one morning as they stood sweating at their labors. "You have to keep track of the exact amount of time that the manioc has been at a boil. If you don't, it will retain some of its poisonous properties."

"I'm sorry," came her daughter's piteous reply. "I'll try harder next time."

Abish was immediately repentant and placed a hand on the girl's shoulder. "It's all right. But just to be safe, I'd better dump this in the waste pit. We don't want to risk poisoning any animal that may come sniffing around. At least," she continued, "we have plenty to spare. Jarum has had so much success with the planting that we'll be able to fill our quota for the army and even have enough extra to sell in the market come harvest. Perhaps that will allow us to buy you a new dress. Would you like that?"

As her daughter shrugged and walked back to the house, Abish felt even more discouraged. Maybe she would try to talk to Teara when she had a chance, but Teara was so busy with her own family that they barely saw each other anymore, though they had enjoyed that nice picnic by the sea a few weeks ago.

She smiled at the memory of Namon hoisting his son up on his shoulders and galloping down the shoreline with Ruth chasing at his heels. She had tried to look happy as she sat by her friend's side, but Teara had sensed something was wrong and asked her what she could do to help. Abish looked down at little Rebekah resting on a mat and then at her friend's growing belly. Her friend's youngest was only in her first year and the physician in her was anxious that she should be expecting again so soon. But the excitement in Teara's eyes was so evident that she kept her concerns to herself. So she told only part of her troubles, about being concerned for the missionaries' safe return. Teara had echoed her feelings, and they left it at that.

As she started to cover up the spoiled manioc with dirt, Abish sighed and looked up at the sun. She would have to wait to go into the market another day so they could finish another batch of bread. But as she laid out more roots to mash, she heard angry voices coming from the house.

"You did that on purpose!" Jarum's cries reached her first.

Rushing to the house, she opened the door just as Miriam started to cry.

"What is going on here?" she demanded. When both children began to speak at once, she held up a hand, telling Jarum to explain first.

Miriam scowled and was silent only until Jarum had blurted out that she had ripped one of his parchments. Then she protested, "I was just looking at it! You grabbed it out of my hands and that's when it ripped."

Abish gave them a fierce look that had them cowering. Then she turned first to her daughter. "Miriam, you've been told this before. You are not to touch Jarum's work. Why can't you obey me in this?"

"I only wanted to look at it."

"Why?" Jarum laughed. "It's not like you can read it."

"Jarum, that's enough!" Abish groaned. "There's too much work to do to have the two of you fighting. As a consequence, there will be no *pah-lech* tonight." It was strange how withholding the sticky honey-candy could still be a punishment, even at their age. She supposed it was because in their harsh existence there were few pleasures. But they *had* to learn not to contend with one another this way! Their consequences meted out, she sent them back to their work.

That night, still frustrated by the events of the day, Abish thought about how difficult it was raising her children on her own. She had to be everything to them—nurturer, caretaker, provider, disciplinarian—with no one physically there to consult with and to support her. As she stared up at the ceiling, she found that her prayers lately had contained far too many pleas and not enough thanks. And tonight's had been no exception. As tears escaped from her eyes, the words echoed in her heart:

Please don't let me be alone forever.

27

"They're coming!" someone shouted from off in the distance.

Abish's head jerked upright. Soon the market was a roar of confusion as people darted to the city walls to catch a glimpse of the returning missionaries. Aaron and Zeezrom had returned a few weeks after the Harvest Festival but had no knowledge of Omner, Ammon, or Corianton's whereabouts. Abish clasped her hand together, almost afraid to look. What would she do if she didn't see Ammon among this final group? What would happen if one of them had been lost?

Finally accepting that she had to know regardless of the outcome, Abish leapt up the embankment as well. As the sun glinted off the river below, she shaded her eyes and began to count. One . . . two . . . three, or was that four? It didn't matter. It was obvious that they must have all returned safely! Running down the main street to the front gate, she saw Namon and Teara walking together through the market and went to them. Teara was approaching her time of confinement—a good thing since she had been having some early labor—and so Abish was also anxious to know of her status as well.

Namon greeted her and reassured Abish that his wife was receiving the best of care. "Not a day goes by when a neighbor does not bring food or offer to tend our children."

"It is like we are part of one large family," Teara added. "And now, our remaining brothers are back with us as well. Come, I know you are anxious to see them."

Abish blushed, wondering how transparent her feelings had become.

They pushed their way through the throng just in time to see Ammon striding among the cheering crowd. Next to him was Omner, and she could also see Corianton's usual brooding face, but there was a young Lamanite boy about Jarum's age by his side as well.

"Ammon!" she shouted. He turned, waved and smiled wearily. But the people were pushing him forward and even with Namon's help she couldn't reach him to stand by his side. She would have to wait with the others to see what they would do next.

The group ended up walking to a nearby embankment and Alma, who now joined them, held up his hands to quiet the mass. After a moment, it was quiet enough for him to speak. "People of Ammon, we left to do God's will, and now are reunited again through His grace. And once my brother, son, and dearest friend are rested, we will share with you more news of our travels and of the many trials and successes that we had."

The crowd looked disappointed, but seeing the haggard look on Ammon's face explained that this was good reasoning. Yet it had been so long since she'd seen him and there was so much to discover that Abish tried to take advantage of Namon's bulk to clear a path through the multitude more quickly. Doing so, however, was easier said than done. At every turn, she was accosted by one person or another—petitioning her to check on their aged parent, asking if some aspect of their baby's development was normal, even a few invitations to come and sup were put before her. Abish tried to smile graciously, but she had already lost Ammon and his party in the crowd and didn't want to wait until an invitation came to visit him in his home.

So she detached herself as politely as possible from the crowd and caught sight of a honey-colored head just rounding the granary wall.

"Ammon, wait!" she called out in desperation. He turned and gave her another weary smile as she caught up. Abish stood silent for a moment, unsure what to say or how to even begin. How could she say only a portion of what was in her heart without saying too much? "You look well. At least, you appear to be in one piece."

"Yes. Physically, we are all intact, though we did have our moments of struggle." He rubbed a hand through his thick hair. "Hopefully all has gone well for you and your family?" She nodded. There was a feeling heavy in the air between them and she wondered if she was doing something wrong. It was then she noticed the finely-dressed boy—perhaps a little younger than Jarum she now surmised—was still hovering in the background.

"This is Malech," Ammon offered, noting her confusion.

Abish gave the boy a welcoming nod, but received only a blank stare.

Ammon took a deep breath. "Perhaps we can talk later. Right now, I need to find a place for Malech to stay."

"We have more than enough room," Namon volunteered as Abish realized he had come up behind her. Teara happily agreed, causing Abish's eyebrows to rise. *They did?* "Yes, we would be happy to take him in."

The boy still had not made eye contact with any of them, but did not resist following Namon toward his home. Abish had no idea what was going on.

"Whose child is he?" she asked.

Ammon's face was pained as he said, "Isabel's."

Abish was so stunned that she couldn't respond. He pointed her in the direction of the council chambers, where, she assumed, he wanted to discuss this in private.

They entered the main chamber room, and Abish stood by the open door and watched as Ammon paced the floor. He struggled to formulate the words, reminding her of when he had told her of his conversion—knowing the story needed to be told, but reluctant to do so.

"After we arrived on the border of the Zoramite land, it was decided that we would cover more territory if we were once again to divide into groups. I offered to take Corianton with me, thinking that, away from his father and brother, I would have the best opportunity to test his mettle. After a few days preaching in Antionum, I thought it was time to go to Sidon. The journey was so promising! I saw a sullen young man stretching to become a soldier of God! Or at least I thought so." He took a deep breath and sighed. "We arrived in Sidon and I immediately sensed the hardness of those around us, but we found Isabel and did everything we could that first day to convince her to abandon her current life and come with us back to Jershon."

"So where is she?"

He turned and his eyes held such sorrow that she could not help herself. She ran and placed a hand on his arm, her eyes beseeching him that, no matter how painful, he must tell her the rest. But when he finally explained how this son of Alma had fallen, Abish slowly dropped her hand from his arm, not sure she had wanted to hear after all.

Ammon's voice caught in his throat. "And then I did everything wrong! I let myself get caught up in my own emotions, fueled by both the guilt of knowing that he was under my care and I failed him and also the memory of my own past weaknesses and the pain of seeing someone fall in the same way. Perhaps anger was justified, but godly anger was not what I exhibited. Oh, Abish." He turned toward her and buried his head against her shoulder. She stroked his hair and murmured soothing words as if he were a child.

"Ahem."

The couple turned to find that Alma had entered the room. Embarrassed, they broke apart and stood like small children caught raiding a stash of sweets.

"I had a chance to talk with my son," Alma said. "I assume that is what you two were discussing?" He clasped his hands behind his back and shook his head, "What a tragic turn of events when our intentions were so good. But I think he understands the seriousness of his actions and will seek every opportunity to repent of his sin. It will not be easy, but God's mercy is matchless and ceaseless." Alma stood, peering, she was convinced, into both their souls. "Everyone involved made their own choice. There is no blame that goes beyond individual action."

"But he was my responsibility," Ammon protested.

"I made the decision to bring him," Alma said. "I thought he was ready and of an age to prove himself. But my blame is that of a parent anxious to see their child test their independence, nothing more. He chose to take that first step."

Ammon was not convinced. "Then what of my reaction? My anger was not justified. I pushed too hard, passed judgment too quickly."

"Everyone made their choice." Alma nodded seriously. "What is done is done."

"And of Isabel?" Ammon said in an agonized voice. "Did she make *her* choice all on her own? Or did I force her to see what she wasn't ready to see?" Abish, who was still standing next to Ammon, glanced up, unsure of what he was referring to. He looked down at her and said, "Isabel is dead."

"Dead?" Abish echoed his words. "How? Why?"

"As we prepared to leave and were gathering our things, there was a knock on our door. I opened it to find Isabel's maidservant standing there. She had a young boy at our side and she said, with venom in her voice, 'It's your fault she's gone. I alone can't be responsible for the boy. He's yours now.' The old woman left him right there on the doorstep, though I ran after her for more explanation. She told me that she had gone in to awaken her mistress and discovered that she had taken her own life. Then she held up a scarf—the same scarf Isabel had worn the night before— and it was soaked in blood: proof of what she said. I was so shocked that I couldn't say anything, but as she turned to leave, she warned us, saying that Isabel was a favorite of the governor and we'd likely be imprisoned after her death was discovered."

Ammon buried his head in his hands. "So like cowards we left."

Alma came and laid a hand on his shoulder. "We may never understand why all of this has happened, but I feel as if perhaps it is for a greater purpose. Do not carry this guilt with you for long, dear friend. It would be yet another unnecessary burden you shoulder. Besides, we have the young boy's care to think of."

"He barely said a word to me on the trip back. And once he understands my part in this, I don't think he would want to stay with me."

Alma frowned. "He is the grandson of Laban and Akah, correct? They deserve to be told of all of this."

"I will do it," Ammon insisted.

"No," Abish said. "It should come from me. After all, I started this all. Perhaps I'm the one who is really to blame."

Alma stepped toward her. "We cannot look back and wish things were done differently. We must look forward and try to carry on." He took a weary breath. "The day is nearly passed and the boy is settled, for now. We should all retire to our homes, to pray and fast. Tomorrow, we will see that all is set right."

But as Abish looked into Ammon's pain-filled eyes, she wondered if anything would ever be all right again.

28

Within the month there was an influx of converted Zoramites to their land, reminding Abish of those early days in Ishmael. Because of this, families like her own and Namon's, to name a few, found themselves supplementing the newcomers. Along with the increased demand for her healing, she was being pushed to her limits and not sure how much longer she could keep it up. As she found herself returning home through the city late one day, she used it as an excuse to go and see Ammon and talk with him about it.

Ever since he had returned from Antionum, he had been drifting away from her again and she was trying to do everything she could to stop it. It reminded her of when she had lost Jared on the ocean—of how she had sat, helpless, reaching out her hand to him only to watch him float away. Of course Ammon had not let his duty to his people suffer; all week he had sequestered himself to his home, praying to know how to handle the angry Zoramites who had threatened to come against them. They wanted the residents of Jershon to stop giving refuge to those whom they had exiled. But her people had refused to abandon them, even promising to give the converts lands for their inheritance. This had angered the remaining Zoramites to where they were now mixing with the Lamanites and stirring each other up to anger.

She waited until the council courtyard was all but deserted, hoping that if they were alone, Ammon would open up to her once more. She headed to the inner chambers but soon realized that more than one voice was coming from within. Abish recognized Ammon's soft tones immediately and then Alma's became familiar to her. Old habits were hard to break and, realizing she was eavesdropping on their conversation, she began to step forward to make her presence known when she heard Alma say, "Are you going to speak to her then?"

"Yes," Ammon said. "I have to."

"You have been putting this off and I think I know why. Are you sure this is the right thing to do?"

"I don't know. There have been so many issues I've been trying to deal with right now. If only I had more time to prepare her and let her know of my feelings—but perhaps we are running out of time." Ammon turned away from the doorway, and their conversation became garbled for a moment. When she could once again hear him, he said, "She has been alone raising her own children for so long that the thought of having one more person added to her family might take some getting used to. But I feel as if it's the right thing. I will speak to her soon."

"Do you think she will accept?" Alma asked.

"I have known her long enough that I believe I know what her answer will be."

Abish felt the blood coursing into her head. *Could it be? At last!* Desperate not to be seen, she managed to make her way back in the ensuing dusk to her house. She prepared the evening meal, and after the children had eaten, Abish ushered them off to bed as if nothing had changed. But as she undressed, her fingers were shaking. Her mind was whirling. She wanted to stay on familiar ground because her heart had told her long ago that finding love again might never happen and so it was better to redirect her hope toward her children and the love that they could give each other. But she had finally accepted that this wasn't enough. Abish wanted to know what it was like to have a man's love again.

Shrugging off her feelings of apprehension, she looked at her children who were sleeping. *I want this for you so much*, she whispered. *But even more, I want this for me.*

* * *

The next day Abish was actually glad to be so busy. She had only thought of Ammon's words a few times, though the nervous beating in her chest had not left her since. But there was nothing she could do but wait. When a lull in activity came late in the afternoon, she used the time to stop by Akah's house to see how Malech was settling in. Though at first Abish had been of the opinion that the aging couple was in no position, physically or emotionally, to care for their grandson, Akah had insisted that family was family and he would stay with them. How she continued onward after each devastating blow, Abish didn't know. Three children had been lost to her. Three children taken away in violent, cruel ways, and yet Akah pushed forward, accepting the next task at hand and looking ahead to tomorrow.

"Greetings, Akah, are you at home?" Abish called, peering into the darkened hut. She heard a voice out back and followed it.

The older woman was hunched over a large pile of corn cakes just retrieved from the ashes. Abish grinned. Either her friend had miscalculated the amount of food that her family had needed or Malech had a voracious appetite! She stood to greet Abish, but not without expending a considerable amount of effort to do so. "Ah, Abish," she huffed, waddling over to her. "You've come for a visit. Are you hungry? I always seem to have plenty."

Abish shook her head after she noticed that aside from the staple bread, there was nothing more substantial in the hut. "No thanks." She reached into her own pack to take out a large wheel of cheese that she'd been given earlier that day. "In fact, I was hoping you could take this off my hands. I've been carrying it around all day and don't think I could take another step."

Akah fidgeted as she reached out her hand. "Well, I suppose. If you don't need it, that is. Cheese would be nice again—after our old nanny goat dried up, we've missed the taste of it."

"Are you doing all right, supply-wise?" Abish probed. With Akah's mental and physical decline and Laban having fallen down a few days before and breaking his leg, she knew this extra responsibility was difficult for them. "I could go into town for you and Laban."

"Oh no, we're fine," Akah shooed the question away like a pesky fly, though Abish wasn't convinced.

"Where's Malech—with some of the other boys?"

Akah snorted. "I don't rightly know. Probably off down by the river again, all alone. I don't think he's made one friend since he's been here."

"It hasn't been long. Perhaps in time." Abish tried to be encouraging, though she had already begun to doubt this arrangement. Malech seemed too much for Akah to deal with.

"Perhaps." Then Akah's face crinkled up in pain. "How can I know what to do with him, when maybe I didn't know enough to raise my own children proper? First Laman and Abnor. Now Isabel. She was always such a good girl." Akah's face was full of disbelief. "Always did what she was told. Never caused any trouble. I don't understand. How did I fail her?"

She looked at Abish as if for an explanation, but there was none she could offer because they had all failed the young girl in a way: Abish, Ammon,

Corianton. They all had had a chance to help her escape the awful chains that had surrounded her. Of course, the ultimate failure had not been theirs. As Abish looked at the old woman across from her, her blue-veined hands twisting nervously in her lap, however, she realized the time for recriminations was past. What was done was done and only God knew the extent of everyone's accountability.

Akah offered her some food once again, and Abish was on the verge of politely accepting when a sudden, crushing thought overwhelmed her. How many times over the past several months had she agonized over Miriam's moods and behavior? She had assuaged her guilt the few times that she'd tried to bring the issue up with her daughter, but the wall that she found herself up against was so strong at times that it was so easy to justify backing down and waiting until Miriam came to her. What if Isabel's walls had been broken down when she was still a young girl? What if someone had had the courage and persistence to fight for her until she knew she was not alone? None of this dreadful tale would have happened.

"I'm sorry, Akah. I will keep praying for your peace of mind. But I should return home. It's been a while since I've left my children alone for so long a time. With Teara at her time of confinement, she can no longer check on them."

A slight smile returned to Akah's face. "That Teara. Never thought I'd see anyone who would try to outdo *me* when it came to children. As for yours, at their age they need to be fending for themselves from time to time. But I know how you worry, so I'll be getting back to my work." She chuckled as she hobbled away.

Glad to leave on a somewhat lighter note, Abish rushed back to her home to find that Jarum was off fishing and Miriam still sat obediently at work. She quickly put her pack away and came to stand by her daughter's side, glad that they were alone. There was no way to speak the words that were in her heart without sounding abrupt, so Abish picked up a skein of yarn as well, sat down and began to wind. They both said nothing at first, and then Abish noticed her daughter watching out of the corner of her eye. The wall seemed to drop between them and Abish seized the opportunity.

"I hope you know how much I love you, Miriam," she began, cocking an eyebrow in her direction. "If not, then the fault lies with me. I want to be close to you, but it's difficult for me because growing up I didn't have a mother that I could talk to. And so I learned to manage on my own and sometimes I think I've treated you like you can manage on your own as well.

But you shouldn't have to. Will you be patient with me as I learn how to do better?" She watched as Miriam's hands slowed down. "Your happiness is more important to me than anything—but lately, I've sensed that you haven't been happy." She put the wool down and turned to face her. "Is there something that's been bothering you that you haven't told me?"

Miriam said nothing, but remained bent over her knitting.

"Please," Abish prodded. "Don't go through whatever it is alone."

Miriam's shoulders began to tremble. "I . . . I don't know how to tell you. I've always tried to do what I was told and I didn't know how to say this. You've been so busy lately and the last thing I want is to hurt you."

Abish felt her heart clench and reached out and took her daughter's hands. "You can tell me anything, Miriam. I am your mother and it is not your job to keep *me* from being hurt. But it is my responsibility to protect you, so please tell me what's been on your mind."

"All right," Miriam gulped. "I . . . I want to be a healer, like you."

Abish took a moment to process what she'd heard. Considering the nightmare that had been formulating in her mind, this was good news! But then the implication of what her daughter was saying began to sink in.

"And I want," Miriam continued, "to learn to read and write like Jarum."

"I had no idea," Abish said slowly, and yet, now that she thought about it, the signs had been there: the restlessness, the times when she hovered over Jarum at his studies and asked Abish for details about her day. Somehow Abish had been too preoccupied to see them. "Are you sure this is what you want?"

Miriam became very animated. "More sure than I've ever been about anything—except that I love you and Jarum and know the gospel is true." She looked down sheepishly. "Yes. I know this is what I want."

Abish still didn't know how to respond. She knew that her daughter was quick and bright and could accomplish anything she set her mind to, and yet was that really the life Abish wanted for her? She knew only too well what it was like to live on the fringe of society: accepted for her skills alone, never really belonging and never fitting in. Is that what would become of her daughter as well? But then she thought back to the lessons she'd already learned, that this was not about what *she* wanted. She had let Jarum find his own path in life; she owed this to her daughter as well. But her daughter had to be willing to see both sides of the river.

"You've seen my life," she began, "and the demands that are placed upon it. It has made it difficult to be both a healer and a mother, let alone a woman.

Aside from Teara and Akah, I have no true friends because people aren't sure what they think of me." She saw her daughter frown, but not wanting to discourage her too much, she added, "And yet I could not imagine my life without you and Jarum *and* my healing. All this completes me. And I promise you, I will help you do whatever it is you need to do to complete yourself as well."

Miriam threw herself into her mother's arms and cried. "Oh, thank you, Mama. Thank you."

Abish pressed her face into her daughter's warm hair and said, "I will talk to Ammon the first chance I get. We will find a way to make this work."

"Oh," her daughter blurted out, sitting up. "I almost forgot! Ammon sent a message for you earlier today."

"He did?" Abish's heart leapt into her throat.

"Yes. Jarum told me about it before he went fishing with Ka-lel. He said that Ammon wanted to meet with you in the council's chambers tomorrow at midday. At least, I think that's what he said. Maybe you can talk about me with him then!"

Abish pursed her lips and said distracted, "Yes. Of course." But inside she was thinking, *Council chambers? Midday?* This was not exactly how she had envisioned things, but who was she to complain? If Ammon had found the courage at last to declare himself to her, she would accept whatever he offered.

29

The next day Abish was forced to agree with Akah that Miriam and Jarum could fend for themselves so she could go meet with Ammon. After repeating her instructions one more time and adding a silent prayer, she set off. She had spent a good portion of her recent wages on the items she now carried in a pouch across her back. One moment, Abish prayed that Teara was at home, and the next, she hoped to discover her gone. What would her friend think? She would have preferred to keep this all to herself, but she finally admitted that without help, her preparation could take more time than she had.

She found Teara with only her two youngest because Namon had left for Gid, a new Nephite settlement by the eastern sea, just that morning. Benjamin had been invited along this time, leaving her friend with energetic Ruth and little Rebekah, both of whom Abish wished were old enough to be more of a help than a hindrance. A woeful smile crossed her own lips as she thought of Teara being left alone with this new arrival so imminent, but her friend didn't seem concerned. "He'll be back in plenty of time for the birth, and with all the help I've been receiving, there's little to do really. Besides, I really just need you here when my time comes."

As she helped Teara to her feet, Abish realized how huge she was getting. "How have your ankles been lately?"

Teara shrugged. "I'm surviving. They swelled up like tree trunks this morning, though. I took some of that medicine you gave me. It's a little better now."

Hoping her request would take her friend's mind off of her discomfort and not add to her burdens, she finally began to reveal why she was there. "I have come with a favor to ask."

Teara cocked an eyebrow. "Anything, you know that!"

Her friend's face opened wide with surprise and she clapped for joy after Abish explained the long-awaited turn of events. "I thought I'd never live to see the day!"

They both burst into laughter as Abish managed to say, "Me either!"

"Well," Teara ordered. "Let's begin."

Even though Abish would be walking into town during the heat of the day, Teara insisted that they also add a contrasting blue linen tunic beneath the yellow silk one she'd brought, which would look striking against the paleness of the sheer fabric. Abish had washed her hair down by the river late last night and applied the precious jojoba oil that she had been saving. Satisfied that her waist-length hair still had a lustrous sheen, she now let Teara weave a braided headband across the crown of her head, tying it at the nape of her neck. With her hair pulled back slightly, her jade earrings would be quite visible. They had been a wedding gift from Queen Aminash, though this was the first time Abish had worn them. She stood still while her arms were adorned with several gold bracelets, but found herself wishing she had rings as well. At least the soles of her sandals were still in good condition, though she longed for some gold embroidered ones like she had seen Hannah and her aunt wear. Lastly, she took out some ground sandstone from a small bag and tried not to fidget as her friend dabbed the reddish color on her forehead, cheeks and chin. Lacking a mirror, she could only guess at her appearance, but Teara seemed pleased.

She took a deep breath. This was it. There was no turning back now.

With a final blessing of luck from her companion, Abish walked to the center square. Though she was trying to be brave, she had a brief glimpse of herself as a child when her father had led her to the palace gates to be a playmate to Princess Anrah, King Lamoni's youngest daughter. "Abi, make me proud," he had said.

"I will try, Father," she whispered, holding her head up high.

It must have taken less time than she thought to get ready because she arrived before the last meeting had dispersed. If she had been naked she would not have felt more on display! Several familiar faces looked at her oddly as she walked into the building and she croaked out a simple greeting. The heat and discomfort soon were making her sweat, and she felt a small trickle run down her back as she stood silently in the corner waiting. *Please*, she gulped, *leave soon*. At last her prayer was answered and the men of the council dispersed. She realized she had been standing as rigid as a statue and wondered if she could force herself forward. A few more of the brethren greeted her passing with a longer-than-usual stare while others were so deep in conversation that they did not even acknowledge her presence.

"Abish," Ammon said as he finally noticed her, "you received my message."

"Yes." Her voice cracked. "I was told you wanted to see me."

Alone now, Ammon sat wearily on the corner of a table, rubbing his chin. "Yes. I am sorry you were kept waiting. The council has been overwhelmed by our continued struggles with the Zoramites. It's been difficult to think of much else."

She walked slowly toward him. "I understand, though I trust that you and the brethren will be directed as to how to handle our problems." Ammon shrugged and looked so uncomfortable that Abish blurted out, "Would you like to go for a walk, down near the ocean, perhaps?" *Maybe if we're alone.*

"No," he sighed, "it would be best to talk here and get this over with."

Abish felt a lump come into her throat. Was this so difficult for him? "All . . . right."

He stood up and began to pace. "I have been putting this off for some time because I was not sure how to go about it, what words to say. Even now, I am struggling to handle this situation because of how many directions I'm being pulled."

"Well," Abish said, trying to be supportive, "perhaps if you just say what's in your heart everything will fall into place."

Ammon smiled, the first sign of hope she had seen. Then he looked at her quizzically. "You look . . . different."

She consciously ran her hands down her dress. Perhaps it had been too much.

"Are you going somewhere after?" Ammon asked.

"Oh, well, I hadn't intended to, but my plans could change."

He shrugged. "I'd best make this quick, then." He stood behind the table, leaning on his arms as if addressing an invisible council.

"It can be difficult," he began, "for people to be uprooted from everything that's familiar to them. We've witnessed that ourselves with all of the incoming Zoramites over these past few months. Before then, there was hope among our people that we could find peace here in this land. Only now . . ." he waved some unspoken thought away. "But that's not what this is regarding."

Finally! She was going to go mad!

"Instead, I need to discuss something with you. Something that will change your life, but I feel it would be for the best if only you would be willing to let your family increase by one. I know it's a lot to ask and yet—"

"Of course!" Abish beamed. "You shouldn't have hesitated to ask. Yes. I will gladly accept."

Ammon looked amazed. "Are you sure you don't want to give it more thought? I mean, you barely know the boy, and from what I've heard from his teachers and peers, he's been very difficult and hard to manage. That's why I decided that if anyone could give him a sense of direction, it would be you. Besides, with Jarum being nearly his age, I thought the two of them could be friends. If only I had not destroyed what little chance there was that I could be an influence on him. I lost the mother—I will not allow her son to be cast off as well."

Abish stood in stunned silence. *What was he talking about?* Had she been so mistaken to think that he was going to ask her to be his . . . *oh no*!

Her face burned hot. What was she supposed to say now?

"I know that Akah insists on caring for her grandson herself," he continued tentatively as if trying to understand to her distress, "but you've seen her. She is too aged to handle such a defiant young man, and Laban struggles to support them. Once I talk with her, I'm sure she'll agree to this. But I wanted to talk with you first to be sure. You are truly amazing, Abish!"

Yes, her mind echoed. *You must think me amazing indeed.* "Give me a few days to prepare my children for the change." Her voice sounded wooden.

Blinded by the tears that immediately appeared as she left the building, Abish somehow found her way to the main pathway. Her mind was still reeling by what just happened, but she wasn't ready to give place to her thoughts. Somehow willing each foot in front of the other, she turned the corner at the main crossroads. Her heart leapt into her throat when she thought of Teara anxiously awaiting her return so they could share in the joy. But the wave of humiliation, anger, and despair was almost too strong, and it washed over her until she could not breathe. She barely made her way back to Teara's house before it engulfed her.

"Abish?" her friend cried out immediately when she saw her. "Are you all right?"

What words could she use to explain what had just happened? So she said nothing as Teara led her into the house. Then she released the floodgates of emotion within her, letting her lost hopes and dreams wash over them both. She didn't know how long they sat there until she was ready to explain to Teara about Ammon's real intentions in meeting with her. When she finished, Teara said just what she needed to hear.

"How can men be so dense?"

If her friend had merely sympathized with her and then told her to be patient—that she should forgive him for his blindness, that she shouldn't have jumped to conclusions—Abish knew she would have continued to ride the wave of her fury until its bitter end. But instead, she felt an uncontrollable laughter bubbling up inside of her. It flowed over her until both of them were rolling on the ground, their eyes spilling over with tears while the little ones looked up at them with amazement.

"Th . . . thank you!" Abish managed to gasp.

"I'm so sorry," Teara said as Abish helped her sit up. "I should go over there and give him a piece of my mind!"

Abish restrained her. "Please don't. I see now that the conversation I overheard had nothing to do with him and me. I made the mistake and imagined feelings where there were none."

Teara pursed her lips. "Are you sure about that? I've seen the two of you together. I've even caught an occasional glimpse of something in his eyes when he looks at you."

"Then why?" Abish said, her shoulder sagging in defeat.

"I think," said her friend sincerely, "that Ammon is having just as hard a time letting go of the past as you once did. Between that and his unflagging sense of loyalty to serving this people, it has made things difficult. I don't doubt for a second that with those two obstacles gone, he would choose you for his own!" She took Abish's hands in hers. "This leaves you with a difficult choice. You can either wait for him to come to terms with who he is or you can make the choice to move on with your life. If you are ready for love, then you should not feel guilty wanting it! You should not have to look to the future and see only loneliness."

"I'm afraid that men have not exactly been stumbling over each other for me."

"Maybe that's because," Teara said as she wagged a finger at her, "they know that you wouldn't be interested even if they did. Open your heart and you might be amazed at how many would like to be let in."

As she wiped the remaining tears from her face, Abish realized that perhaps her friend was right. Perhaps it was time to move on.

30

Moving on was not as easy as Abish had supposed. Ammon had felt the need these past weeks to check with her constantly on how Malech was coming along. Though he never came to the house, afraid his presence would upset the boy, he confronted her every time he saw her passing through the market or caught her on the main trail leading to and from the city proper. She tried to greet him as if no misunderstanding had occurred—and tried to remind herself that he was oblivious to her pain—but she knew that her overriding goal now was to protect herself. Every word she spoke to him was carefully measured out; every look was veiled so that he would see nothing of her heart. And though it took a few times to discover the exact physical space that she needed to have between them to avoid rekindling the fire she'd begun to feel when he was near, she finally learned how to keep her distance.

One day, she thought, her heart might learn how to keep its distance as well.

But there were many things in her life to keep her mind occupied, especially with their new addition. Jarum had taken instantly to the idea of having another boy in the house—to balance the scales, as it were. Of course, the only other *benefit* that Malech had brought to her life was that, compared to this interloper, she never again felt as if Jarum were uncooperative and disrespectful. He was an angel compared to this young boy that Abish found herself frequently thinking was the devil himself come to tempt her.

She had to remind herself often of his upbringing to keep from throttling him. What kind of life must he have had in Siron with a mother who made her living as a harlot? Was he left alone with an uncaring nursemaid most of the time? Did he know what his mother did, where she went? She thought back to her own upbringing and the mother that had often held raucous parties where male guests had shown little respect for her marriage vows—and where, unfortunately, her mother had exhibited little respect for them as well. Later, when Abish found out about the abuse her own mother had suffered at the hands of some wicked priests it helped to explain, if not completely justify, Saranhi's immoral behavior. But it did not change the fact that Abish had suffered because of it as well.

After Akah had agreed to transfer Malech into her care, she had sat down with her children to gain their approval. Miriam had wrinkled her nose—not sure if she wanted another brother—but Jarum had been very accepting. At least now she felt that her son had matured enough to where she trusted him to *influence* Malech and not just *be* influenced.

Abish glanced back at the house where some skins had just been waterproofed and were hanging to dry in order to make another cloak for the upcoming season of rain. Having another member of the family had also meant supplying him with all of the necessities of life. Apparently Malech's nursemaid felt she was entitled to most of her charge's belongings, because he had been sent away poorly equipped. Ammon had offered to arrange for anything the boy needed, but Abish was insistent that Malech receive only what she could provide him with. This would mean no fine-spun linens or cottons; their hand-woven fabrics would have to suffice. Thin, decorative sandals had been replaced with rough leather ones. And because Malech was a handspan shorter than Jarum, this was going to mean a lot of handed down clothes. He needed to learn right from the start that theirs was not a life of ease.

Abish stretched her back and looked up at the sky. *The skins should be dry by now*, she thought, heading back to the house. But as she drew closer, they continued to glisten in the sun. Perhaps she should have moved them closer to the house, where the radiating heat would have had them ready to stitch together in no time. She reached out a hand and touched one, only to find that her hand clung to the soft skin. Confused, she rubbed her fingers together and sniffed.

Honey! The skins were coated with the sticky substance. *But who . . . ?*

It was obvious who the culprit was. The only question now was how to proceed. Well, she reasoned, sometimes life provided the best consequence. While the others stayed warm and dry this summer, Malech would learn what it was like to be drenched to the bone in the daily rains that would come. But that was still weeks away, and she was itching to teach him a lesson now.

Since it wouldn't be proper for a boy of his age to share a house with a young woman who wasn't his sister, Malech had taken up residence in the stable. Her son had immediately begged to join him, thinking it an adventure, but she somehow knew Malech saw it as a punishment.

"Malech!" she said loudly, knowing that he was probably lurking somewhere around it. It took a moment before he appeared, leaning up against the wall with a smirk on his face. He was still attired in the only outfit he had—though it was becoming worn—and his dark eyes flashed in defiance as he stood there. Abish didn't give him the satisfaction of knowing that she was angry; instead, she went to the pot of congealing fat and dumped in a bucket of ashes. "This needs to be stirred down into soap. If you start now, it will be ready by dinner. When it becomes too thick to move the ladle, let me know, and I will help you pour it into the forms," she instructed, holding out the long wooden stirring stick.

"But that's women's work!" He frowned, crossing his arms across his chest.

Abish didn't back down. "I have plowed a field and butchered animals: all men's work. There is no differentiation between the sexes when there is work to be done, especially if it ensures your survival. We all do our share around here, and you will complete this task or you will not share in the benefit of our labors with us."

With that, she turned and walked into the house where Miriam was unstitching the hem on her old dress to accommodate her growing frame. They were both growing so fast; it wouldn't be long before they were gone! That was the last thing she wanted to think about. She went to her daughter and praised her work, receiving a glowing smile from Miriam, who, after her work here at home, would be off to her private tutor.

Abish had no trouble discussing her children with Ammon if it meant their happiness, so it had been arranged that while her daughter could not attend the boys' school, Miriam could study separately with one of the teachers—one with five bright, capable daughters—that Ammon felt was sympathetic to Abish's plight. Jarum was finishing the soldier's tally for the year to ensure that no more reckoning was due and would be home soon. She was so proud of them both. How could she ever feel the same way about their new resident? Maybe Ammon had overestimated her.

With a quick turn to the window, Abish was not surprised to see the pot outside unattended, but she still prayed that Malech would begin to accept his place in their lives.

Later, when it was time for the evening meal, Abish called her children in to wash up and take their places. Malech followed in slowly behind them and plopped down, ignoring the bowl of cleansing water for his hands and feet. On the small woven mats in front of them, Abish dished up ample portions of beans and squash for her children. She had even made small bundles of corn meal steamed in banana leaves, this time with seasoned venison inside—all of Malech's favorites.

Only, she did not put any of the food in front of him.

As the others began to eat, Malech burst out, "What is this? Where is my food?"

"If you do not work," she said evenly, "you cannot expect to eat."

Malech's mouth dropped open. Without another word, he stomped from the house.

* * *

Over the course of the next few weeks, Abish's own little world seemed to only mirror the chaos around them.

First, tension between the people of Ammon and the Zoramites continued until a portion of the army of Captain Moroni had been recalled from Manti to assure his troops would be sufficient in number to protect the inhabitants of Jershon. But word had trickled down through the people that perhaps the strength of the Lamanites and their new allies might be too great for the Nephite faction to defend against. If so, that could mean only one thing: another war.

On the heels of this trouble, Teara had a long and difficult labor that left her weak and lethargic. The little boy was welcomed eagerly into the world and Abish had never seen Namon prouder—as if *he'd* gone through the labor! After much deliberation, Abish suggested that Teara would not have sufficient energy to suckle little Enoch herself and that perhaps a wet nurse ought to be found. Her friend vehemently opposed such a thing at first, but finally saw reason and left it up to Abish's discretion.

A nearby Zoramite couple had recently given birth to another child, a healthy baby boy, and the woman agreed without hesitation to take the other newborn for a few weeks while Teara recovered. But Abish soon wondered if this arrangement was the best thing. After the child was taken to live with the other couple, Teara immediately sank into a deep despair. Abish had often seen new mothers experience intense sorrow because of the birth of a child, but now it was evident that without her new baby by her side, Teara could not be happy. So Abish talked with the Zoramite woman, Zaharah, about perhaps living in the house of Namon for a while. Not sure how receptive her idea would be, Abish was pleasantly surprised when the woman readily agreed. And since the woman's other son was close in age to Benjamin, they had both agreed to go and help Zaharah's husband with the harvest, thus providing more room for the new additions.

If only all of Abish's concerns were as easily remedied.

As far as Malech was concerned, if breaking down his defenses was her goal, it was going to take some time, Abish realized. Malech eventually began doing his chores, reluctantly and with as little effort as possible. But as soon as he finished and was fed, he found some unknown place to hide until the next day. She wanted more than a change in his actions—she wanted to know his heart was changing as well. The days passed and it was proving yet another sore trial for her faith.

One day, Abish decided she was desperate enough to see Ammon for his advice.

As she found Ammon in the council chambers, however, she was disheartened by what she saw there as well. He looked so tired. Their leader's usually confident frame was slumped over his desk, his shoulders sagging under yet another unseen weight. But he gave her a weary smile upon seeing her and sympathized with her methods as she explained life with Malech.

"His stomach was the first to surrender, and I'm sure his determination will follow shortly behind," Ammon encouraged.

"I hope so, because sometimes I wonder if I'll be the first to break."

"You must stand firm. If he gets his way now, imagine what he'll be like as a man."

Abish cringed, seeing another Laman or Abnor in the making. "I won't give up on him. But, if you will, pray for me."

Ammon looked into her eyes in a way that made her forget the resolution she had made to keep her distance. "I always do."

The remainder of the day did nothing to calm her unease. Malech had sulked and refused once again to finish the soap properly, forcing her to do it herself before the pot of congealing fat attracted too many unwelcome visitors. Now it was late and she had an early morning trek to make to a new Zoramite tent settlement just north of the city. Finally with a sigh, Abish went inside and began to finish her preparations for bed. Hopefully she could put it all behind her and get some rest.

As she stood behind the privacy cloth, changing into her sleeping gown, Abish noticed a slight flicker upon the wall and turned to see what looked like a thousand fireflies shimmering outside. Pushing the barrier aside, she walked over to the window. From here, she had an unobstructed view all the way to the stable, and she could see that the sputtering light originated from there. Still confused at what she was seeing, though, Abish made her way to the front of the house. She only had to take a few steps into the yard before her heart leapt into her throat at what she saw.

31

"Jarum! Malech!" Abish shouted as she ran to the stable. "Wake up! *Fire!*"

The nearest stream was a hundred paces away and so instead she grabbed one of the leather cloaks that had been hanging abandoned on the fence. Dousing it in the nearby rain bucket, Abish rushed again toward the stable, which was now spewing thick smoke through its thatched roof. "Jarum!" she once again screamed as she threw open the door, only to have living darkness spring toward her. She began to choke on the black air but pushed forward, kicking at the flames that licked at her feet and curled down from the damp reeds above. Abish thanked God that it had rained the night before. If the drought had held, the entire edifice would have been engulfed in fire by now.

She saw a small bundle in the corner and ran to it. The figure sat up, coughing, and she saw that it was Malech. Grabbing him under the arms, she dragged him from the stable and dumped him on the ground, sputtering and disoriented. He kept muttering something over and over again, but she hadn't the time to process what it was. Assured he was alive, she looked back at the fire. *She had to find Jarum!* And quickly. But when she tried to reenter, she found that the flames had spread up the back wall and the heat had become so intense that it seemed to melt even the words that she kept yelling. Scrambling on her knees to escape the worst of the smoke, Abish pawed around on the ground, ignoring the bales of straw and extra supplies that they thought would be safe there but which now fueled the fire's hunger.

"Jarum!" she rasped. "Where are you?"

Please, Heavenly Father. Help me find him!

Her senses became attuned and somewhere beyond the crackling and popping of the reeds she heard a groan. Shuffling toward it, Abish pushed back a portion of the fallen roof to discover her son lying unconscious in the blackened debris.

"Thank you," she cried to the heavens above as she struggled to find enough strength to remove her son from the crumbling edifice.

It was only later as they both lay face up in the still, fresh air that she realized that her hands and feet had been burned. But Abish didn't care what injuries she had sustained, only that Jarum was safe beside her. She propped herself up on one elbow and leaned over him. "Son? Can you hear me? Please wake up."

Jarum groaned again and his eyes flickered slightly. After a few coughs, he was more alert and looked up at her. "Mama, what . . ." he began coughing again.

"Shh. Lie still," she ordered, remembering that Malech was just a few cubits away. She could see his form in the light of the now-spent fire and determined that he was not seriously injured. And so she returned to Jarum, who was breathing heavily and struggling for each breath as if his insides had been scorched by the fire as well. "Malech," she called out. "Help me bring Jarum into the house."

She didn't know what she would have done if Malech had been un-cooperative and refused to come to her aid. But he came and took Jarum's legs as they carried him to safety. By now, Miriam had been awakened by the shouts and commotion and stood in the doorway. "Mama, what happened?"

"A fire," Abish panted, "in the stable. They're both all right."

"Take my hammock," Miriam cried. Without being asked, her daughter retrieved a wet cloth and began to wipe the soot away from Jarum's brow. She then tipped the small bowl of water to clear his throat. Abish stood and watched for a moment, proud of her daughter's control and confidence. But Jarum was in need of her own advanced skill and so she went to her basket of medicines and began to make a paste. The mere process of grabbing the pestle, however, made the burns on her hands throb with such excruciating pain that she cried out.

Miriam was immediately at her side and took one look at her hands. "You must tend to those," she insisted. "They're already blistering. I can help Jarum and Malech."

Abish nodded in defeat and plunged her hands into a basin of water, cringing as the coolness hit seared flesh. She watched as Miriam used her fledgling knowledge to administer to the two boys and once again felt a rush of pride that her daughter was following so competently in her footsteps.

After bathing her hands a few more minutes, Abish dried them off as gingerly as she could and began to apply the aloe paste that her daughter had made. Then she allowed Miriam to bandage them up. The worst of her burns tended to, Abish turned to Malech, since Jarum was in too much pain himself to speak. "What happened? How did the fire start?"

But Malech only grunted and turned away from her to the wall.

Abish shook her head as weariness overcame her. "Under the circumstances, it would be appropriate for us to stay together the remainder of this night. Miriam, take my cot and I will sit vigil over my son."

* * *

Abish was unaware of when the throbbing subsided enough for her to sleep. When dawn broke through the window she sat up and was reaching for Jarum's sleeping form before the memory of her own injuries returned. She clasped her damaged hands against her chest, frustrated that she could not even reach out and stroke back a lock of the hair that had fallen across his cheek. She looked over at Miriam, who had fallen asleep leaning against the wall. Malech, on the other hand, was nowhere to be seen.

She stumbled from the house and immediately saw the charred remains of the stable. Though her heart sank at the loss, she needed to focus on finding Malech. But a quick glance around the vicinity of the house did not reveal where he had gone. She returned to find Miriam rubbing her eyes.

"Malech is gone. Will you watch Jarum?" Abish whispered.

Her daughter nodded, so she left.

Where could he be? If it had been Jarum, he could be anywhere. But she had known Malech long enough that she knew he would not have stumbled off blindly into the jungle to places unknown. Though he tried to act brave, he was really a scared child who would most likely run to the only protection that he knew: Akah's house.

The brief journey gave her enough time to consider how she should handle the matter. Not sure if his flight was indicative of fear or guilt, Abish knew that something had happened that he wasn't telling her. After the ordeal she'd been too tired to think of anything. But now she had time to think about the words she'd heard Malech repeating to himself, as if a mantra, *"I didn't mean to. I didn't mean to."* And she wanted answers.

Sure enough, she anticipated his behavior perfectly and found him cowering in Akah's arms. The older woman was stroking his head and soothing him. "It's all right. Don't you worry, it will be all right."

"I'll be the judge of that." Abish stood towering in the doorway.

The look on Malech's face was all she needed to see as he huddled even closer to the old woman's ample flesh. "I didn't do it! It wasn't my fault."

Abish frowned. "Why should anyone think it was your fault, Malech? Is there something you want to tell me?"

"The boy's been through a terrible scare," Akah protested. "He needs to rest."

Abish held up her bandaged hands. "We've all been through a terrible scare. The most frightening of which was that I almost lost my son last night! So I think I deserve an answer from Malech about what happened."

Malech looked to his grandmother again, not sure if there was enough sympathy to prevent what he believed was going to happen next. "Go on," Akah finally ordered. "Tell her that you had nothing to do with it."

Left on his own to speak, he quickly broke down. "It was an accident! I . . . I was just playing with the flint block, trying to see if I could start a small fire on a leftover piece of soap. I didn't know it was going to splatter like that," he moped. "Before I knew it, sparks started flying all around." He looked up, terrified as if reliving the moment. "I tried to put it out! Honest I did. But it was too much, too soon."

"Why didn't you come and tell me immediately so I could have helped?" Abish demanded.

"It happened so fast," he said, looking down, "I thought I could handle it and no one would know. But then, the smoke got so bad that I couldn't see. I tried to wake up Jarum, but he wouldn't wake up and I couldn't see where the door was anymore. It wasn't my fault!" He suddenly broke away and ran out of the house.

Akah tried to get up and follow, but Abish bade her stay. "I will go talk to him." The old woman nodded.

Outside, she found Malech sobbing against a nearby ceiba tree. If it had been one of her own children, she would have gone and put her arms around him and waited until their sorrow had all spilled out, but she still felt like this boy was a stranger to her. He had put her family in danger and she wasn't sure what would happen to this arrangement after tonight. But he suddenly looked so small and frail. All the bravado was gone from him, and Abish wondered if he were truly sorry for what he'd done or only that his secret had been found out. At least she owed him the chance to reveal which.

She went and put a hand on his shoulder to try to get him to look her into her eyes. But he pushed her hand away and sobbed even harder. "Malech," she said firmly. "Please turn around and look at me."

"You're not my mother!" he yelled, pushing her away.

Abish took a calming breath. "No, I'm not. I'm just trying to understand what happened last night. Jarum will live and the stable can be rebuilt. But I taught my children long ago that by lying to cover their mistakes, they would lose something very precious: another's trust. How can I trust you after what happened unless you accept responsibility and feel remorse for it?"

"So now you hate me!"

"Hate is a strong word. I'm angry and upset and tired. But I'm willing to give you a chance to make things right."

Malech turned slightly, wiping his nose with the back of his hand. "How?" he sniffed.

"You can apologize to me and Jarum and help us rebuild what you have destroyed. But most of all, you can ask God for forgiveness for trying to hide from your actions."

"Ask God for forgiveness?" he sniffed. "How do I do that?"

Abish smiled. "We're going to have to have a long talk."

* * *

The prophets spoke in the scriptures of a person being "reborn" when the gospel was shared with them. Abish had witnessed this happening so many times that it shouldn't have surprised her when Malech seemed to change overnight. After she had sat by his side and explained to him the miracle of forgiveness and how Christ would come and make that possible, she literally saw a glow spreading across his face—she felt the anger leave him, though it was replaced with a certain sadness.

Malech had wrinkled his face when she tried to explain that God was his heavenly parent and loved him and would never leave him. He asked, "Why did Mama want to leave me? Didn't she love me?"

"No matter what, I know your mother loved you," Abish explained. "But for some reason, she felt as if she couldn't take care of you anymore—not because of anything you did, but because she felt too much despair to go on." Abish thought of her own mother, who tried to drown her sorrows in sleeping draughts. "Please try and forgive her, though. Our parents aren't perfect—sometimes they make mistakes that we have to be brave enough not to make ourselves."

"Mama tried to tell me once that what she was doing was going to make a better life for me. But nothing ever changed. Nothing got better!"

"I think," Abish said softly, "that your mother didn't understand that it wasn't money or power that was going to improve your life. That you just needed her love and the love of a family around you."

"Will you . . ." Malech stammered. "Will you be my family now?"

Abish smiled. "Yes. If that's what you want. We will be your family now and always."

32

They all tried to be patient with Malech in the days to come as they began to repair their lives. At times, the "angry" boy would leak through like water from a cracked bowl; Abish could handle him, however, with a little firmness and consistency. Namon, Ammon, and several of the brethren had quickly rebuilt the stable, and they could almost imagine the fire hadn't happened. Malech had settled into the routine of chores and study and exhibited a quick mind for learning things that were new. Most of all, he hungered to learn the gospel, so Abish took this opportunity to have Ammon work with him. At first it was awkward for both parties. But gradually their defenses began to melt away to where one day when Abish went to walk Malech home, she found the two of them bent over a scroll as Ammon traced their lineage back to Adam.

"And then Abraham begat Isaac, and Isaac, Jacob . . . do you see?"

"Ahem." They both turned as she entered.

Malech rushed toward her as Ammon stood and dipped his head slightly in greeting. "How did your lesson go today, Malech?" she asked.

"Good, but I'm hungry!"

Abish grinned. Ever since his self-imposed fast, he seemed to be trying to make up for it. She handed him a measure of copper. "Then go and grab something from the vendors and then we'll head home." She cocked her head to one side, wondering why Ammon seemed more intent on gathering up his precious scrolls than turning around to talk to her.

"There's going to be a council meeting tomorrow night," he finally said, his back still to her. "To discuss how to handle the latest rumors about the Lamanite army. Perhaps you'd like to come."

Abish smiled. Ammon had always understood her need to be involved. "Perhaps. I'll see if Akah will come and watch the children."

Ammon finally faced her with a wry look on his face. "Are you still not comfortable in leaving the boy alone?"

"Not yet. He's come a long way," she said, slowly stepping toward him, leaving the door behind her open, "but I have to keep my family safe. He'll regain my full trust in time."

"Your caution is wise." He took a step toward her as well. "Trust must be earned. How are your hands?"

Her calloused feet had healed quickly, but Abish looked down at the puckered flesh on her tender palms. The skin was still red and a few blisters had yet to burst; she was still unable to use them for some tasks, but they would heal in time. She realized that Ammon had taken one of her hands, gently testing the scarred ridge with his thumbs. "You could have been seriously hurt."

Abish found it hard to think with her hand in his. "The thought never crossed my mind when I knew that my son was in danger."

"There's nothing quite like a mother's love."

"How is your own mother?"

Now he let go of her hand and turned away again. But he couldn't disguise the emotion in his voice. "She is trying to be strong, but the pain in her abdomen increases daily. I wish . . . I wish that you were there to care for her."

Abish sighed. "I'm not sure I would have any more answers."

Just then Malech came whooping back into the building. Not only had he purchased the fruit, Abish realized, but used the remainder of his funds to add another annu stone to his game collection. She frowned. Now she would have to add a lecture on stewardship to her list. Looking back, she saw that Ammon had already gone back to his work and so they said their farewells and left for home.

* * *

The new year came with little celebration. The days had been unseasonably hot and dry and emotions were strained as Moroni's army continued to grow. There was only one explanation—one that nobody, however, cared to voice.

Abish wished she could hide away in the small world that revolved around her children and home, where mutual respect and love had made a haven for them. Perhaps then they could forget the intruder that hovered on their doorstep.

"Tell us another story," Malech urged one night as they huddled around the light of a small lamp. Bedtime had come and gone hours ago, but still they urged this childish pastime to continue. It was their favorite way to escape.

"All right." She waved up a hand in defeat. "But this must be the last one."

"Make it the one about Moses," Jarum begged.

"No," Miriam cried. "Rachel and Jacob!"

Abish wagged a finger at them, "I think it's Malech's turn to choose."

"Tell us about Alma and the sons of Mosiah again."

She tried to work past the lump that suddenly came into her throat. The look on Malech's face was so sincere that she knew there was no ulterior motive to his request other than to hear about their miraculous transformation. Trying to keep that in mind, she rehearsed the events of the wayward boys who, while seeking to destroy the church, were visited by an angel and then turned their hearts back to God. It was such a simple story that she often wondered if the generations after them would even believe that it had happened. Once they were all gone, would anyone believe any of this at all?

"It's time for bed. No more delays," she said amid groans and protests. Then she went outside, where the air was cooler and brought with it the fresh tang of the nearby sea. The last touches of evening light were rimming the mountains off to the west, but the stars were already so bright, like a million fires spread across a backdrop of darkness. She had always wondered what those brilliant specks of light were. Her people had once believed they were the eyes of the gods looking down on them; her father had instead told her that it was the souls of those who had passed on. She liked to think that. Perhaps he was looking down on her, even now.

A rustling in the nearby bushes alerted her to Namon's approach.

"You're out late," she said, worried. "Are Teara and the children all right?"

"They are well. Sleeping. I thought you would want to know of something."

"What?" She stepped away from the protection of the house toward him. "It's not . . ." she was hesitant to speak the words as well.

"There will be a council tomorrow, of only the leaders. In fact, Alma has secretly come to be with us. We decided it was for the best to keep this matter as *contained* as possible for as long as we can. But I think that nobody would protest your being there as well."

Abish wrapped her arms around herself as if the air had grown cool. "Yes. I will be there."

Suddenly, her haven had become as fragile as the skim on a bowl of milk.

* * *

The next morning Abish went to the council meeting as invited, greeting Alma and Namon before waiting unobtrusively in the back. But by the time it ended, however, she almost wished she hadn't agreed to come.

Her family was waiting unawares at home, though nothing could compare to Ammon's job of telling all the rest of their people what had been decided. Now not only had they made an enemy of their brethren, the Lamanites, but the Zoramites had joined them as well and were planning to come against them as one giant scourge. Because the city was still relatively new compared to other surrounding cities and had no defenses, Captain Moroni had thought it best to have the Anti-Nephi-Lehies leave the land and give place instead for the armies to fortify the city and attempt to ward off the impending attack.

It appeared that their land of inheritance had been lost.

At least Namon could break the news personally to Teara. She watched as the burden already caused Ammon's shoulders to sag. Now she felt guilty thinking that her little problems of the heart were worth spending energy on when, once again, her people were being forced from their homes.

She waited until the remaining members dispersed, leaving her and Ammon alone. Then she went to him and crossed her arms angrily across her chest. "Why? Why does this keep happening? Where will we go now?"

"I don't know." His voice was like an echo.

"Well," she reasoned, "it had best be soon. In a few months, the rains will begin and make travel more difficult. Of course, if we're pushed further north into the land Bountiful, we won't have as rough of a terrain to deal with. But going west would give us more natural water sources and has already been well-scouted." She blushed, realizing she'd been telling him what to do. "I'm sure that whatever you decide, we'll be fine."

"I hope so," Ammon said grimly. "But I won't be there to know. This time, I'm not going with you."

All sounds ceased but her breathing. Abish's mind could not formulate the words to speak. Her heart could not accept what he was saying. It had to be a joke. Ammon was making fun of her, waiting to see how she might fall apart at the thought that he could be leaving—for good. But the look on his face told her that it was all true.

"But why?"

Ammon was having trouble looking her in the eye. "I had a feeling that we would be forced to leave once again and so I worked it out in my mind last night what I would do if we did. I decided that I needed to be home . . . with *my* family. My mother is dying and my brothers are only a sporadic part of my life. For too long I've been without them." Now he looked at her, his green eyes pleading with her to understand. "Perhaps it's better if you went on without me. All of you."

Abish felt a familiar, intense sensation start low in her stomach as the memories of another time came to mind. Another time where he'd left her to face something difficult on her own. But this time it wasn't a matter of her going back to find her people, but to travel with them to yet another strange land. "How can you leave us like this? We need you now more than ever!" Then, she finally spoke the words she'd longed to say. "I . . . need you more than ever."

His knowing look was pained. "Sometimes I wonder if you've ever needed me—"

"That's not true," Abish cried. "Maybe the real truth is that it's only me that you're trying to leave. In which case, I should be the one to go."

He grabbed her by the arm as she tried to walk away. "I'm sorry. Do not let us part this way."

Abish shook her head. "I can't stay! It hurts too badly."

"I never wanted to hurt you, Abish."

"No," she said wearily. "The truth is you just never wanted me."

Ammon groaned. "You don't understand. There is so much you don't know. I want to tell you, but . . . I'm just afraid . . . afraid that . . ."

"What?" This time she couldn't just let him hurt her and walk away. So Abish pushed him to finish his sentence. "What are you afraid of?"

His reaction was so quick that she didn't have time to think. His hands were on the sides of her head and he pulled her to him. He stroked her hair with such tenderness, and she found herself lost in the depths of his green eyes. She felt the warmth of his body against hers and took in a deep breath of anticipation. But then, suddenly, like the beat of a hummingbird's wings, it was over.

"That," he cried, releasing her to stumble backwards, "is what I'm afraid of."

33

The next day as Abish returned home from the bedside of a new supplicant, she began to walk more slowly, trying to recapture the moment of Ammon's touch. The look in his eyes as he had held her. How ironic that his passion for her would be the thing to keep them apart. But he would never choose to be with her as long as a part of him was afraid of her.

Now she was left alone to ponder the question of their departure. Which of all the known lands of the Nephites would be the place where *she* wanted to raise her children? As she took a breath, the scent of the jungle and the life growing therein was heavy in her nostrils. She also couldn't mistake the freshness and tang of the sea air not far away. And then it occurred to her. Only one place had ever felt like home and ever could: the rolling pastures of Melek, the gentle hills sweeping down to the ocean where she had come to know of God's love for her. That was where she wanted to go. But who was she to decide? Once again, they would have to take what they were given.

The next day Abish went with her family to gather with the others. Standing on a high wall by their unfinished temple, Ammon looked a little like she imagined King Benjamin had but without the unanimous reception. There were many who could not bear thinking about another journey. Others were anxious to settle anywhere they were led and were desirous to leave at the thought of another war. Amid the confusion, Alma took his place and told them of his travels in Melek—how he had never witnessed a more righteous city. Though the journey would be long and arduous, he also made his feelings clear: no matter where they settled, they would be blessed for their righteousness. But he reminded them that even considering the people of Ammon's unique background, as many as were able should stay together to strengthen one another and give all manner of support.

Abish marveled at his words. It was as if he had read her mind last evening! But a hush fell over the people as they stared at each other like lost sheep. Abish couldn't blame their reticence. They had been told that this would be their land, an inheritance for their children. And now they were being told they had to leave. How much more could they endure? As confusion surrounded them, Abish secretly hoped Ammon would change his mind and once again stand as their leader, but he remained silent. So for the second time in her life, Abish went and stood before her people and tried to find a courage she did not realize she had.

"I do not know what our future holds any more than you do, but I will continue to do whatever I can to find a place where my children and their children can live and hopefully find peace. We owe that to them and to ourselves. And we owe God our continued devotion by doing His will. We have been through so much together, and as Alma said, we can only be *strong* together. Who will stand with me?"

A ripple of approval swept through the crowd. Then she found Namon at her side.

"I will." Then Teara took his hand. "And I will!"

Soon other prominent citizens had joined them in agreement. As she looked at the faces of those she had served and learned to love over the years, she knew that together they would survive. Somehow they would find a way. Soon a murmur of approval went up and the people cheered.

"Yes, Melek! We will go!"

* * *

Standing on the hill above Jershon, Abish realized that she had two vantage points: first, the land that they had called home for the last two years behind them and, second, that of the wilderness, which held their future in its dark expanse before them. Soon the sun had broken through the haze of morning, and it felt as if everyone were just delaying the inevitable. Namon had already made a tally of the crowd below her and organized the people into camps. He had only to give the signal and the mass would surge through the jungle—into the darkness, into the unknown.

Once again she looked at the people who had stood by her side. She saw her family, her friends, and her neighbors waiting patiently for the journey to begin. Of course, there were many she did not see among the gathering. Ammon and Alma had already left the day before for Zarahemla. And some of her people had chosen to stay behind in the land of Jershon, including many of the old and infirm, who said they would rather have their bones interred in this temporary sanctuary than strewn across the land. Sadly, Akah and Laban had chosen this course, and it had been with many tears she had said farewell. The convert Zoramites who also agreed to stay had based their decision on another set of reasoning: there were still many of their own people who were being driven out of their land and who were making their way to Jershon. If they left, who would welcome these repentant brothers? Besides, they had not entered into the covenant and could take up arms to defend their families. But even then, some had chosen to join the exiles. Abish looked over at Teara and her companion, Zaharah, standing with their infant sons in the distance. She took a breath to reassure herself and then realized Jarum had come to her side.

"Are we ready, Mama?" he asked with a serious expression.

I have to be strong for you. I have to be strong for them. "Yes, my son. We are ready."

Namon turned toward Jarum and asked, "Would you like to sound the command?"

Jarum's face brightened as he took the large conch shell in his hands and blew. The noise echoed off of the surrounding trees, causing everyone to turn like stalks of wheat in the wind to look at them. And then, swinging an arm over his head, Namon gestured them forward.

Land of Melek
73 BC

34

"I finished the weaving," Miriam's voice drifted in from the doorway.

"Thank you," was Abish's weary reply as she stirred the contents of the boiling pot. It was difficult to find the energy to do much more than put one foot in front of the other and she was glad for all of the strong backs she could find to help with all the work. Since their arrival in Melek two months ago, there had been little time during the day to think about anything other than the amount of work there was to be done in this harsh new place.

Even though her people had been welcomed with open arms and offered the choicest land by the Melekites, they had refused. There was an unspoken understanding among the people of Ammon that the Nephites had been generous to them—even to the point that they had lain down their lives for them—and that this ragged group could ask for little more. So instead they chose a small, rocky valley in the south, far away from the main trading route where, hopefully, they could live out their days unmolested. But since the rains in these lowlands came less predictably and over a shorter period of time, the ground was even more difficult to farm and there was not enough free-flowing water. Jarum had been working tirelessly to create an irrigation system. Afraid he was overdoing it, Abish had ordered him to take some of the other young people down near the shore. Naturally Miriam had insisted on staying behind with her. But looking at her daughter's sagging shoulders and sweat-stained tunic, now she insisted.

"You've worked hard today." She brushed a lock of thick, dark hair from her daughter's face. "Go and see your friends! Malech and Jarum left for the seashore hours ago." She watched as Miriam frowned at the idea of going, though, obviously not wanting to leave her side. But then she bit her lip, glancing in the direction of where the other young people had gone. Abish managed to give her another reassuring smile, at which point she eagerly hurried off as well.

Soon the sun burned high in the sky and still her children had not returned. Exhausted, Abish poured a gourd of cool water over her head just as a figure came into view. She raised a hand to shade her eyes from the blinding light and saw that it was Teara, and she waved back in greeting. Her friend approached and held out a small pot, and Abish was amazed as she lifted up the lid to look inside.

"Namon found a honey tree," Teara explained.

With a huge smile, Abish thanked her. The children had gone nearly mad for want of sweets. "You have enough for yourself, I hope? You have a tendency to give away more than you keep."

"There was plenty. It is hard to see so many wanting, though."

Abish nodded in agreement. Continually starting over had begun to take its toll on the people. For most, this was the third time that they had left everything behind to travel to a new land where they would try to start a new life. Some had not even moved out of their tents while back in Jershon and had forgotten what it was like to live in a house. Reminded of her present task, Abish rushed back to the steaming pot and retrieved the last skin she'd been soaking to expand their own lodging. While the boys had agreed to sleep unprotected, Abish felt better knowing they at least had some safeguard against their backs until their new permanent dwelling was completed. Once that was done, she could possibly consider traveling into Melek to try to find Jacob and Sarah.

Over the years she had told her children many times about the Nephite foster family that she had stayed with as a young woman, and they were anxious to meet them as well—probably to find out the truth of some of the stories she had told or neglected to tell them. But there had been too many pressing demands to even consider leaving her family to make the half-day's walk to where they lived.

"Are your children doing well?" Abish asked. "I feel as if I've been so busy that I've hardly seen you."

Teara sighed. "I feel the same. And we are doing as well as can be expected, though there are days when I wish the youngest were a little more independent."

"Enjoy this time when they need you. Soon it will be you needing them. That's why I convinced Miriam to join the other young people. Between her chores here and working as my assistant, I'm afraid it might become too much." Together they tossed the last leather up over the line. "I certainly haven't been able to give my children an easy life." She sighed.

Teara rested a hand on hers. "But you've given them so much more."

Almost immediately the air came alive with whoops and girlish squeals as the youth came running through the trees. Abish unconsciously identified that all of her children were present and then smiled at their enthusiasm. Their own conversation interrupted, the two mothers listened as their children related the adventures of the day. Apparently there had been some unwelcome dunkings and small creatures deposited down the backs of tunics. But the two women knew that the girls' protests were shallow indeed; they had enjoyed every moment of attention. In fact, Abish noticed that in the entire time that Ruth stood by her mother's side, her eyes had not once veered from Jarum's direction. At first it shocked her. Her son was nearly thirteen years of age and Ruth, barely seven, and yet, she had such a look of adoration in her eyes that it was hard to miss. Of course, Abish reminded herself, childhood infatuations were like summer storms: intense and quickly passing.

The friends said their farewells and went off in their separate directions. Jarum had wanted Teancum and Hagoth to stay, but a raised eyebrow from his mother reminded him of the unfinished project of this morning. Like the obedient son he had become, he accepted that the festivities of the day were over and began to contemplate the work at hand.

"I appreciate all of your efforts," Abish said to him after Miriam and Malech went back to the house. "You do the work of a man already." Jarum said nothing, but she noticed he stood a little straighter as they walked along. Not wanting to see him too puffed up with pride, she changed the subject. "Did you have a good time at the seashore?"

Jarum shrugged. "I suppose."

"Did something happen?" His response had her confused.

"Well." She could see him looking at her from the corner of his eye. "It's just, uh, that daughter of Teara's. She was being a pest."

"Ruth? A pest?" she echoed.

"Yeah." He kicked at a rock as they went along. "I could barely walk without tripping over her. It was a little annoying."

Abish tried to stifle her smile. "I think she's fond of you."

"Me?" Jarum groaned. "She's just a little girl." Then he dashed off ahead. *Ah. But little girls grow up, son.* Abish smiled after him.

* * *

Finally!

After two more months there was a break in the rain and Abish was able to make plans to travel to the northern border of Melek and see if she could find Jacob and Sarah. Certain she would remember the way, even after so many years, she left a list of chores for her children and kissed them good-bye. Packed light in order to travel quickly, she made good time. Within a short while, she had moved from the rolling, rocky hills of their isolated basin to the jungle-clad valley that held the city of Melek. Early morning light crept down through breaks in the canopy, effusing the scene with verdant shades of green. Abish moved along a small river and soon began to encounter the inhabitants who had so graciously welcomed them.

Good memories began to flood back and she remembered how protected and safe she had felt when she first lived here. She had been truly happy for a time, though a part of her still felt as if she hadn't really belonged. Though Jacob's family had taught her the gospel and treated her as one of their own, she had always felt as if her life would take her in a different course. When Ammon came to Melek as a missionary, she had let herself believe that he would be a part of that life. But look how that had turned out.

Soon she was in the city square and she saw the temple, grand and imposing. Other impressive, though smaller, edifices lined the main corridor as well, and Abish would have liked to take time to tour it more closely, but her heart was set on its original goal, so she hurried on the way. When she was finally on the outskirts of the city, she sought for any familiar landmark to remind her of the correct direction to take: a familiar hill, an aging tree. Was she on the right path? She questioned a few of the other travelers, and they only shrugged apologetically. There was no Jacob and Sarah of Melek that they knew of. She would have to persevere.

The sun began to dip in the sky and, still unsuccessful, Abish grew anxious that her trip would be for naught. In all likelihood they might have moved into the city, or even away from the city, though she could not see why. They had always had everything they needed: fertile land, a humble home, the support of friends around them. Why leave all that? But then, just when all hope seemed lost, Abish realized that the best way to retrace her steps would be to go back to the source: not where she had found them, but where *they* had found her.

She easily located the sandy shore that she had walked so many times during those first few years. At first, as she daily prayed, it was with the hope that Jared would miraculously come walking toward her one day, saved from the depths of the sea. Later it became the scene of her salvation, where she had risen from its depths after having her sins washed away. The same copse of trees stood off to the left—a miracle considering how often they were demolished by summer storms.

From here, she let memory guide her inland and soon saw a curling line of smoke rising off in the distance. Her heart leapt into her throat, and she ran to it like she was coming home.

35

Abish quickened her pace until the house came into view. The small adobe dwelling had been slightly extended off to one side. *They must have needed the room.* The stable still looked to be in good repair, giving her hope that it was being cared for by its original occupants. The tiny garden to the side of the dwelling was bursting with ripe squash and fragrant herbs. *How Sarah loved her garden!* She could see in her mind Sarah kneeling and kneading the bread: kind Sarah, gentle Sarah. Soon Jacob would come striding in from the fields, with his first smile for his wife before sweeping her into his arms and spinning her around. She had learned so much of love from their example. The children would no longer be there, she knew. Helaki and Nephi would be grown men by now, with families of their own. Rachel must be married—what a beautiful child she had been. Even little Esther would have found someone to care for her by now. But maybe they lived nearby and they could all be reunited and sit around the fire, telling stories and thinking of those days.

Nearly bursting herself when she arrived, Abish gave herself a moment to catch her breath before rapping on the door. She stood there anxiously.

But no one answered.

She rapped again, a little harder this time. Still, no one.

Pursing her brow, Abish meandered around to the side of the house. Some fresh laundry was drying on the roof and so obviously someone lived here and must be nearby. Walking toward the small garden, Abish wasn't sure who was more startled—her or the woman with curling auburn hair who was walking back to the house with a basket on her head.

Sarah?

Surely her eyes were playing tricks on her. This woman was much too young.

"Greetings," Abish said with a smile, trying to overcome her surprise. When she realized that she was not the only one surprised, she quickly added, "I'm of the people of Ammon who have recently settled on your borders. I hope I didn't frighten you."

The woman visibly relaxed. "Oh, I'm sorry. I'm not usually so skittish, but we see few visitors out here. I thought, well, you . . ." Now she was embarrassed.

"I understand." Abish tried to sympathize. After all, finding a strange Lamanite woman on your doorstep would be unnerving. But she was anxious to get to the task at hand. "I have come looking for someone. Two people actually. Their names are Jacob and Sarah—I used to know them some time ago. In fact, you look so much like—"

"You're Abish!" came the delighted cry, cutting her explanation short. She was astonished. "How do you know me?"

"My parents spoke of you from as far back as I can remember. I was just a baby when you left, but they never forgot."

Who this woman was dawned on her and it was almost more joyous than she could bear. "Esther?" Her hand flew to her mouth. "You're grown up and . . . you look so much like your mother."

Though their first meeting had been tenuous, now Esther broke into a huge smile. "Please, you must be thirsty and tired. My husband will be coming home soon to eat. You must stay and eat with us."

As she was led back to the house, however, Abish couldn't help asking, "Where are your parents? Do they still live here?"

Esther stopped, turning toward her with sadness evident on her face. "Both of my parents are dead. I'm so sorry," she said softly. "I know that must shock you. After so many years, I have come to accept it."

"How," Abish choked on her words, "did they . . . die?"

"Of an illness. Shortly after my son was born."

As if on cue, a young boy of around seven or eight years came whooping toward them. "I found more, Mama!" He held out his grubby hands to show her the roots that, by the state of his clothes, he'd obviously dug up himself. But he stopped wide-eyed when he noticed Abish standing there.

"We have a visitor, Lib." Esther stepped reassuringly behind them. "A friend of our family who knew your grandparents."

"That was a long time ago. You must be old! I just got baptized!" he said proudly, reminding Abish so much of Jarum at that age.

He was quickly ushered off to clean up after that. Esther then guided Abish into the house, where she set down the basket on her head. Sorting through the contents, she explained, "Many of our people became sick in that year, especially in the inner city. We believed that we would be more protected out here in the countryside, but it eventually found us, too. Rachel was the first struck down—" At the terrified look on Abish's face she hastily added, "No. My sister is alive! She and her husband live on a neighboring farm. But our mother was by her side night and day, so she was the next to become ill. It was the height of the planting season, and my father knew that we all might starve if he didn't finish the sowing, so he hated leaving her side, but he had us all to think of."

Even after so much time, Abish recognized the pain of remembering on Esther's face. "You don't have to go on if it's too painful."

There was a faraway look in her new friend's eyes. "It was the one thing that my father always regretted—that he was not there to say one final good-bye to her. For days afterward he worked like a madman in the fields until, finally, he sickened himself. I stayed well enough to tend to him, and his last words were of her. My parents were very much in love," Esther said.

"Yes," Abish said softly. "I know."

Abish offered to help with the meal in any way she could. But Esther was an accomplished cook and the complexity of the recipe was such that she quickly felt inept, so she instead volunteered to wash off the roots that Lib had found. It was good to be alone for a moment to take in what she'd been told, anyway. Though she felt an instant kinship with Esther, knowing that Jacob and Sarah were gone had come as quite a blow.

As she turned the corner of the house on her way to the nearby stream that she hoped was still there, she saw an unusual sight behind the old ceiba tree that had stood long before anyone's eyes had seen this land. She walked over to it, curious. A gentle breeze drifted across the land and brought with it the familiar scent of the flowers that Sarah had loved. She took a deep breath. Then Abish discovered what had drawn her toward the ancient tree. At its side, she saw the two small mounds and a pile of rocks that marked the spot where Sarah and Jacob were buried. She felt her legs weaken, and she collapsed to the ground.

Running a hand over the dirt, she released the tears she had been holding inside while in Esther's presence. It was a wordless cry, the kind filled with such anguish that it defied earthly utterance. And once again she felt so alone. Sarah had been like a mother to her, and considering how brief a time she'd had with her own mother, Abish longed for the bond they'd shared. Her mind was also racked with guilt. Jacob and Sarah had died shortly before she had come back from Siron so ill. What if she had been here instead? Could she have saved them? It was too much to consider, but now she felt doubly sad at the loss.

Afraid that Esther would worry if she lingered, she sought to regain her composure. But before she returned, in a gesture that had become familiar to her, Abish removed the seashell necklace from around her neck and placed it lovingly upon the ground.

"I promised to return it to you one day, Sarah." *I'm sorry it was too late.*

She felt her neck. It was now bare—a reminder of all those she had lost. Then she hurried to the stream to wash away her tears.

* * *

The setting sun was now just a thin line on the horizon. Though anxious to return to her own family, Abish had accepted an invitation to stay the night, which allowed her to meet Esther's husband, Eliab. The next morning, she tactfully excused herself after breaking her fast with them. But as she scurried up the hill, she knew that it wasn't just the thought of her family waiting for her return that had hastened her departure. There was a familiar pang of jealousy at the happy family scene, of the husband and wife smiling lovingly at each other while their children played at their feet. Abish had promised that she would return and she would. It was the closest she would ever be to those she had loved and lost.

At least everything seemed to have gone well in her absence. Jarum was anxiously awaiting her return to let her know he had come up with a new idea for watering the crops—regardless of the rainfall. If all went as planned, he would have it ready for the next planting. When Abish heard what was required, she bit her lip, thinking of the cost. But Jarum assured her that both he and Malech could complete it on their own. And when she went inside, Miriam couldn't stop talking about how well she'd done at her studies that day. Abish listened patiently for a while before realizing that a tired body wasn't the best home for an attentive mind.

Having tended to her children's needs, Abish then made her own preparations for bed, but was immediately overcome again by the thought that she was alone. Her spirit was heavy. She had no husband, no mother, no father to listen to her talk about *her* day—to listen to her excitement about new discoveries and comfort her over her losses!

But as she fell wearily to her knees in prayer, she realized that wasn't entirely true because she always had a Heavenly Father who was concerned for her. And yet her heart still, perhaps selfishly, longed for someone she could see and touch. Someone who could hold her when she felt like life was more than she could bear.

36

It was the first Harvest Festival to be celebrated in their new land—the first of what the people hoped would be many. While so many had struggled to tame the native soil and they knew they would have to beg for sustenance from their neighbors during the upcoming dry season, it was more the *spirit* of the celebration that they were enjoying.

Jarum and Malech, along with Benjamin and Zaharah's eldest son, Hagoth, had already left hours ago to make sure they didn't miss entering their prize goat in the judging. Abish and Miriam had been put in charge of finishing up some mats that morning that would be sold at a special section of the market today. It was an idea that Teara had put forth for the less fortunate among them, knowing that few would accept outright charity, but would be willing to work at these designated booths for a portion of the proceeds at the end of the day. Though it meant that some would not be free to enjoy the entire day, it would give them a sense of dignity when the day was done.

Frantically working to finish the mats, Abish looked up and saw Teara and Ruth appearing like angels of mercy with little Enoch and Rebekah in tow. Two more hands were just what she needed—though Abish wasn't sure Teara had two free hands. Teara immediately sat down by her side, but when Ruth found out that only the women had remained, she began to bite her lip nervously.

"May I go on ahead?" she said timidly. "If I hurry I can catch up with Father and . . . the boys."

Teara frowned slightly at the loss of her eldest daughter's help, but gave her permission, while Abish had to force back her knowing smile. Left alone, the two friends talked of their children as they worked.

"I wish Ruth was as responsible lately as Miriam," Teara sighed. "One moment she's deep in thought and the next I can't seem to keep her feet on the ground."

Abish finished the last row on her mat. "She'll come around. Miriam went through her own struggles."

"I hope so."

But Abish was soon to notice that in spite of the excitement of the day, her friend was even more quiet than usual. "What's wrong?" she demanded to know. "It can't just be Ruth's flightiness that has you troubled."

Teara dropped her mat and wrung her hands together. "I am with child again." Abish's eyes widened before she could hide her fear. "Don't tell Namon, not yet. He will just worry as well."

Abish perused her friend, so small and delicate-looking. Her last delivery had been so difficult that Abish, in a moment of fear, had advised her against any more children. King Mosiah must have been right—it was the size of the spirit that controlled the body; Teara had never seemed strong enough for the work she did. But somehow she had already born four children. Yet the thought of a fifth had them rightfully concerned.

"I will be right there by your side," Abish said as she tried to comfort her. "We'll get through this together."

"I know," was the small reply. "For some reason, this time, I feel anxious. As if something might go wrong."

"Most mothers worry until they hold their child in their arms."

Teara pursed her lips. "You're right. If only he or she were already here. How Namon would love another son."

Loading up their supplies, their group was now able to join the throng that surged along the main pedestrian path that led toward the "center" of their establishment. Though it consisted only of a few permanent buildings— such as the council chambers for their newly elected leaders—the layout for the city had already been established. The large clearing in the center would be for their temple. The rise that had been cleared of rocks would be a public area for recreation. Numerous other mounds indicated where the educational and civic districts would be. One day. It was this anticipation of what was to come that fueled the day for most of the attendees.

Zaharah met them at the crossroads and Abish mustered up her most sincere smile, knowing she would have to stop thinking of this new addition as an intruder upon her small circle of friends. After all, they now had one more "mother" to help with all the children. It was a beautiful morning as they walked along, but Abish was not completely at ease.

"Are you sure you are up to the demands of the day?" she whispered to Teara, knowing how difficult these first few months could be.

Her friend shrugged as she walked along beside her. "I hope so. But I couldn't bear the thought of sitting at home alone."

Somehow the city elders had arranged for a showing as grand as anything Abish had remembered in Ishmael—well, almost. Though she realized that most of the participants were their own people, somehow their cumulative abilities had been showcased in a fashion and with an enthusiasm that made up for any lacking skills and resources. Their children, young and old, were already standing with their mouths agape at the jugglers and fire-eaters in the square. As the scent of cooking food filled the air, she realized that somehow her people had managed to accumulate a bounty of tasty treats to tempt the spectators. There was ripe melon and corn cakes seasoned with lime and chile, *pah-lech* for the children and sour cactus fruit for the more adventurous. The children were immediately clamoring for some sweets but, to Abish's surprise, both Teara and Zaharah shook their heads.

"I'm afraid not," Teara said. "I brought our own meal for later, though."

Abish realized immediately what the problem was. Certain that the others had no money with which to pay, Abish's first thought was to offer to treat the children to whatever they wanted. But then she remembered Teara's feelings on outright charity. Devising a solution, Abish whispered in Teara's ear, and a smile broadened her companion's face as Abish turned to the older children.

"Oh no! I should have filled my water sack full today. Would you like to go and fill it at the well? In return, I'll buy you each a small piece of *pah-lech*."

As the terms of the negotiation sank in, Rebekah quickly nodded, and Zaharah's two children followed suit, though the youngest most likely didn't understand what it meant. As Abish watched the water sack being dragged across the dirt and then bouncing up the stairs to the local well, she only prayed that it wouldn't have to be fished up from the bottom. As the mothers went for a closer inspection, Abish grimaced as Kalem ended up being doused in at least half of the precious liquid before the goatskin pouch was handed back to her. Not sure she had any more water now than before, Abish praised their efforts.

"Well done!" She led the children to the vendors, where they were handed their reward. Now Enoch seemed to understand the consequences to their actions and he reached for the water skein again. Abish let out a hearty laugh. "I think I've all the water I need for now. But by this evening, I may need a fill-up again."

Satisfied that another sweet lay in their future, the children rushed back, sticky and satiated, to their mothers' sides.

The day was very enjoyable and it was good to laugh and smile again. As midday came, however, Abish had been well-reminded of the constant demands of little children, so she volunteered to check on the three older boys, whom they had not seen all day.

Left on her own to navigate through the ever-growing crowd, Abish surmised there were only so many places to go and she was sure the boys would be located before long. She came across the stockyards and found that, as she'd suspected, the judging had come to an end long ago, but she was impressed with the selection herself and stopped to take a look. There were goats and asses and oxen whose coats had been combed with nettles and horns polished with oil. She ran a hand along the fence, wondering if so many were for sale because their owners had to decide between feeding their livestock or their family. This almost convinced her to get another nanny goat, though it was the last thing she wanted. *Between the milking and churning, it would just be one more task for Miriam to do.* Of course, Akah always had three or four such animals and always managed to keep them producing. So maybe the fault really lay with her.

That unexpected memory of those they'd left behind rushed back to her, and Abish found her eyes welling up with tears as she took a deep breath to try to contain them. It had been a wise choice—many would not have completed the journey—and yet, contemplating what they might be enduring if the Lamanites continued to target the land of Jershon weighed heavy on her heart.

Abish was so deep in thought that she almost didn't hear the commotion behind her.

Abish wiped the tears from her eyes and turned to see that the owner of a magnificent ox was having trouble with a cumbersome yoke. She frowned. *Why did men think they had to do everything on their own?* He was in obvious need of some help, but Abish wasn't about to volunteer—she'd never been fond of any animal that stood above her knee. He would have to fend for himself if he couldn't admit to his male companions that he barely had control of the situation. She looked back to the goats, trying to decide if she preferred the milky white one with spots on her backside or the pure black one that was happily chewing away at some nearby leaves.

Suddenly, a great shout went up. She heard a crash of timbers and a great bellowing noise. Everything happened so fast. There was no time to think. In a blur of movement, she found herself thrown to the ground.

The weight upon her was immense and the breath had been all but knocked from her body. Gasping for air and trying to push the shroud of her own hair from her face, Abish gasped, "Get . . . off . . . me!" Finally escaping out of the darkness, she looked up and saw a man's face above hers.

He seemed almost as stunned as she, but managed to sputter, "I apologize, I—"

"Please," she begged. "I can't . . . can't breathe!"

The man rolled off to one side and it was then Abish could survey the chaos around them. Now several men had come and roped the enormous ox, though it continued to buck and writhe. The stockyard fence had all but been destroyed, allowing the smaller creatures to take advantage of the freedom they suddenly possessed. Abish watched as a white streak went scurrying past her and began nibbling on a nearby vendor's wares. The woman shrieked and tried to pull the piece of linen from the goat's mouth, but to no avail. Watching the struggle, Abish began to chuckle.

It was then she realized that the man beside her had not moved. "Are you all right? Are you hurt?" she asked, concerned he had injured himself.

"Yes," he blinked up at her. "I mean, no. I'm not hurt. I . . . let me help you up."

He gave her his hand and lifted her off the ground as if she were as light as milkweed seeds in the wind. For a moment she found herself pressed up against him and quickly stumbled away from him for propriety's sake. When he did not immediately speak again, she took a moment to study him. There were no markings upon his body and he was attired in a simple tradesman's loincloth and leather jerkin. He was exceedingly tall and muscular, with hair the color of ripe wheat, a fair complexion and eyes that were blue as a stormy ocean. She realized that his features were quite pleasant to look upon. "Thank you." She cleared her throat. "I suppose you saved me just now."

He cocked his head. "Something tells me you probably would have been fine on your own. I hope I didn't hurt you, though—I'm afraid my instincts took over."

"Well then, I thank your instincts."

They both smiled.

"My name is Abish."

"And I am Lamech."

Now what? She stood there awkwardly assessing the situation, realizing that *she* was now the subject of scrutiny. In a gesture she thought she'd outgrown,

Abish found herself tilting her face to one side to show off her better features. At last Lamech broke the silence by asking her to accompany him to see the archery contest. It was tempting, but she still hadn't found Jarum, Malech and the other boys. After a deep breath, she had to find even more courage to tell him that she had three grown children and was looking for two of them.

He stood without speaking, digesting the information, but then announced, "I will help you find them, if you'd like."

It was too late now to deny that she wanted to be near him. "Thank you. I'm sure it won't take long."

"I would not mind if it did," said the deep voice beside her.

* * *

Abish lay in the darkness but couldn't sleep. For hours she had found herself rehearsing the events of the day.

After they had found Jarum and Malech, she tried to act as casually as possible, not sure how to explain the man at her side. She succeeded, somewhat. But the look on Teara's face when she saw the handsome stranger nearly caused her to cringe! At least her friend's own attempt at matchmaking served one purpose: by the end of the day, Abish knew practically everything she'd wanted to know about this new acquaintance, *without* having to ask a single question herself.

Lamech was a stonemason by trade and a Zoramite by birth, converted by Alma before leaving everything he knew to join the people of Ammon. Through Teara's none-too-subtle questioning, they also learned that he was unmarried and the only member of his family to accept the gospel. He was now commissioned to begin work on the new temple, and already had some standing among the people.

But it was what she *didn't* learn that was keeping her awake tonight.

Had he felt it too? There had been an undeniable reaction between them, something she hadn't felt in a long time. It was exhilarating, exciting, and it also scared her to death.

The day had taken its toll both emotionally and physically, and Abish fought off thinking any more about him. But as she lay in the darkness, the loneliness that usually lay dormant during the day returned and she felt it like a weight upon her. Struggling to breathe, she wrapped her arms around herself and rolled over onto her side, thinking about how she had struggled to be strong all her life. Left alone, moving from land to land—somehow she had managed to survive. And yet, there was a difference between surviving and *living*.

And perhaps she'd merely been surviving for too long.

37

Abish had known all day that something was wrong with Jarum.

He had been sullen that morning as they broke their fast and impatient with Malech out in the fields when a section of his canal had collapsed in on itself. Abish bit her tongue, knowing the last thing he needed was a reprimand, and she herself offered an apology to Malech later on. But when he criticized Miriam for overcooking the corn cakes that evening, she decided it was time to confront him.

"Jarum," she said sternly as he drew a portion of water from the rain barrel behind their new house to wash up. "I did not like the tone you took with your sister tonight. She has done nothing to you and you hurt her feelings deeply."

Her son continued to look down. "I'll apologize to her. I'm sorry. It's just that, well . . ." He seemed hesitant to continue.

Abish looked at this boy who was becoming a man before her eyes. It was hard to see him struggle over the years, but aside from occasional lapses, like today, she was proud of the person he was becoming. Whatever was bothering him now, he would work it out. But the mother in her couldn't help but know the cause of his distress. "Is there anything I can do?"

He looked up at her with pleading eyes and said, "Could you talk with Aunt Teara for me, please?"

She was confused, "Why? Has something happened?"

"Well, maybe," he said, shuffling his feet, "she can talk to Ruth." Abish raised an eyebrow as he let his problem pour out. "Yesterday Ruth told Miriam that she was going to marry me. Teancum overheard and spread it around and now all of the boys my age know and they tease me whenever I'm around. I don't know what's wrong with that girl—she's acting crazy."

Abish tried to stifle her grin. What had seemed like a momentary infatuation a few months ago now took on a more serious tone. "I'm sure it will pass in time.

She's young and looks up to you. Not that I'm biased in any way, but you are the smartest and most handsome in your class."

"Oh, Mama, stop." Jarum squirmed, confirming that at his age he was too old for such mother-coddling. "Will you talk to her, please? Tonight? Maybe if Ruth doesn't say anything like that again my friends will forget it."

"I still think you're making too much of this. Ruth is a beautiful girl."

"That's right . . . a girl! And I'm a man." He puffed out his chest.

"But you don't mind playing with Benjamin, who is also quite a bit younger than you."

"He's a boy," was his reply, as if that explained everything.

Abish had the feeling this conversation could go on interminably. So instead, she agreed to talk to Teara.

"Can I go work now?" he pleaded, as if digging in the dirt were preferable to continuing their conversation.

"You've been working all day. I think you should rest."

Jarum scowled. "You know if I don't figure out this project I'm working on, this year's harvest could be worse than last year's. I'm so close and should be able to start planting soon—if it doesn't collapse again."

Abish relented and released Jarum on his way. Even though there wasn't much daylight left for traveling, she knew she could make it to Teara's and back before it got too dark. And after borrowing Tuk, the dog that she had finally agreed to get, she at least felt a little more confident going out into the night. Hopefully Teara would have the good advice she always seemed to possess. But when Abish arrived, it was evident that the last thing Teara needed was another crisis. Apparently Rebekah had been trying to help with dinner and had gotten too near the cooking fire and burned her hand. Amid her cries, Enoch was trying to scurry up his mother's legs while she tended to the wounds. Abish almost sighed with relief that she was not the only one to have one of *those* days.

"Let me help!" she said as she rushed to her friend's side. Nephi was quickly dispatched up into the air with a squeal of delight.

"Thank you," Teara said. "Namon had a meeting tonight and Ruth and I had everything under control until Rebekah hurt herself. You must have known I needed you!"

Abish grimaced, wishing that was the reason for her visit. "Will Namon be back soon?"

"Yes, the council is trying to agree upon the design of the adjoining prayer chamber for the temple. It shouldn't take long." Teara cast a sly glance in her direction. "Of course, most of the work depends upon Lamech's opinion of what is to be done."

Determined not to blush at the mention of his name, Abish scrutinized the bandage being wrapped around Rebekah's hand. But Teara had remembered her skills and did an excellent job. "Do you miss it?" Abish asked, diverting the attention from herself.

Teara shrugged. "At times. Of course, with my family, I'm not allowed to think of anything besides them too often! There." She kissed her daughter on the forehead. "I think you deserve an extra honey cake for your bravery." The reward worked and she scampered off into the house. Teara turned back to Abish. "I doubt you heard this chaos all the way over at your house. What brings you here then?"

"Do I get an extra honey cake too?" she joked and then her face grew serious. "I speak to you as one mother to another. I'm afraid we have a small situation on our hands." She explained about her and Jarum's earlier conversation.

Teara cupped a hand under her growing belly. "I knew something of what was going on. After all, he is all she ever talks about lately. 'Jarum said this today,' 'Jarum did this.' And I can't blame her; you have a fine son."

"Ah, she said, using much flattery!" Abish laughed.

Teara joined in softly laughing. "What should I do? She follows after him like Tuk does at your heels. I did speak to her one evening about how young she was and that a lot could change before she is old enough to be married."

"What did she say?"

"That true love should be patient and she would wait if needed."

Abish eyes widened. "You have a philosopher on your hands, my friend!" The small girl's words struck her deeply. It *was* true. But it was the waiting that hurt so much.

"I'll speak to her again," Teara offered.

Abish thought for a moment. "No," she said. "I'll talk to Jarum again. I think perhaps he is the one who needs to see things differently."

* * *

Nighttime had deepened, casting shadows and lengthening the darkness to where Abish wished she had brought along a lantern. She kept Tuk close to her side, since he had the tendency to try to chase after the numerous lizards and snakes that abounded in the land. At least the larger predators would avoid the open spaces of this rocky terrain and the smaller knew enough to scurry away at the sound of her approach. That is, most creatures should have been afraid. A rustling in the distance almost convinced her otherwise. Tuk began growling deep in his throat, putting Abish on guard until she saw what or rather who it was.

"Oh, it is you." Abish let out the breath she had been holding. "How are you this evening, Lamech?"

"Much better now." A smile broadened his handsome face as he came toward her. "Now that I see the face of the intruder that caught my attention. Why are you out so late, and in the darkness, no less?"

"I'm often about at this hour," she said defensively, omitting the truth of her earlier nervousness in the process. "And I was on my way straight home. Besides, Tuk has been trained well."

"I do not doubt that." He chuckled as Tuk continued to growl. Abish hushed him. Lamech was close enough now that she could see the glow from his lamp reflected in the black of his eyes. "I suppose you wouldn't need an escort if you're used to traveling about in the night," he ventured.

Abish immediately cursed her bravado. When would she learn to stop being so independent? "Actually, it *is* later than I had supposed. I thought when we neared spring solstice that the sun was supposed to stop vanishing so early."

He did not respond to her flimsy explanation, but kept pace silently by her side. She listened to the crunching of the dry grass beneath their feet and the occasional whisper of the wind through the trees. Although they had seen each other several times in the months since their first meeting, their encounters had been brief and respectable. This was, Abish realized, the first time they had really been alone and the darkness created a level of intimacy they had never experienced before. Now the sound of her beating heart joined in the bevy of sounds, though she tried to keep her breathing even so as not to give away her true feelings. Thinking what to say, however, was nearly impossible.

"How has your family been?" Lamech rescued her once again.

"Fine," she said.

"Is Jarum nearly finished with his studies? We could use a bright mind like his on our project."

Abish frowned. "I'm afraid that unless something is related to farming, it tends not to keep my son's interest for very long."

"That is to be commended," Lamech said in a voice that at the same time was so soft and yet as solid as the stones he worked with. "A man needs to have a passion for something in his life. Mine has always been shaping the rocks that grow up out of the earth and your son's, for starting life in the ground beneath them."

She was surprised by the poetic nature of his words. "Were you always a stonemason back in Antionum?"

For a moment he was silent, and she turned to see his jaw clenched firmly. "Yes," he finally said. "I was a stonemason, building synagogues and altars for the priests of our city—places where I was then not allowed to enter. But," he took a cleansing breath, "that was the past. Then I came to know the falseness of our beliefs."

"Something we have in common," she added.

He smiled down at her. "Yes, the first of many things, I hope. Now," he insisted, "tell me about yourself."

Unsure how much to reveal at first, she rehearsed only a few of the basic events of her life, from her childhood in Ishmael to her final conversion many years ago in the land in which they now lived. But when she began telling of Jared's death and the persecution that her people had gone through, her voice choked up. At some point during her revelations, Lamech had taken her hand in his. They walked through the stillness of the night like that, drawing strength from one another through their simple bond. Soon her only distress was when she realized that they had almost reached their destination and would have to say good night. They came near the perimeter of her own land, and Abish could see the flickering lights in her hut.

"Well," she said reluctantly after they waited a few moments more. "I had better go. It is late."

But as she turned to leave, Abish's foot caught the edge of a protruding rock. She stumbled and would have fallen to the ground if Lamech had not been at her side, holding her up. His arms were like a vise around her; she could not have pulled away even if she had wanted to. Her heartbeat quickened as his hands ran up her arms to her shoulders. One hand cupped her chin while his thumb skimmed over her jaw line and then brushed across the scar on her cheek.

"I'll expect you to tell me about this one day as well," he whispered, his breath on her face. "I want you to tell me everything."

She could feel the warmth of his body near hers and, blushing, she stepped away. "I . . . I had better check on the children."

Lamech smiled and she could see his white teeth in the dim light. "Until next time." And then he turned and walked away, striding like a powerful creature into the night.

Abish felt her knees tremble and she placed her fingers against her skin where his hands had been to find it still burned hot. With a deep breath to calm herself, she went into the house.

38

The time of planting approached yet again and still the drought continued.

Everyone was suffering and working night and day to survive, so this gave Abish ample excuse to avoid seeing Lamech again, and he had not come to her. This suited her, since she still did not know what to say to him. Even more, she was not so sure anymore what she might *do* around him.

There were many reasons, though, why she needed to stay clearheaded— the most important one concerned the progression of Teara's pregnancy, though the thought of failed crops should have been foremost in her mind. The Melekites had been most generous, but the people of Ammon could not subsist on their charity forever.

Discouraged one day, Abish scanned the cloudless sky and decided to visit Esther and her family. This time, Rachel had come to visit her sister and had brought her husband and children. One was the spitting image of Esther's brother, Nephi, when he was a boy, and Abish said so. The two sisters agreed, and to her relief, Abish found it was good to talk of some memories. There were other reminders of those days. She was amazed that the indoor plumbing system that Jacob had built was still functioning; Ammon would be happy, she sighed, remembering his role in it. The grove of avocado trees where she used to climb still stood, and she debated giving it a try for memory's sake then thought better of it. She was too old now. Well, much older than she had been then. Perhaps it was time to put away childish things and act like the adult she claimed she was.

And that meant facing Lamech and proving that she was in control when it came to him.

This time, Abish decided not to skirt around the city the next day as she went home but instead to head straight toward it. With a quivering in her stomach, she guided her steps to the rising temple in the main square. It was nearly finished and just needed the final coating of stucco before it could be painted and decorated.

Lamech was impossible to miss. The sweat on his bare torso glistened in the sunlight and caused enough of a stir to make several women stand at the base of the structure and gaze longingly up at him. The fact that Abish could laugh at them gave her confidence that she at least wasn't completely overcome with feelings of jealousy. She had no claim on him. He had given her no token. And yet as she approached the group as well, his eyes seemed to immediately turn to look down at her. One of the women turned and saw her and frowned slightly. This gave Abish a rush of pride, which caused her to regret her earlier confidence.

With a few broad leaps, Lamech was at her side. Now that he was up close she could see where the sweat had attracted the fine particles of stone he'd been chipping away at. It created dark streaks and reminded her of the soot that had always covered Jared. Though it caused her some pain, she let herself compare the two of them: both laborers, men of sweat and work. They dealt with their hands and their pride was as tough as the steel and stone they worked with. And yet she had never felt fear when she was around Jared. But as Lamech sought her gaze, she felt a tremor of something akin to it.

"I was hoping to see you today." He grinned. "Come, I have something to show you."

Without waiting for her to respond, he grabbed her by the hand and dragged her into the underbrush. Soon they were immersed in the dark green canopy around them and though light occasionally flickered down, she felt as if she were traveling down a long, dark tunnel.

"Lamech, I . . ."

But still he dragged her on.

Finally they came to the quarry where much of the stone had been retrieved for the temple. There, he showed her what he had been working on. The carving was very intricate, as was the Zoramite way, with numerous pictoglyphs surrounding the area of focus. She tried to discern the images she saw, but was baffled. Surmising this, Lamech began to explain.

"This is a representation of the coming Messiah, as indicated by his quetzal feather headdress and the serpent at his feet. Also, I have surrounded his image with representations of all of the reigns of the kings that we have known. But naturally," he said as he puffed out his chest, "the image of the King of Kings had to be more prominent."

Abish tried to smile. "It's very . . . striking."

"You don't like it?" Lamech frowned.

"Well, I guess I don't see the artistic side of things like you do," she said, trying to recover. "With this new art form, it seems like so much is required to say so little. I suppose I am accustomed to plainness over such . . . splendor."

Lamech laughed heartily. "Then it is a good thing I am the one commissioned to finish this stela for the temple because such *splendor*, as you call it, is the best way to show our devotion to God. It will be magnificent when finished."

Abish had no reason to dishearten his attempts and so she smiled more enthusiastically this time. This turned his attention away from his work and he took a few steps toward her. "Now," he said, "if it is splendor that you are referring to, I don't have to look much further than what I see in front of me."

Before she could react, his lips were on hers, gentle at first until he sensed her responding as well. And she was responding. Then his attentions became more insistent. Abish allowed herself to sink into his embrace, disappearing in the breadth of his chest and power of his arms, wanting to sink even deeper until she was no longer sure where he ended and she began. She reveled in the feel of his body, so warm and strong, against hers—how long it had been since she'd felt this way!

But the emotions playing through her began to feel overwhelming. When she felt the rough stone of the wall behind her it startled her for a moment. All reason fled. How could she have possibly thought to control this? She could not think. Could not remember what she had sought to prove. Her world was this moment and his hands upon her.

And then she heard the sound of men's voices nearby. Trembling, she pushed him away. "I have to go," Abish gasped. Tearing herself from his arms, she ran toward her home. Toward safety, which meant *away* from Lamech!

With a large ceiba tree blocking her from view, she rested and yet felt as if her face was still flushed with desire. Where had her control gone? Her sense of decorum? She had acted like a young woman confronted with love for the first time! Abish knew she had come perilously close to succumbing to the deluge of passion that had swept over her; how easy it would have been to let go. Her mind taunted her. What would have been the harm? She was a grown woman and had denied herself these feelings for so long, would God have judged her that harshly?

No harsher, she realized, than she would have judged herself when it was over.

She knew so little about Lamech and yet, for a moment, was willing to give him so much. When it came to desire, it was difficult to judge what distance was safe, and she had trodden much too closely to the edge; in doing so, she had jeopardized her own spiritual security. And even worse, that of her family. Because how could she raise her children in righteousness when she was teaching them one standard and living by another?

* * *

They were going to survive!

As if a sudden miracle had blessed the land, rain began to drench the ground, making their struggling fields blossom in abundance, and for the first time since their arrival, there was hope among her people. She sensed it as she went among them each day. *We will survive here*, their eyes seemed to say. *We have come home at last.* And to Abish, Melek was finally starting to feel like home. She began to imagine growing old here, perhaps even dying here. Of course, she still wished that their home was located closer to the sea. But they were now so established here that it didn't seem likely that would ever change. When she was homesick for it, however, all she had to do was visit Esther. She took comfort in the memories there: both those of days past and those that they were now making.

After returning from one such visit, Abish found Miriam outside waiting for her. She instantly knew something was wrong.

"Teara needs you. She is—"

Abish began to tremble. "But it's too early!"

This was not the time, however, to let fear overcome her. She dropped everything and ran into the house. Preparing for the worst, she had already gathered everything she needed and merely had to grab her pack.

"Let me go with you," Miriam begged.

Abish hesitated briefly, knowing that every moment was precious. "All right." Together they rushed to Namon's house.

They found Teara lying on her bed behind the privacy sheet, writhing in pain. "Something's wrong," she groaned as she saw the three of them enter.

Abish knelt at her side. After a few questions, she discovered that her friend had begun having pains the night before. They weren't strong and regular like she thought they should be and she didn't want Abish to have to be bothered so soon. But by midday, a flood of darkened water convinced even her that something was not right.

"She's trying to be brave." Namon had come to stand by her. "But this has become more than she can bear."

"I'm sorry I wasn't here for you. I promised—"

Teara raised a trembling hand to stop her. "You're here now."

Abish motioned for Namon to take the children away from the house so the three of them could be alone. He hesitated, obviously wanting to stay near them, but Abish said she would call him if he were needed. She hurried and washed up, using the brief moment to catch her breath and say a prayer. Strengthened, she returned to her friend's side.

When she examined Teara, she was confused that there was little progress. Why the delay? Abish shuddered. This wasn't good. The baby needed to be moving downward. "Can you get up and walk around, my friend? We can help you."

She helped Teara to her feet and they walked around the small house for a while. Amid the pain, Teara tried to speak, "Abish, if I don't . . . if this becomes too much, will you take care of Namon and the children?"

"No! That's not going to happen, Teara. Let's keep moving. This baby *will* come and you'll be fine."

Only when it was obvious that she could no longer continue did they return to the bed. Abish again felt for the baby's head. There was none to be found. Instead, she felt something else.

No!

39

Abish's worst fear was coming true. The baby was trying to be born the wrong way! She had faced this problem many times before and shuddered at what it meant. Her daughter had worked by her side long enough to realize its meaning as well, and Abish tried to send her away. But she refused.

"I know you can do it," Miriam encouraged softly. "And I want to be here to help."

Suddenly, Teara cried out and arched up from the bed with the intensity of the next contraction. Her body was trying to push the baby out anyway!

Abish shouted orders to Miriam. "I need some of the purest oil and find me some twine and a knife. Teara needs us all. The baby is struggling and it's been a long time. Together we will do this." The girl did as she'd been told while Abish continued to talk to Teara and distract her from what needed to be done. "Just think, soon Ruth and Rebekah might have another little sister to play with. Or another son for Namon. We don't want to disappoint them. You know by now that your baby is trying to come out the wrong way. We'll have to help it along some, so be brave. You'll be fine."

How often words were said in comfort to another when really they were meant to comfort the ones who had spoken them, Abish thought.

For hours they struggled: a huge pain crashing over Teara like a wave trying to drown her with suffering, Miriam kneeling by her side and moistening her lips with a wet cloth, Abish trying to do what needed to be done to end the ordeal. Finally, when it seemed like her friend could not take another blow, the baby turned and its head appeared—then it was out to its shoulders! Abish had a soft cloth to catch it in, though it took more encouraging to both baby and mother until it was free of its watery home. She cleared its mouth and soon a tiny cry, like a baby lamb bleating, filled the room, though Abish was sure that the much louder cry was her own.

She held up the fragile baby for Miriam to see, and then, to Teara. "You have another daughter."

But her announcement was not heard, for Teara was already drifting back into that realm of unconsciousness that seemed determined to claim her. Abish shook her hard.

"Teara? Teara, don't do this!"

It was like a nightmare unfolding. Her friend was dying.

"What?" Miriam cried in alarm.

Abish stared in horror at the stain that spread out across the bed like a crimson flood. "Keep the baby warm!" Abish cried as she handed the slippery newborn to her daughter and ran from the house. "Namon!" she sobbed. "I don't know what to do. She is dying!"

Namon rushed to where his wife was. Teara's face was pale, drained of the life force of her body. But her husband remained calm as he said, "I have something that *I* can do."

Abish watched as he placed his hands upon Teara's head. He knelt at her side as if he had all the time in the world. And when he finally spoke, Abish felt as if they weren't the only ones in the room.

"Oh, mighty God! Thou who didst lead us to this promised land by Thy grace and benevolence. I come before Thee, unworthy to be called by Thy name, and yet by the power I have been given I have anointed the head of Thy daughter." Abish marveled at the words he next spoke. They were full of such power and yet compassion. And then he finished. "But, as always, Thy will be done."

As his words trailed off, Abish watched in amazement to see what would happen. It was a subtle change, but perhaps there was a little more color in Teara's face. Yes! And her eyes flickered, just for a moment. She groaned and turned her head toward Namon. A slight smile crossed her lips before she was still. Abish knelt down beside her and felt her heart. There was a movement. And her breathing was shallow, yet steady.

"She will live," Abish whispered.

* * *

As the months passed, Abish found that it was easy to be both grateful and sorrowful at the same time. With their storehouses full of food for the year to come, the people were constantly offering up prayers of thanks.

But at the same time, Teara's new baby girl was not thriving and Abish could not figure out how to help her this time. Zaharah had been indispensable in providing support. Though the close bond between the two women had once made her jealous, Abish was now grateful for all of the extra support she could get. She knew that the situation was difficult for Namon as well. As she met him at the crossroads one day, his face clouded with fatigue, she tried to reassure him—and herself at the same time.

"I appreciate everything you have done for us, Abish. It is in God's hands now."

It was as if he were already trying to accept the inevitable and she had no defense against his fatherly intuition. But then she discovered that this was not the only burden pressing upon him. She encouraged him to tell her what else was troubling him. He did.

"There are many troubles again in Zarahemla. Soon, they may affect us all."

Namon went on to explain that a man by the name of Amalickiah had conspired to lead away many of the Nephites and become their king. Many believed him and joined with him. But they were no match for Moroni's armies, so he led his followers instead up to the land of Nephi. There they set their efforts to stirring up the Lamanites to join them. Amalickiah was so successful that the newly elected king of the rogue Lamanites issued a proclamation to all the city-states that they were to join him in war against the Nephites. The king would head up the army that would be gathered together, with Amalickiah as one of the lesser captains. But this was not enough power for such a cunning man. Instead, Amalickiah ingratiated himself with the Lamanite army until they began to have more loyalty to him than to their king. Now, all he had to do was replace the current commander of the Lamanite army and he was well on his way to his ultimate goal.

If she had heard the rest of the story from any source other than Namon she might not have believed it. But he had been in the council chambers when the Lamanite king's own servants had come to beg for sanctuary within their city's walls. Still, it shocked her greatly to hear Lehonti's name once again, so much that Namon led her to sit on a nearby wall. There she waited in nervous anticipation for Namon to finish the tale—of how Amalickiah had asked thrice for Commander Lehonti to come and meet with him. Thrice, he refused, but must have grown curious and accepted when the other leader eventually condescended to come closer to him. It was the last mistake Lehonti would ever make. No one would ever know how much poison was used to finally cause his death, thus leaving Amalickiah to take his place.

He was dead!

Abish struggled with her own emotions. Was it wrong to be glad she was rid of him? That she would never have to be afraid that she would come across him again one day? In her heart she knew the answer to that question. Lifting her own tear-stained face to heaven, she asked yet again for God's grace and for mercy for her many weaknesses.

As the day wore on, Abish found she was still having to process what had happened and the new concerns that it had brought. Where was her mother? What would happen to her now that her husband was dead? Abish was torn between wanting to try to find her and knowing that she was responsible for staying with her own children.

She heard a rap on her door near eventide and sighed, having enjoyed only a few moments of peace in which to think. Her children were still at their studies and nobody had come to her for healing in days. Then an unwelcome thought formed. *What if it's Lamech?* She knew she had to tell him once and for all where she stood, even though the thought of being near him again still unnerved her. So if it was him, she wouldn't let him pass the threshold. They would talk outside.

But when she jerked open the door and saw who was standing there, she gasped. Surely this was a ghost in front of her! Some image created by a still guilty mind! Trying to compose herself, Abish started to stumble backwards. "Isabel?"

"Am I to be invited in?"

"I . . . I . . . yes, of course." Abish found her tongue. "But I was told you were—"

"Dead?" Isabel removed the cloak she was wearing, revealing a beautiful gown underneath. "That is what I'd hoped would happen."

"But why are you here? How did you find us?" she finally managed to ask.

Isabel gestured to a nearby cushion as if asking permission to sit, and Abish could only mutely nod as the woman told her story.

"I left Siron the day after my . . . encounter with Ammon. For years I wandered about the land: barely surviving and yet not caring because I longed for death. Then I found myself in the city of Nephi. It was so large I thought I could get lost there and no one would know who or what I was. But old habits are hard to break. Soon I found myself in Nephi, living in the palace as a *companion* to the king." She played with one of the bangles on her wrist. "When he was murdered, I was with the servants and saw what happened, so I had to flee with them from the city. We heard that Melek was taking in Lamanite strays," she said a bit sarcastically. "It didn't take long before I heard your name being spoken and found out that Malech was with you."

"So you came to find us?" Though she tried to remain calm, her words came out more fearfully than she'd hoped. What did Isabel's coming here really mean?

But Isabel ignored the question. "You have done well for yourself." She stood, posturing as if to defend herself. "Do you know what it is like to raise a child alone? If you did, you'd understand why I did what I did. When Ammon came and condemned me, I think for the first time in my life I was truly afraid. I had convinced myself that whatever god existed wouldn't punish me for the life I was living. After all, I was a creature of another's making." She flicked her wrists and the bangles on them created a tinkling noise. "But then I started to doubt—to wonder if perhaps my current situation was not so much a result of my will being taken from me as it was my decision to never take it back. And so I did what I could at the time."

"You gave your son to Ammon to take back with him and told your servant to lie about your death."

She nodded. "It was better than my son staying with someone like me." Her voice trembled when she next spoke. "Is he well?"

"Oh, yes," Abish's voice confirmed. "He is with my son, Jarum, studying at the temple school. He should be back soon."

A momentary look of terror crossed Isabel's face. "Then perhaps I should go."

"No!" Abish jumped up and restrained her. "He needs to know that you are still alive. Please. He is different—a good boy. He won't reject you."

Her eyes glistened with tears. "But how can he ever accept me? How can your people accept me?"

Abish took Isabel's hands in hers. "They are your people too. And Malech is your son."

"Then it is not too late?"

"It is never too late," Abish said. And this time, her voice did not waver.

"Someone else told me that once," Isabel responded pensively. "There was a woman in the palace in Nephi that was as close to a friend as I've ever had. She was a lot like me and, in a way, we understood each other. She said that even though she had been unable to accept the Nephite god, her husband and daughter had found some measure of happiness in it. She told me that perhaps he could help me find the peace she'd never had. At first I didn't believe her—after all, she was married to one of the most wicked men I'd ever met. But then she told me that it had been her *first* husband that she'd been referring to."

Abish held up a hand to stop Isabel. "This woman you speak of. What is her name?"

Isabel seemed taken aback by the intensity of Abish's response. "It was just a woman that I knew in the king's palace. Because her husband was the commander of the Lamanite army, she was often in the capital city and frequently stayed in the palace."

"Yes," Abish cried. "But her name!"

"Why, it was Saranhi."

Abish clasped a hand to her breast. *My mother.* "Please, you must tell me about her," she begged. "The woman you mention is my mother."

Now Isabel was the astonished one. "Then you are the one she often spoke of! It all makes sense now. At first I couldn't believe her when she told me of her daughter's faith and courage; I thought she was merely a parent bragging about her child. She was . . . proud of you."

Tears came to her eyes as Abish realized that she was finally going to get the answers she'd been searching for. "Then you know where she is? Is she still at this palace in Nephi?" When she saw the look on Isabel's face, Abish realized she had seen that look before and began to tremble. "Please tell me. No matter what, I must know."

It was then Isabel that explained that Abish's mother had been in the throne room as well when Amalickiah had come to greet the king. Upon hearing of her husband's death, she was obviously stunned at first. "But when Amalickiah stabbed the king, we realized that he was not a friend to any of us, so we began to flee, but your mother did not go! Instead, she tried to call for the guards outside the throne room door and tell them the truth of what had happened. Amalickiah's men stopped her."

"Then is she"—Abish choked back her tears—"dead?"

Isabel nodded sadly. "It was swift. She did not suffer. I had never seen such bravery," Isabel proferred. "The rest of us ran like scared mice, while she stood her ground and did what she knew she had to do."

Abish took what solace she could from Isabel's words as the knowledge that she would never see her mother again sank in. But then a slight smile crossed her face as Abish also realized that this same person she'd vowed for years not to be like had, in the end, become the exact type of person that she'd always wanted to be.

* * *

Abish waited as patiently as she could with Miriam and Jarum outside by the well. Isabel and Malech had been in the house for a considerable time. Everyone had their own thoughts going through their minds, she was sure. She wondered if any of them were thinking like her that perhaps now Malech would be taken away from them. *I don't want to lose my son,* she agonized. But that was a faithless thought to have. No one could take Malech away from her. He would always be a part of her family.

When the door finally opened and Abish saw Malech walk out, she started toward him. But when she saw the emotion written on his face, she knew he needed a few moments by himself, so she let him go off by himself to think.

Gesturing to the rest of the family, Abish entered the house alone. She tried to discern by the look on Isabel's face what had happened. Had Abish spoken truly? Had Malech been able to reconcile himself in that short amount of time? Or had the shock been too great to where he couldn't accept her back into his life? Unfortunately, tears were never a clear indication. So she had to wait and watch as Isabel wiped hers away and then spoke.

"You have raised him well. I could not have asked for a better son."

"Then he . . . he will be all right?" Abish probed.

"He told me that he loved me! It's been so long since anyone's said that. I asked him if he wanted me to stay."

"And?"

Isabel smiled. "He said he had never wanted me to leave." She grabbed Abish's hands and held them tight. "Thank you. Thank you for teaching him and for giving him that kind of strength."

Abish found her own eyes welling up. "I was not the only one who taught him about strength."

They discovered that Miriam and Jarum had been waiting anxiously at the door. They were ushered in, and together they shared an evening of rejoicing.

40

As Abish prepared to leave to visit Esther and her family a few weeks later, she had much on her mind. Isabel had been settling in quite well. And even though she occasionally felt a tinge of jealousy when Malech began to turn to his true mother for answers and excitedly sought her out when he had found success at his studies that day, it was as it should be. She would have to accept that. Even more difficult was hearing how quickly Saranhi and Isabel had developed a relationship. It was almost as if in Isabel Saranhi had found the daughter she could finally relate to.

These numerous thoughts that kept circling around in her mind must have kept her from hearing the voice calling her name. Abish turned when she realized someone was approaching the house.

It was Lamech.

She took a calming breath as she stood in the doorway. Since that day she had managed to avoid him—or perhaps they had both been avoiding each other. As they stood looking at each other now, she felt a mixture of feelings. The physical attraction she had for him was still as strong as ever, but her conscience was stirred anew and she had to will her feet toward him.

"I've been meaning to talk to you," they both said at once.

Their discomfort was as thick as morning mist between them and she wondered if he would rescue her again by speaking first. He didn't, but his eyes spoke volumes. "We should talk about . . . what happened between us," she said.

"Yes. What *almost* happened," he echoed.

"I can't explain my behavior." Even now her face burned. "It was very unlike me to be so brazen. I'm embarrassed to think of it."

Lamech took a small step toward her. "And I should be embarrassed as well. But I can't stop thinking about you. Every time I hit one of those stones," he gestured at the temple, "I try and rid myself of these feelings I have for you. But I can't."

He reached out for her, causing her to take a step back into the house. "No, Lamech. It isn't proper."

But he wouldn't relent, and the words he said next filled her with memories. "Why deny ourselves what we feel, Abish? What are you afraid of?"

What are you afraid of?

The very words Abish had spoken to Ammon at their last meeting came back to chasten her, and suddenly she knew part of the reason why he had gone back to Zarahemla. He wasn't ready for the powerful emotions he'd felt, and they had pushed him away from her. But she also knew their relationship had been more than that—they could have had a life together—whereas a life with the man in front of her could never be if virtue meant so little to him.

"I'm sorry, Lamech. If you're so willing to forget what you've learned, then there can be nothing more between us." She pushed her way past him.

Abish had almost composed herself by the time she reached the house of Eliab and Esther. With a calming breath, she accepted that she had made the right decision. But doing the right thing meant that once again she would be lonely. Seeing a plume of smoke curling up from the cooking stove out back, at least Abish knew that they were home. A few hours with Esther's gentle and understanding spirit and she would feel rejuvenated.

They had long ago told her that she was considered a member of the family and did not need to stand at the door and wait. This time she took them at their word and merely pushed the door aside as she called out a greeting, "Is anyone home? It is Abish."

As the large group inside turned to glance at her, she looked for Esther's kind face. Instead, she found two eyes, green as the River Sidon, staring back at her.

"Abish! Abish!" Lib came running toward her, distracting her from her shock.

As she sought to disentangle herself from the child's excitement, she couldn't help but glance again in his direction. *How is it he had not changed?* Sidetracked again by the tugging on her shift, she reached into her pocket and retrieved the annu stones that she made a habit of bringing. Lib cheered and quickly ran and added them to their game.

"How nice of you to come," Esther said, rising from her mat. "And what a perfect time. There's someone visiting that I think you might like to meet. After all, it's not often we receive news directly from Zarahemla."

Ammon rose from the ground as well. "We've already met."

"Yes," she tried to reply evenly. "You look well."

By now, the other occupants of the room must have sensed that something more was going on. What could she say to explain? Ammon seemed to take his cue and turned to his hostess. "I won't impose upon your hospitality any longer. Thank you for the refreshment and, again, my condolences for the loss of your parents. They were good people."

Esther smiled sadly as her guest hastily retreated to the door.

The scent of him lingered in the room, and Abish stood there, unsure what to do. Her friend came to stand by her side and whispered. "I sense that the two of you know each other well."

Abish sighed. "I used to think so."

* * *

No matter what she did over the next several days, Abish could not escape the shock of seeing Ammon again. Of course, she said nothing of the encounter, leaving her children to surmise that each was responsible for her moodiness. Miriam offered to take over even more of her healing work, and Jarum worked more furiously in the fields. Even though Isabel and Malech had finally found lodging closer to the city, Malech still made daily visits, and his visits always brightened Abish's day. With her family acting as near to perfect as they ever had, she would have thought she could quickly gain her equilibrium again. But it eluded her, and she felt like a newborn colt on wobbly legs.

Men! she thought as she sat at the side of the river, furiously plunging in the last of the laundry. *What trouble they cause! Why did Ammon come here anyway? Why didn't he stay in Zarahemla where he belonged?* It took a moment for her to realize that she'd been pounding the rocks so hard that she'd worn a hole in one of Jarum's tunics. She slumped down onto the soggy ground and would have wept if not for the other women nearby. Gathering up her wash, she balanced the basket on her head and started for home.

But she cursed the empty house she had to return to. Her children were so busy now and often gone. Where she had once longed for peace, Abish now missed their constant antics and prattle. She felt more alone than ever. Throwing the laundry over the thatched roof to dry, Abish tried to decide what to occupy her time with next. The house had not been swept for a while, so she gathered a handful of dried rushes and listened to the sound they made as she whisked them across the floor. She noticed that Miriam had left out her weaving again, and she bent down to examine the intricate pattern. She would have to start one herself one day before her fingers forgot how to weave entirely. In order to keep the fabric protected from moisture and insects, Abish had allowed her daughter to keep it tucked away in the small stone box that had been built to replace their old one. Now, as she lifted the lid to put it away, she found how easily memories could be stored as well.

Abish saw the bejeweled dagger in its sheath, a silver bangle from her childhood, and the small metal plate that Jarum had inscribed at his studies. She noticed another object as well. She picked up the wood carving with her name on it that Ammon had given her those many years ago right before she made the decision to go to Zarahemla with him. Though she still couldn't read the symbols on it, they had given her strength many times. She heard the crunching sound of footsteps outside and, hoping it was one of her children returning to keep her company, Abish went to greet them. Words failed her when she saw who it was.

"So this is where you live," he said as he peered at her with emerald eyes.

"Yes," she said proudly, "this is my home."

Ammon walked with his hands clasped behind his back as if examining a property for sale. She was glad for the rows of stalks out in the fields—it was evidence of their abundant harvest to come and meant she was doing well on her own. But she somehow sensed that he was really examining it all to try to avoid looking at her. He seemed to be searching for something, though, something he was unable to find as he looked off into the distance. With his attention elsewhere, she couldn't help but look at him, and she found that in reality he had aged as she had. Grey flecked his temples and there were lines more firmly etched around his eyes and mouth. Some of the energy had gone out of his stance as well. But they had both changed that way.

Finally she couldn't take his silence any longer. She wanted to show him that regardless of how he had abandoned her, she had stayed strong. "What are you doing here, Ammon?" she asked, with a hint of irritation in her voice.

"I am looking for Alma." He turned, his eyes troubled. "He left months ago without so much as a word to me about his destination. Hannah will not say anything about it, but when he didn't return in time for the reconvening of the judges, I knew that something must have happened. So I have been searching for him. The only thing I have discovered is that he was traveling toward Melek."

"But why would he come here?" she questioned. "And why should you be so concerned for him? He is God's chosen prophet. Surely God would be watching over him."

Her response dumbfounded him. Finally he managed to say, "Yes. Yes, of course."

His eyes pleaded with her as if she somehow had the answer. She wasn't sure she did. But he at least owed her one. "Why are you really here?"

His green eyes looked earnestly at her. "I don't know."

It was then she realized that she still had the small carving in her hand. She looked down at it and then handed it to Ammon. She hoped he didn't notice that her hand was trembling.

Ammon looked at it. "You've kept it all these years?"

She nodded. "It gave me strength during many of the difficult times of my life. I would see it and remember that you had the courage to face your enemy—could I be any less courageous?"

He clenched his fist around it. "The last thing I've been lately is courageous." He stared down at the carving again. "I believed that the only way I could repay God for all of the damage I had done would be to serve Him, so I found contentment in serving your people in my service to Him. But in doing so, I also felt as if I had to deny myself the very joy he had created me to receive."

Abish thought back to her encounter with Lamech that morning and knew why he had felt this way. "Perhaps that was because you did not understand back then the difference between pleasure and true happiness," she said softly. "Pleasure comes quickly, while happiness can take time."

"But so much time has passed and I have been so unfair to you, Abish. Is it too late now to think you could still care for me?"

She smiled. "Someone very wise once taught me that it is never too late."

"So we are friends once more?" Ammon smiled, his green eyes now full of love and hope.

"Yes," she said, cupping his face tenderly in her hands. "Friends *always*."

Ammon looked at her quizzically, as if her answer had left him wanting more. So she leaned toward him and gently touched her lips to his. The joy in his eyes was all that she needed to see.

Land Of Melek
64 BC

41

Abish looked off in the distance and saw that the small mounds that dotted the landscape were already topped with green, conjuring up the welcome thought of another abundant maize harvest. Several hired hands toiled clearing another field as well—which was fortunate considering how many men preferred building walls and fortifications for the Nephite army—but it was Jarum who caught and held her attention. He was so tall. Tall and straight, with a commanding figure and serious expression on his face.

She watched as he worked, directing two of the men to make sure that the beans that were also being planted were placed deeply enough so as not to be scavenged by small animals and that the hills of dirt that were built up around them were not so high that they would not give place to the steady stream of water that would soon flow around them. Her son had amazed her with the irrigation system he had finally contrived, which was more efficient than any she had ever seen. They had been able to stretch out their planting season and increase nearly ten-fold the bounty of their crops! Soon her son found himself in charge of a group of men twice his age, but somehow, even though he was nearly twenty-and-two years old and was still unmarried, he had found a way to engender respect from his much older companions.

Abish strode into the field to try to persuade Jarum to take a break from his efforts; he had been hard at work since dawn. A boy his age should have other, well, interests, she surmised. But it was still harder than tearing palm fronds to get him to focus on anything that wasn't related to farming.

"It looks like you have things well in hand," she said, coming upon him.

Jarum shrugged and then said in a low-toned voice that suggested he didn't want to be overheard, "I suppose, though some of the men are not earning their keep. I may have to replace them."

Abish was concerned. "Which? I am acquainted with most of them and know that some of their families are struggling."

"All the more reason for them to put in an honest day's work." But then seeing his mother's face, he added, "There are many others who are suffering, Mother. Should *they* not be given a chance to feed their wives and children?"

This was not the first time that her son had said something that revealed his strong nature. But still, he had a lot to learn. "Do what you feel is necessary. Just remember that you are dealing with a person's livelihood. That is not to be taken lightly."

"I won't. Mother?" he asked as she turned to leave.

"Yes?"

"That rocky patch on the south end, the one that we've never planted, do you think you'll ever want to do anything to it one day?"

Abish shrugged. It hadn't compared to the soil where they now planted and so she had given it little thought. "Did you have a plan for it? One of your systems, perhaps?"

Jarum looked a little sheepish. "Well, I had some plans. I'll discuss it with you some other time. It looks like Miriam has come for a visit."

At the mention of her daughter's name, Abish clapped her hands for joy. It had been weeks, and Abish was anxious to hear how Miriam had settled in. As she rushed back toward the house, she couldn't help but notice how grown-up Miriam looked. Where was the little girl who used to tag along at her mother's heels? With a confident stance and self-assured smile, her daughter looked more ready than she had been at that age to take on the world.

Throwing their arms around each other, Abish led Miriam by the waist into the house. "I'm so glad you've come," Abish said. "I was beginning to think you'd never get away."

"I have been busy." Miriam sighed. "But a good busy. There is so much to be done in the city."

Abish tried to hide her frown. It was hard to accept that two years had already passed since Miriam made the decision to move into the heart of Melek and begin training other women in the art of midwifery. Ever since the day that her daughter had stood with her by Teara's side, she had been passionate about learning everything she could regarding childbirth. In order to do so, she had even gone to Zarahemla for a time to work with the wisest healers there. Of course, upon her return, Miriam explained that wisdom and open-mindedness did not mean the same thing! The city had taught her many things, her daughter said, but Abish blessed the day that she had decided she had learned enough and come home to them.

She was proud of Miriam's intelligence and drive. She would make a wonderful wife and mother one day. If only . . . well, there was a time and place for everything.

Abish beamed, nearly forgetting her manners. "You must be parched. It's been so hot this year."

Her daughter looked toward the fields. "Jarum has been busy. It must be a relief to know that you aren't always at nature's mercy now." Abish nodded her agreement as they went into the house. "You'd think with all the effort he is investing that it is his own fields he's managing!"

"If he ever comes to his senses where Ruth is concerned," Abish said as she poured two cups of nectar, "he just might one day. I'm happy to give him a portion for his inheritance. He's more than earned it. Of course, Malech would be included in that arrangement. That way he would always have the means to care for his mother."

"But he will always think of you as his mother as well."

Abish held her emotions in check. "And I will always think of him as my son."

Her daughter tactfully changed the subject. "When did Ammon return from Zarahemla?" Miriam asked, draining her cup.

"Day before last—and he has spent most of that time conferring with Captain Moroni and the city council."

"Those few years of peace we had seem so distant. But war has found us from the east to the west now."

Abish smiled wearily. "I know. Ever since Ammoron attempted to attack us, we have had little rest. We were fortunate to have the armies of Moroni to protect us, though."

"But that was a while ago and now he is commanding the army in Bountiful," Miriam reminded her. "What if . . ."

Abish placed a reassuring hand on her daughter's arm. "We can't think that way—we must have faith. At least Ammon has been by our people's side again through all of these struggles."

"And by *your* side. You waited for someone for so long," her daughter said wistfully. "Did you ever give up thinking you would find love?"

Her mother's heart knew the source of Miriam's question. "Love is worth waiting for. You must never give up."

* * *

As the season of harvest came and the people of Ammon found the Lamanites nearly on their doorstep again, they began to take what measures they could to defend themselves. Those who lived on the outskirts of their land now grouped themselves closer to the city center, abandoning their fields and newly constructed homes in the process. The available food was being rationed and kept in granaries and storerooms. There were groups of men who braved leaving the security of their valley to secure fresh fish or meat, and as Abish received her own family's share one day, she was grateful for their sacrifice.

But looking down into her basket's meager supplies, it reminded her too much of those lean days in Ishmael. Right before the Lamanites attacked. Right before Jared . . .

She was not the only one to notice the similarities. As she stopped by Teara's on her way home from the market, Abish noticed the strain it was having on her friend as well. The thought of another war had taken something out of Teara's usual bright smile.

"There's not much meat left," Abish said, finding how often their talk turned to unpleasant things. "I would have gotten you some as well, but they record each family's name."

"I was planning on going as soon as Enoch returned from his apprenticeship. I never realized how much I would miss having him here with me during the day."

Abish nodded. "It is difficult when the last of your children hops from the nest, isn't it?"

"Especially when," Teara answered softly, "for a time, he wasn't the last."

They sat in painful silence as they both thought of the tiny baby girl with beautiful black eyes and hair who would have been nearly eight by now. But death was a part of life, and the living had no choice but to look ahead. Still, Abish regretted that there hadn't been more time for her to have spent with those she'd loved. And even though Malech and Isabel still lived nearby, she felt the loss of him as well. Her little family was shrinking and she wanted to stop time!

"I wish there was some place we could go and escape from it all," Teara sighed.

"If only it wasn't so dangerous to go to the seashore. How I miss the fresh tang of sea air and the warm sand beneath me."

Just then Enoch appeared on the nearby path, and Abish saw the smile that had been missing from her friend's face suddenly appear as she saw her young son. Sensing that this would be a good moment to make her escape, Abish waved farewell and continued on her way.

A slight breeze tugged at her shift and she breathed deeply. Somewhere off in the distance came the cry of a howler monkey, followed by the screech of a bird. A flock of brilliant macaws burst from the canopy above, and Abish watched their synchronized dance as they circled in a patch of blue sky. It was her attention to the beautiful sight that allowed the figure to step behind her, undetected. When two arms wrapped themselves around her body, she instinctively tensed until a familiar scent joined the jungle's aroma.

"Am I your captive now?" she asked.

"How is that possible," said a voice in her ear, "when you are the one who has captured *my* heart?"

She smiled as Ammon took her hand and walked by her side. How glad she was to see the gleam back in his eyes—and she hoped it was as much for her as it was for the fact that he was so needed again. "Was the meeting with the council productive?"

"I suppose," he said cryptically.

"I know, I know. Or at least, I should know better after all this time to ask for more details."

"There's no reason for both of us to worry about what may happen."

Abish pounced on his words. "So there *is* something to worry about?" His green eyes flashed a slight disapproval. She kept dutifully silent, for a while. "How is Helaman enjoying his visit?" she finally asked.

Now his eyes narrowed in confusion. "How did you know . . .?" And then, realizing that he'd been outmaneuvered, he grabbed her and swung her around. "Why you—!" He stopped and took her face between his hands. "I promise that you will be one of the first to know what will happen. I won't leave you in the dark any longer than necessary."

He pulled her to him, and she rested her head against his shoulder. She felt so safe in his arms, and yet a part of her struggled to let her fears go and have faith in what was to come. That was probably a product of having been on her own for so long. Complete trust in another was difficult, even if that person was her husband.

42

Ammon was correct in saying that she would be one of the first to know what their fate was to be. But she did not learn it from his lips in the quiet stillness of their home the night before. Instead, it took the gathering of the entire city the next morning to make that decision. This time, Ammon wanted to hear the people's thoughts before he made a judgment—and Abish didn't see this deference of power as weakness in her husband, but as a wise leader's recognition that the people had the right to help decide their own fate.

All but the youngest children had assembled in the temple square and, listening to the discussions around her, Abish knew she was not the only one prone to speculation as to what they should do. She gave a smile to Miriam at her side and was glad that Jarum had decided to step away from the fields to join them. She then watched with pride as Ammon stood up on the steps of the temple. He was dressed in a royal tunic of deep purple with a turquoise sash about his waist, reminding the people of his lineage. Because of his familiar spirit, it was easy to forget that their leader was really the son of a former king. But as she had helped him dress that morning and sensed his nervousness, she had been more aware than any of them that he was also just a man. A man who had suffered with them so many times before.

Helaman stood nearby—the keeper of the records—and yet at this moment, he deferred to his father's friend as the true heart of the people he addressed.

"My dear people," Ammon began. "It is with great consternation that I have asked you here today. I wish that we did not have the decision to make that we do. But I have been directed through my prayers and much fasting that it is a decision that we need to make together." He paused to take a deep breath.

"I also have had it made known unto me that our land would not be in this position had it not been for the many dissensions and matters of intrigue that we have allowed to come among us. Now, in stating 'we,' I mean the Nephite people, to whom you have been adopted through your righteousness. I only wish all of our people had remained as steadfast in their faith as you have. But this has not been the case. And as such, the Lamanite army has come perilously close to our land again and placed us in dangerous circumstances."

A murmur went up among the people. Abish felt her heart quicken as he continued. "But we cannot criticize our brethren too much, for it has been through their efforts that we have been able to stay true to the covenant we made. They have borne our arms for us and suffered many tribulations because of this. For this we are eternally grateful. It is with great sadness that, in order to stay in this land, we may have to ask them yet again to do so."

For a moment a hush fell over the crowd, but then the sound of voices began to swell until it sounded like a swarm of bees. Finally, several voices sought to be heard above the din, and their message was in accordance.

"How can we do this?" was their cry. "How can we ask more of them to die for us?"

A shout of approval began to rouse the people from their fear. Now other voices went up, pledging that they would defend their land and their liberties. Though most of these volunteers were Zoramites, who had not taken upon them the vow, a few of them were the people of Ammon. Abish couldn't completely blame them. They had all grown tired of these constant threats and of the many sacrifices the Nephites had made for them. Amid the tumult, Helaman came to stand at Ammon's side. He raised his hand, requesting silence.

"People of Ammon!" he said in a voice of authority. "I beg you not to break your oath, lest by doing so you should save your mortal bodies but lose your immortal souls. We will find a way to protect this land and still preserve you in your righteousness."

But how? the people seemed to ask. *How else can we save ourselves?*

They stood there like a group of lost sheep while Ammon and Helaman began to confer amongst themselves. While they waited, Abish sensed a motion at her side. *Jarum? Where was he going?* Confused, she watched as her son walked up the steps to stand by the man who had been a father to him these past eight years. At first she thought that he had gone to his side to let him know of his support. Little did she know what he had planned.

"Please, listen to me," her son said timidly at first. It took a while before the crowd settled down to hear him. And then, as if bolstered by some unseen courage, he spoke more boldly. "I was not yet born when many of you faced the first trial of your faith back in Ishmael, but I know something of it and am not a stranger to the losses that have been endured as a result. You entered into a covenant in order to save my life." He placed a hand upon his chest. "And the lives of many of those whom I call friends."

Abish watched her son with a strange fascination. She had never seen him be so bold. *What was he doing?*

Jarum now swept his hand out over the crowd. "However, *we* did not enter into such a covenant. We are therefore free to defend your lives, the lives of our mothers and our fathers, of our sisters and of the elderly. We will take up the cause of liberty. Yea, this will be *our* covenant, to defend our land even to the giving of our lives!"

As his last words echoed through the crowd, a great roar went up as thousands of voices shouted their support. Abish began to tremble. This couldn't be! When did her son lose all possession of his faculties?

She pushed her way to the head of the crowd, only to be deterred by the number of young men who rushed forward to stand at Jarum's side. "Jarum!" she cried out, her voice lost in the tumult. "Ammon!" her eyes pleaded with him. *Please don't let him do this!* Ammon stepped forward and waved frantically at the mob, trying to calm them down. Abish breathed a sigh of relief. He would talk reason into these boys.

"People! My people, please!" Ammon shouted. It took an incredibly long time for the crowd to quiet enough for him to be heard. "I am overwhelmed at the sacrifice these young men are willing to make. I have never before witnessed such courage." *Yes,* Abish wrung her hands, *now tell them they can't go.* He turned to address the boys. "I have to ask you how you can consider such a thing. You have never known war, have never gone to battle. How then can you have such faith?"

Jarum sought his mother's eyes out in the crowd. "Because," he said in a voice so soft she felt as if only she could hear, "we have *seen* such faith."

Oh, my son! Abish felt her heart both breaking and bursting inside of her.

* * *

It was quiet when she returned to her house. Abish numbly opened the door and walked into the small confines. The walls seemed to close in around her. She knew where she was and the year in which she lived, but a strange feeling had come over her, as though she had been transported back in time. It was the first attack in Ishmael—all over again. Only this time, she would not be by Jarum's side as their attackers came upon them.

Thus was her frame of mind when Jarum entered the room. And for a moment, she saw Jared's face transfixed upon his and her heart filled with such love for him that she could not breathe. Could not speak. He sensed this and came to her.

"Mama, please. I know you're worried."

She grabbed at the hand that was on her arm and clung to it as if it would keep her from sinking to the ground. "What if you don't come back?"

"I *will* come back."

"Your father didn't."

The words hung in the air between them. It was true. God gave no promise to His people other than that they would be saved in the last day if they obeyed and endured. But this was almost beyond enduring for her!

"Mama. When I was very young, you put me on your lap and taught me of Christ and of His great Atonement. You let me know that God was with me and would give me strength." His voice began to quiver. "And now, even though I don't want to leave you, somehow I'm not afraid—of the future, of what we'll face. Or even of death."

Abish threw her arms around her son and sobbed. "Your father would be so proud of you." And then she took his face between her hands. "And I am so proud of you."

Wiping her tears, Abish walked over to the small stone box. She opened it and took something out. When she handed it to him, he smiled. "I remember the day you got mad at me for playing with it."

Abish watched as he took the dagger from its sheath. The jeweled handle gleamed in the sliver of sunlight that came through the open window. "And now I give it to you with the hope that it will protect you as well and bring you home safely. Oh, my son!" she cried. "Be strong! Have faith and God will be with you!"

43

The days began to pass more slowly than ever now.

Abish removed the sluices from the canals; a few more weeks and the crops would be ready for planting. Though the days of rain had not been generous to them, they no longer had to fear. She could almost imagine the fields of maize bowing in the breeze like the ocean itself. She smiled. It was as if Jarum was still caring for the land.

Three moons had waxed and waned since two thousand of their sons had followed Helaman into the wilderness. *Stripling warriors*, they had called themselves. Helaman had called them his sons. But only the heart of a mother could truly feel the agony that came from sending the fruit of her womb into harm's way. Abish watched the life-giving water flowing down the trenches and felt as if her own life somehow was flowing away as well. But, she sighed, she was not the only to be suffering this way.

The morning when their sons left, she had stood with Teara, Zaharah, and Isabel, their arms wrapped around each other. Their faces wet with tears. It had been decided that only those who were unmarried and between the ages of fifteen and twenty-five would be allowed to join, so the women watched as Jarum, Malech, Benjamin, and Hagoth marched with so many others in uneven lines toward the horizon. What a difference those few years made: some looked like mere boys while others towered like men. They were trying to look stately as they left, but were so unorganized and ungainly looking that it would have caused a few smiles had it been under different circumstances.

And then the mothers stood, alone, wondering if the departing figures had somehow taken with them all of the faith their sons claimed they had. Faith now seemed the most precious commodity, and in that moment, it sent all of them to their knees in a common prayer.

Father in Heaven, watch over them. Bring them home to us.

She had not allowed herself to cry again since that day. Ammon understood her need to appear stronger than she felt and was content to watch her internal struggle for a while. But then that evening he came to her as she sat on her favorite ridge, watching the sun set in the distance. He sat on an adjoining rock and placed his hand gently over hers. She kept her eyes on the horizon, reluctant to give a sign that she acknowledged him there, instead rubbing a hand over Tuk's bristly fur. She had promised to take care of the pet for her son, but somehow, she knew that the animal would not live to see his return. The realization was like a wave crashing over her; a great sob escaped and her body began to shake. Ammon lifted her up and placed her on his lap and rocked her like a child, letting her release the pain she had been keeping inside. When she was depleted, he had wrapped an arm around her and led her home.

***

The next day after she finished her work, Abish glanced at the setting sun—a sign that Ammon would be coming home soon. Miriam said she would have the bread cooked by then. Abish sighed. How ironic that this war had caused her daughter to move back home to be with her. At least she knew one of her children was safe.

Abish headed back to the house only to find she had a visitor.

"Teara!" she said, delighted. "How wonderful to see you. But, isn't it late to be out?"

"Namon said he would walk home with Ammon and then escort me back. I told him that I needed to speak with you."

Abish was immediately concerned. "What about?"

Teara seemed to read her thoughts and said quickly, "No, I'm not with child again. But it does concern one of my children. And . . . one of yours."

Now she was quite baffled. She led her friend away from the exposure of the night and into the quiet, glow of the house. Miriam had everything set for their evening meal and gave a warm smile when the two of them entered. When Abish explained Teara's presence, Miriam tactfully excused herself, saying that she had to check on the squash in the fire pit out back. Alone, Abish waited patiently for Teara to begin. She did, but with a question.

"Has there been any new word?" They both knew of what she spoke.

"None that I know of. I vowed to flog Ammon within an inch of his life if he kept anything, no matter how painful, from me," Abish joked. "So all we know, still, is that they were heading toward Antiparah. But whether the army of Antipus has joined them in battle or whether," her voice caught in her throat, "they fight alone, I know not. All we can do is continue to pray."

Teara smiled. "Yes. We are all praying. Some, it seems, more than others. And perhaps with good reason." She reached into a small bag and pulled out a piece of precious ficus paper. It was very costly, and Abish wondered why her friend was in possession of it. Teara handed it to her, though Abish was unable to read the words. After she saw the writing, however, she recognized Jarum's script immediately. With a questioning look, Teara explained the mystery.

"I showed it to Namon this morning and he told me what it says. I'll try to remember the exact words, but it's more the sentiment that matters:

> *My beloved, I fear that in leaving I may gain our freedom but lose what has become most precious to me. Do not forget me. Think of me when the mist wraps itself around the distant hills and know that I am longing to wrap my arms around you. I will be thinking of you always.*
> *All my love, Jarum.*

"Jarum!" Abish cried out. "But what . . . who . . .?" She was at a loss for words.

Teara folded the paper gently. "I found this in Ruth's sleeping cot. She had it hidden between the folds of her blanket. I was not prying, only trying to hang the linens out to freshen. It fell on the ground and, well, I couldn't resist looking at it." Abish still had not regained the use of her voice as Teara continued. "I think it's obvious what it means. But, if you have any hesitations at all, then I'll under—"

"Hesitations?" Abish clapped a hand over her mouth. "Do you know how long I have waited for my son to come to his senses? I could not be happier."

Now Teara seemed awestruck as well. "Oh, I'm so glad! I was afraid that you might think Ruth was too young still or have some other apprehension regarding her. But when I found this, it seemed like an answer to *my* prayers."

"I know it will be a good match. Do you know what this means?" Abish asked. "We will be family! As close to sisters as we ever could be."

Teara wiped away a tear. "You have always been like a sister to me. When we first met back in the palace of King Lamoni, I knew that somehow you would always be a part of me. I must admit that at first I was a little jealous of how quickly the queen took to you, yet I have learned over the years that it's only because you possess an inner strength that is so rare in most. But I have been honored all these years to be called your friend, and I will be even more honored to be part of your family."

"And I, part of yours," she said as they embraced.

"I'm so glad I don't have to keep Ruth's secret anymore! Now we have even more to pray for!" Miriam squealed, revealing that she had been listening at the door.

Yes, Abish thought. *And to be thankful for.*

* * *

The days continued, however, and still there was little word. As they approached the second year of their sons' departure, they began to receive information in bits and pieces. What torture it was to hear of the skirmishes that occurred near Antiparah and Cumeni, and then Manti—to know that even though Helaman's army had triumphed each time, there was no news as to who was injured and none as to those killed. All their people could do was pray.

Ruth had been spending more time at their house in Jarum's absence, and Abish welcomed this girl who would one day, God-willing, be her daughter-in-law. She found that Teara's daughter had turned out to have a keen mind and gentle spirit. Even though she was quiet and unassuming, that didn't mean she wouldn't stand up for herself when provoked. Content that she complemented her son well in nature, all Abish could do now was wait and hope for a future that would include them all.

One night after the two families had shared a meal together, Abish and Teara went for a peaceful walk outside. Ammon had constructed a small bench by a nearby stream, and they eventually sat and listened to the calming sound of water flowing over the stones. They didn't immediately broach questions that couldn't be answered—they didn't want to talk of things that hung heavy on their minds.

"Rebekah thinks she wants to be a teacher," Teara said proudly. "Who would have thought we'd come to have such independent children?"

"I suppose that comes from having independent mothers." Abish sighed.

Her friend chuckled. "And Enoch has gone from wanting to be a farmer, like his father, to sailing the ocean, like Hagoth seems inclined to do—much to Zaharah's consternation."

Abish joined in her amusement. "Well, I imagine he will change his mind when the actual time comes." But then she tilted her head, puzzled. "Isn't Enoch afraid to swim?" she asked.

"Yes." They both doubled over in laughter. It felt good. When they regained their composure, Abish added, "It can be difficult to raise them, knowing that the end result is to send them off into the world alone. It seems a cruel trick of nature."

Teara agreed. "It reminds me of how our Heavenly Father must have felt sending us to this earth, only to watch us struggle and suffer—perhaps never to return to Him." They were both struck with the reality of what that meant: What if *their* sons never came home?

"Sometimes," Abish thought aloud, "I wish that I had the power to control and change things."

"But you do, when you heal people," Teara said matter-of-factly.

Abish shrugged. "I suppose. But more often than not I'm reminded of what little control I have over anything. I remember that time when you nearly died, how frightened and helpless I felt. But then Namon came and gave you a blessing and you were instantly healed. Sometimes I'm envious of that—I feel as if, because I'm a woman, all I can do is watch and wait. What power is there in that?"

Teara smiled. "Don't you understand? We've been given one of the greatest powers of all. We have been given the power to create life on this earth—to work hand in hand with *our* Divine Creator. Never forget that . . . we have been called to be *mothers*."

44

Abish grimaced, convinced that another mirror was the last present she'd wanted in celebration of the fiftieth year since her birth. In fact, Abish was of a mind to forbid any more celebrations of this kind. Marriages . . . yes. The birth of a grandchild? She would shout it from the rafters! But reminding oneself of an increase in age seemed as pointless as it was painful. Why would anyone want to see more clearly her graying hair and the wrinkles around her eyes?

Ammon at least had guessed right as to her needs. The leather pouch he had made her was the perfect size for all of her healing implements and she knew he must have fashioned it from a few of his own. And yet he had seemed a little disappointed when he'd given it to her. She'd asked why, to which he'd cryptically answered, "It wasn't the gift I was hoping to give you." But she had kissed him before he went off to his meeting and assured him that it was perfect and she could think of nothing else she would have liked better.

But that wasn't entirely true.

As she cleared away the morning's meal, she knew that more than anything, she wanted to hold her son in her arms again. Another season had passed since they'd last had word, and soon the days of rain would be upon them. With them would come visions of her children sloshing through knee-deep mud and enduring nights of unending downpours. After so long a time, the mothers knew that whatever supplies they had sent with their sons had been used up and that they were probably subsisting on whatever they could find or were being generously given. Did that mean they were walking barefoot by now? Had their oiled cloaks begun to unravel and fall apart, leaving them exposed to the elements?

It was too much for her mother's heart to think about.

Not that the inhabitants of Melek were faring much better. The numerous wars had continued to cause the once-heavy flow of trade between cities to cease like a river during drought, which left the people of Ammon once again dependant upon their own devises. Both she and Miriam had tried to develop new ways of weaving "cloth" from old roof-thatching or dried plants, but the result was often painful and, at the very least, uncomfortable. And they were all tired of the rations of maize and beans and fish that had made up their daily fare for months. But even though she longed for meat to the point where her mouth watered at the mere thought of it, she knew they shouldn't complain. Most of the land was in even greater distress.

A number of people had fled to Melek to escape the battles in their own cities, bringing with them bits of news from their own lands. Thus, she learned that Nephite cities, such as Gid, Mulek, and even Bountiful, were changing hands like sticks in an a-ul game—from Nephite protection to the mercy of the Lamanites and often back again. And while the Nephite armies held to the centuries-old law that forbade the taking of women and children as prisoners, the Lamanite armies had no such honor. Even Moroni's recent request for an exchange of prisoners had been denied. She shuddered at the thought of what her people endured.

It took all of their faith to sustain them.

But while they were poorer in body than they had ever been, the people of Ammon had found a strength of spirit that came only through hardship. There was no rich among them and so they were poor, together. And they did not succumb to envyings or strife. Each man shared his goods with another—which was why Abish had received the present of the mirror, in exchange for a pair of reed sandals that Miriam had laboriously made. More grateful for the thought than the gift, she set the mirror back in her stone box.

Going to the window, Abish wondered if the day would ever end. Miriam probably wouldn't return from the supplicant's bedside for hours—another "gift" she'd bestowed today by allowing her mother an entire day that didn't require her to attend to anyone's needs. It had been thoughtful of her daughter, but Abish quickly realized that leisure time was highly overrated. With Ammon at his meeting, she'd considered visiting some friends. But Teara and Zaharah were busy fashioning dresses out of remnants so their youngest daughters would be prepared for their betrothment celebrations. Abish had been asked to join them in their preparations, but she felt awkward when the three of them were together. The other two women had so much in common still and she often just sat there smiling, trying to discover how she fit in.

Looking around the room, she saw the plate that Jarum had inscribed and which now hung on the wall where all who visited could see. One of Miriam's weavings was next to it, and the deep, rich colors formed a striking pattern that showed off her daughter's imagination and skill. Malech's carving of a deer sat on the table where Ammon worked. Her eyes moved from the pile of scrolls that Ammon had left out the night before to one of his tunics that lay draped over a chair. She went and picked it up, breathing in the now-familiar scent of him, and found herself overwhelmed by her emotions. This was her home—her family! She knew that in this place, where there was love, she truly belonged.

And yet she couldn't completely be at peace. With a sigh, Abish decided to work in the garden or at least create some work to occupy her troubled mind until Miriam or Ammon returned. The smell of the earth as she turned it over wafted up, and she thought about the promise of the potential life she was planting, feeling as if she were just on the verge of understanding something for the first time—something that was new and exciting. Crouching down, she patted the soil back into place and went to dig another hole. She decided to plant a flower, thinking it might brighten the days ahead. But she stopped. How did she even know the seed would grow? How could she be sure of anything? Abish thought of Jared and Malech and the army marching across the land of Zarahemla. She considered her own people's future and the future of God's church among them. Why couldn't she know that everything would be well? Why couldn't she *know* that her sons would return home? And then something Ammon had tried to explain to her days before as he quoted the prophet Alma's words suddenly came into focus as if she had finally learned how to open her eyes.

Sometimes there could be no sure knowledge, but there could always be hope. She could not know that this tiny seed would sprout into a living plant and certainly would never know what her future held. And yet she had hope for her children, her family, and especially her people. So much hope that there were times she felt as if she knew things in her heart and could not doubt them. Perhaps that *was* the true essence of faith: to hope and believe enough until that overcame all doubt.

"Abish!"

The voice called to her, reaching around the corner of the house. *Ammon must be back from his meeting*, she thought as she wiped tears of gratitude from her eyes. She struggled to stand after being on her knees for so long.

"Abish!"

His voice was now more adamant, so she hurried to the front of the house. "What is it? I think the whole village can hear you."

Ammon came rushing toward her and thrust a handful of papers at her. She was about to remind him that she couldn't read when he said, "They're coming home!"

Now she frantically scanned the marks on the pages as if by will alone she could understand the words. "When? When will they be here?" She clutched the papers to her chest.

"If all goes well, tomorrow, perhaps the day after—"

She didn't hear much of what he said after that. *Tomorrow. Jarum and Malech could be home tomorrow!* Her thoughts stopped cold as sudden fear gripped her heart. "Does it say . . . were any . . .?"

Ammon smiled. "Here. Let me read some of this to you. It's an epistle Helaman sent to Moroni. It will explain all." He held up the papers and began:

> *My dearly beloved brother, Moroni. We received your epistle releasing us from our duties, and following your orders, I will return my sons, for as I had ever called them my sons (for they were all of them very young), to their land forthwith. But I have somewhat to tell you concerning our warfare in this part of the land.*

Ammon's eyes scanned the paper until he found what he was looking for, then he continued.

> *And now I say unto you, my beloved brother Moroni, that never had I seen so great courage, nay, not amongst all the Nephites. We had much success, and my sons truly believed that our God was with them and that He would not suffer that they should fall. And behold, to my great joy, though injured every one, there had not one soul of them fallen to the earth.*

He paused again, searching, and then read on.

> *And we do ascribe it to the miraculous power of God and to the exceeding faith in that which they have been taught to believe. Yea, even have they rehearsed unto me the words of their mothers, saying: 'We do not doubt our mothers knew it.'"*

Ammon looked up, eyes glistening. Abish took the papers carefully into her hands, caressing them as if they were hope itself. And then, looking into Ammon's smiling green eyes, she wept tears of joy.

Epilogue

There. Another part of my story has now been told. I do not blame those who may judge me or think me a foolish, weak woman. After all, I struggled the remainder of my days with pride and stubbornness. That I should merit any mention after my bones are laid in the earth . . . I suppose that will be left to God.

At least this part of my weaving is finished, but my hands have grown so tired I fear it will be the last one. If only my grandchildren and perhaps their children will remember and think of me from time to time or perhaps will be told of me when they wonder how they came to this land. But will they understand? Will they know how it feels to see two husbands go to their rest before them? Will they comprehend how painful it is after four-scores of years to see the lands they love continually ravaged by war? I can only pray that their generation will find peace again. I pray that they will have joy and perhaps see the face of their Redeemer descending from the heavens. That will be my biggest regret. But my body is tired, and I will not live to see that day.

And yet I learned something of forgiveness during this time of probation. Something of patience, for I believe the two are intertwined. And most of all, I have learned the importance of faith.

About the Author

K.C. Grant grew up in rural Idaho but has spent most of her life living in Northern Utah. She served a Spanish-speaking mission to southern California and upon returning, finished her bachelor of arts with a double major in English and Spanish at Weber State University. She has traveled extensively throughout Mexico, even taking the opportunity to study Hispanic literature and history at a local college in Michoacan, Mexico. Over the years, she has been a frequent contributor to several family/home-oriented magazines, such as *LDSLiving, Natural Life, Parents & Kids, Latter-Day Woman, The Washington Family,* and *BackHome.* She also enjoys participating in various writing organizations, such as the League of Utah Writers (where she's been a chapter president for three years), LDStorymakers, and the Association for Mormon Letters.

You can learn more about K.C. Grant by visiting her website, *www. kcgrant.com.*